Black Apples

belladonnapublishing.com

Black Apples

Edited by
Camilla Bruce and Liv Lingborn

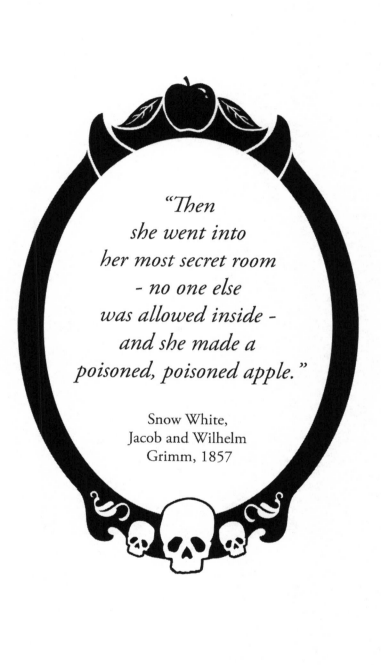

"Then
she went into
her most secret room
- no one else
was allowed inside -
and she made a
poisoned, poisoned apple."

Snow White,
Jacob and Wilhelm
Grimm, 1857

978-82-999548-0-8 ISBN

Contents

Snow Child

Molly Pinto Madigan

The city is full of mirrors - shining skyscrapers, polished police cars, flat-faced fountains, and glass that throws your faults back at you on every street corner.

Some mirrors lie, and some tell the truth, but all of them are telling me the same things these days: my time is up.

When I met your daddy, I was young and sad. He said I was beautiful, and I was. His skin was light and his hair was dark and I liked the contrast, but it wasn't like yours. Yours was magnificent. A curse.

He didn't tell me about you until I loved him, which didn't take that long I guess. He was a real prince, bringing me blood red roses and giving me his sweater when I shivered in the movie theatre.

His hands were narrow, with fingers slim as ballpoint pens, tracing territory on my skin. Freckled skin, murky skin. Not like yours. But my ring shone like ice in the August heat waves, when everyone had to loosen their collars to let the steam out, when cubed ice was as precious as diamonds. I felt the weight of the ring as a promise, and I didn't take it off, even when the heat made my fingers swell.

Then, there was you.

I couldn't even say your name right. Wrong emphasis, your daddy said. Yukiko. Snow child.

Your mom was Japanese, a beauty. Like a flower, he said, and as ephemeral. Sometimes I wish that I were less hearty, less va-va-voom, as he put it, so I could know that kind of beauty. I have more flesh than I know what to do with, all sunspots and tan lines and streaked hair in need of a touch-up. My roots are showing, Yukiko, and there's gray in the mud.

You put that there. You and your daddy.

My mother warned me about men who like Asian women. Asian girls, really. It's an ugly stereotype, so don't you listen to it.

You were anything but weak, and you certainly weren't submissive. You were so strong, a minx. So why'd you let him do it, Yukiko?

Not even a month after the wedding, a band of hot gold welded to my finger, I found the blood on your sheets - the Power Ranger polyester that made me smile, because you wanted no part of all that frilly stuff your friends liked. You were so young then, your breasts unbudded, body hairless as an Egyptian queen, but so pale. You were strong, though, so why did you let him touch you?

My mind was filled with darkness and hot breath, whispers and burning hands. Those slim hands on you, and your skin like February's deep snow, unblemished, sparkling, and sullied.

It made me sick.

And I was angry, but not just with him.

I went to him: Henry, what did you do? I stammered, and he spotted my weakness, turning the whole stinking mess onto me. How could I think that? What was wrong with me? Then, he kissed me, but it tasted sour in my mouth. It tasted like a lie.

But I heard him in your room, and it was my fault because I should have stopped it sooner. I sensed the lies and chose to turn away. It shouldn't have gone on, Yukiko, and I'm so sorry. I let him ruin you.

I waited for him in our bedroom because I'm a coward and couldn't bear to see. I waited on our king-size bed, and boiled by the brass headboard where my grandmother's rosary beads hung.

He hit me when I said it, as if bruising my mouth could force the words back in, but his eyes spilled their secrets. He left me on the floor.

He kept a pistol in his bedside table. No safety lock. Typical.

The gun felt leaden in my hand, but my arms didn't shake. I wasn't weak, so I wouldn't look it. I imagined that my eyes were dark and full of poison, so he'd know that I wasn't kidding.

When I came into the kitchen, he was eating, his slim fingers picking through yesterday's lo-mein. He always picked out all the pork and vegetables, leaving me with only spit-slick noodles and scallions, and suddenly

I hated him for it. My finger itched on the trigger.

I told him to leave, and he did, and he hasn't been back.

The next morning, when you asked, through a crunchy mouth of Kix, where your daddy was, I told you he was dead. You were so brave, you didn't shed a tear.

Neither did I.

You and me, we're survivors. I recognized this in you early on, before I even got your name right. This one, I said, she's a fighter. I just didn't realize that it was me you'd be fighting against.

I was angry. I was angry with myself for not being enough, and angry with him for leaving me with you - a black-eyed girl that, at ten, was already turning heads. Now, at thirteen, you're stunning. A curse. Competition.

I've tried to love you like the mother I'm not, but you've taken so much from me. Not just your daddy and the others, but my youth, my beauty; there's no getting those back. As I watched your pale radiance grow like the moon, mine waned. My skin thickened like leather - crow's feet, cellulite, sag. As boys honked at you from their tinted muscle cars, I wanted that, because then I would know that it wasn't all gone. I longed for a lone catcall, anything to show me that I was still desirable.

Your body was slender, smooth, taut white chocolate that never puckered or sweat. (Why the hell don't you sweat?) You never broke out like all your friends from school, even though you guzzled coke and lunched on cheese curls dipped in Fluff. No "bacne," no blackheads. Your body looked airbrushed even in the harsh lights of dressing rooms, and I wanted that. I still do.

What kind of screwed up society do we live in today, where a grown woman wants the body of child? Yours was a clean beauty, and next to you I started to hate my dimpled hips and cheesecake thighs, even my heavy breasts that had once lured men's mouths like flies. I hated them, and I hated you for making me hate them, Yukiko.

Then, there was Woody. And he wanted me. He called me his beauty, and through his eyes, I was. All the mirrors in the house, which I'd covered up with stale sheets and blankets, were unveiled. I was transformed, ravishing, a bona fide tabloid queen. But not as lovely as you.

Woody was a good man, a quiet man, smelling of cigar smoke and pine. He had these great big hands that were rough from working and would chafe my skin until it felt pink and new. Young. But not as young as you.

You were a fox, tempting him, smiling lewdly with those pearls. I wanted to knock your teeth out, because next to yours my smile flickered like a subway fluorescent. Why would he want me when he could have you, as dazzling as the sun shining off of the snow?

Why did you take him, Yukiko? It's like you wanted it, that kind of trouble, when I'd spent all those years trying to protect you.

The scratchy couch. Woody moaning like an animal. I could have killed you then. Your lips were carmine-kissed, and I was back to that day when the blood screamed off your snowy skin, hair throbbing black.

Who seduced who, Yukiko?

It doesn't matter; either way, I was betrayed.

He begged to stay, you know. He begged to stay with me, but how could I look at him after that? I hated you, because I still wasn't enough, not for him, not for your father, and not for you. I saw the way you looked at me, minx. Like you'd already won.

And you had.

The mirrors were covered up again, but there's no escape in the city. Sharp, shining, cruel: they're everywhere. I saw my hideousness in every glass's gleam, and it was torture, especially next to you.

There you were, shining like a constant beacon of my shame. A red and white CITGO sign advertising my inadequacies. And you reveled in it, you broken beauty.

I tried to avoid the mirrors, but they were shouting my name, and they all said the same thing: I had to do something, for your sake as well as mine.

You knew you were breathtaking, and it poisoned you. You and your posse of seven beauties (but not quite as beautiful as you, of course) prowled the halls of school, leaving carnage, breaking boys, and sitting on sidewalks in July dripping ice pops down your camisoles.

You had to be stopped.

I bought you t-shirts two sizes too big that dwarfed your body, hiding your hard apple breasts, and I gave the sexy shirts you loved to Goodwill. You didn't complain, but it backfired when you cut deep plunges out of the necks and tied up the waist in a knot that exposed your slender midriff.

So I cut your hair, shearing it to your ears, hoping that without those inky ribbons your beauty would be dampened, but you slicked it and came off looking like a manga femme fatale. That drove the boys wild.

So I cooked for you. Belgian waffles, maple pecan scones, and your favorite: apple pie made with ruby red delicious and thick cubes of butter that disappeared into the filling when I baked it. Sugar, cinnamon, and calories galore. Full-fat, à la mode.

I watched you gorge yourself while I nibbled on butterhead lettuce and choked on celery strings, and then, miraculously, you grew.

Your hips widened.

Your breasts plumped.

Your marble stomach softened.

You started to bleed.

It was like magic. There was even a pimple on your perfect nose.

I drank red wine and delighted in what I thought was your defeat, and for the first time in years, I felt young again.

SNOW CHILD | 11

It didn't last long, though, because at the end of the tunnel, you were even lovelier and so very fair, and you never lost sight of that. Your hips curved gently, and you swung them as you strode. Strutted. Your breasts bubbled over your push-up bra, as tempting as steamed buns. You stole my makeup and powdered your nose clean again, adding cat eyes and candy apple lips. As if you needed them.

You can paint your pretty face all you want, Yukiko, but I know you; I see the bitterness, and I know the canker inside of you. We're not so different.

You embraced your new skin with a passion that baffled me. I didn't understand. But be careful, Yukiko, because men are fickle shits and you won't be young forever. One day you'll wake up, and you'll be old, and if you go on letting the hurt corrode your insides, you'll be left with nothing.

I tried to protect you, you know, from yourself and from them. And I do love you, in my own way. I thought that I hated you once, but I don't. You make me hate myself, which is close, I guess. But that's not your fault.

The city's full of mirrors, and not the nice kind, either. Nasty ones, like the one in my bedroom, but I can't even cover them with sheets or scarves, and every glassy storefront throws back fat thighs, flabby wings, jiggling flesh. I can't help but look. I can't look away from the washed up beauty I've become. Past her prime. Ephemeral. Caught in mirrors, twisted, stretching, I've felt my heart fester like an open sore. And I don't want that to happen to you, snow child.

See? I do care.

I've consulted silverware, and sunglasses, and grimy cab windows. Puddles, and doorknobs, and empty TV screens. They're all screaming your name. I know you're a teenager now, fierce and lovely, and you don't want to hear it from me, but there's no one else who knows you like I do. The mirrors, they all speak the same truth, Yukiko:

Beauty is fleeting.

Twelve Sisters, Twelve Sisters, Ten

Karen Heuler

The sisters, all twelve of them, rushed down the corridors, looking at the mirrors, not to see themselves but to see each other. Artemis, short-haired; Bethamis, short-browed; Chloe, red-cheeked; Doloreen, smiling.

They wore wide skirts and silk shoes and belts made of crystals. Ellerence wore a velvet blouse, Glorene, satin; Helena, brocade; Ingelise silk.

"Oh, my feet are drunken," Kittilette declared, lifting up half of her mouth in a smile - she had practiced it all afternoon, that half-done smile. "I can feel them getting tipsy."

They were outside now, Bethamis helping Artemis, the eldest, whose thin back was bent, whose fingers were curled.

Ellerence and Fiorence, joined at the wrists, faced each other, sliding into the night. Their faces were taut, strangled with bitterness, joined as they were against their own wishes. All those years of crying out, "To the right!" only to be stymied. Imperious, outraged, they dragged each other sideways.

Lotte, the youngest, skipped ahead, her breasts like small gloves; she leapt up and spun, her long hair snapping. Too, too glorious to be sixteen, the youngest, the fastest, the best. She reached the water and curled her foot out of her shoes; behind her the sisters were calling, in muted shouts, in telescoped whispers: "Hold on! Not so fast! Get your hands off me! My turn, mine!"

But she didn't wait for them, at sixteen, why wait for anything? and she swayed into the water, sliding in like a snake, ages ahead of the stragglers, years ahead of Artemis, forty-six if she's a day, brittle and gray and knife-eyed while she was soft as good firm dough.

Her head was under water, hair pulled by waves, and she turned, saw a sister's foot break through and descend, then foot after foot, an ankle, a calf, a hem touched with green, the moon's strong light like a million lamps strung along the lake bottom.

They were all through now and even Artemis was lighter again, un-humped, her eyes lively as her waist - they skimmed down the avenue like a cascade.

No one looked back; no one saw a man push his startled face down through the flat of the water, his tongue sticking out, he looked such a fool. He drew back, he was cautious, having followed so carefully, he was willing to take his time.

Hired by the king, their father, that man strangled by daughters, all of them virgins, he swore, he swore; none of them willing to leave him, free him, get married and be gone. Why won't they marry? Suitor after suitor has come, some of them even clever, some of them even young, but none of them accepted and half of them sent to their death before they were gone.

Girls. The great disappointment of his life, girl after girl. He'd drowned the first few, but after that he'd let them live, curious as to how far the joke would go, replacing the wives instead. Now he merely wanted to be rid of them. He was nearing 80, and his girls had long ago stopped fearing him, if they ever had. When Martin appeared, young and with in-sufferable eyes, asking to see his daughters that he might choose one, the old man's heart had surged. This one looked steadfast. He sighed. "They will not marry," he said finally. "None of them."

Martin filled his lungs up with air; a little tail of a smile appeared. "I will choose one and leave her no choice," he said handsomely.

"A tithing of my gold will go to you if you succeed." And with that agreement, the king began to tell all that he knew: time after time he had glimpsed them all in a line in the moonlight, and they had laughed at him when questioned. A line of twelve daughters was not a thing to be han-dled easily, so he had thought he was mistaken, or that it was some secret women's business, and he cared nothing for that.

"I will find out, first, where they go," Martin promised; "and break them of the habit. And the one who thanks me for it will be my wife." He was used to enchantments and he loved to break them.

Martin combed the countryside for the former queens and found two of them living together in a cottage on the edge of the woods. "I have come to woo your daughters," he said, "and I wish to please them. But they disappear in the moonlight; will you help me win your daughters's love?"

Nigea, the elder, sat inscrutable and unyielding; she said, "My daughters choose their own way; I won't help you deceive them."

"Of course not," Damiel said, but she winked at Martin, one eyelid shutting up and down furtively. "My daughters will be unwed and unprotected for as long as they choose."

Martin thanked them cordially and left, walking slowly and before long Damiel slipped up behind him and said, "You will marry one of my daughters, the twins, for they need someone to provide for them, sweet as they are, the world is cruel. Here, this is a reed that will allow you to breathe underwater. Follow them wherever they go, and kill whomever they meet. They won't be free until you do."

In town he purchased a great cape with golden seams, and a wide brimmed hat with a single pearl; and a knife as thin as a hair. He was bathed and perfumed, and he strode into the rows of daughters as their father's guest, their heads bowing in abbreviated courtesies. They had seen suitors before.

That night they went out as usual in the moonlight, in ones and twos, the youngest racing forward, the eldest lagging behind. "I heard something, I heard something," Artemis said, pulling herself up.

"Some creature in the woods," Bethamis assured her, pulling her forward. Already Lotte was in the water, the balloon of her skirt not yet dropping down, and they raced to catch up with her, going too fast for Glorene, who stopped to free her hem from a branch and thought she saw a foot, a human foot with a human shoe, dart back into the shadow. "Ingelise!" she cried to her nearest sister. "I saw a man's foot!"

Ingelise laughed. "I've seen a lot of them, Glorene. Nothing to worry about." She mounted one of the underwater horses that always waited for the sisters. "Hurry, Glorene, the others are miles ahead!"

Martin, who had no horse, pushed himself carefully along a trail of lost coins, breathing through the reed, which lengthened and shortened automatically with the depth of the lake.

He heard music, eerie blurred sounds, and began to see a brightness up ahead. He came upon a great house, and peered in through the windows to a good-sized room, with a polished floor and corridors going off like arms.

The dancers sprang up with the beat of the music, raising their arms and stiffening their legs, floating up together, and when they reached the highest point, they spun around together, partnered up, the women twisting their ankles round the men's legs, twirling together.

Martin could make out the eldest - Artemis - now lithe and arching in the dance, and the youngest one, not as good as her sisters and inclined to tangle in her clothing. He could see their bare legs, their pointed toes, as they sprang up and slipped back, and his face was grim as he noted how closely they were held, how intimately entwined. All were shameless, save for the bumblings of Lotte, who kept drifting apart from her luckless lover.

He watched as Artemis first, then Bethamis, then Chloe, drew their lovers away from the dance, and window to window he followed Chloe and her lover down a hall to a room, to a bed, dressed in underwater ferns.

He watched, only drawing away when they were done.

At dawn the dancers bid adieu, and the sisters mounted their horses and sped back to shore, where they put on their shoes and went home to bed.

Martin took longer, walking, mindful of the reed he breathed through, but he too returned above and hastened to the king.

"Your daughters go to a house beneath the water," he said, "where they dance and fornicate and defile your good name."

"All of them?" the king asked.

"All save the youngest," he said, "and that only because she has not yet found a partner. She is the only one I would marry; she is the only one left pure."

"Then the others shall die," the king said.

But an unnoticed servant heard this, and whispered to Artemis, whose crooked spine seemed to straighten in fury. "Sisters!" she whispered hoarsely, going from room to room. "We have been betrayed!"

That night eleven sisters went down to the lake, but this time they avoided walking in a line, and the sister who always seemed forgotten - Doloreen - hid behind a tree to see if they were followed. She saw a man's form slip through the shadows and wait till her sisters had gone to the water, saw him pull the reed from under his shirt, and follow.

She kept close but out of sight. He was cautious as he neared the great underwater house, slowing down so much that Doloreen hurried ahead of him. She nodded to her sisters and climbed a tree, wrapping her skirt against the trunk where it branched. She watched him as he peered through windows, fingering a knife tied to his side, shifting his weight.

One, two, three of the sisters danced in plain sight. Doloreen could see him shifting, trying to look into the near side of the room, counting four and then five.

Suddenly he felt fingers at his ears and legs. Unseen sisters - two of them, ten of them, how could he tell? - blindfolded him and tied his arms behind, tied his ankles together, careful to leave his reed undisturbed.

At last he was bound, and they put him on a horse and rode far away, and then they tied him to some coral, near a shore he couldn't see. They made sure he had his reed, and they left him.

They went back to the ball and gathered. "Sisters," Artemis said, "this is not going to end well. Our father insists on marriage, and he can order our deaths if he chooses. We must consider what to do."

And they set to planning. Marriage seemed inevitable if they were to stay their father's wrath. "It's a pity," Fiorence said, "that there isn't a son. He would ignore us entirely then. Too bad one of us isn't a boy." She trailed off, and her eyebrows lifted, and she looked around. The other sisters looked around, too, and began to laugh. And their plan was born.

The very next morning, a cry arose from the sisters' quarters, and Artemis hastened to her father's room with a letter in her hand. "Father, father!" she cried breathlessly, falling at his feet. "That man - Martin - has proven himself a liar and a thief! He has taken Lotte - this is her farewell letter. He has promised to protect her, and wed her - but why would he steal her away then? I'm afraid he will dishonor her and kill her."

"This is shocking," her father said. He sat back abruptly in his chair. "The scoundrel." His bones looked heavier, and he looked weary.

"And liar," his daughter added.

"And liar," her father agreed.

Relieved, the sisters continued with their plan. Lotte waited for them under the lake while the sisters assembled a valise with two sets of garments, with shoes and a cap and jacket, all of which they took down to the lake, along with scissors.

"Come Lotte, it's time," Chloe said when the sisters met her at the ball.

"Must you really cut my hair?" she asked regretfully.

"Hush, Lotte, you know we must."

"Must you really take away my skirts, and my petticoats?"

"Hush, Lotte, you know we must."

"Must I really wear these clothes?" she cried as they dressed her in a loose shirt, and a vest, and trousers.

"Yes, yes, of course you must," they told her. "And your name is Loren and you are good and fast and glorious, you know that, don't you? Your father will adore you and your sisters will be forever in your debt. You'll still have your life here, Lotte. When you come here you can wear your skirts and we'll save your hair for you to wear, but look at you now," they said, coaxing her to a mirror.

She looked at herself critically. She looked a good boy - slim and agile. She turned and saw the effect, approving it. "I'm ready," she said, and they mounted up again, eleven sisters and their brother, and rode to shore.

"New shoes," Lotte said, observing the pair along the water's edge.

"And your name now is Loren," they reminded her, and slipped off to their old rooms.

In the moonlight, Lotte stood, the last time she would be known by that name. She was the youngest, judged easiest to pass as a boy, and she mourned the loss of the life she had envisioned and began to imagine herself as a boy.

By morning she had it fully in her mind, and she strode off to her father's house - wide strides, sharp impetuous looks, sneers aimed at squirrels and woodcocks.

Loren demanded immediate audience with the king. "Sir, I am your son," he said. "I only recently found out my mother - your last wife - had been pregnant when you banished her." He bowed deeply.

"My son!" the king cried, leaping to his feet and grabbing the boy by the shoulders to peer at his face. "Yes, yes, I see it. The resemblance is there. A son!" He was beaming. "I shall murder the woman."

"Sire, she is my mother. I would hardly like to mark the day I found my father with the day I doomed my mother." Loren's mouth was firm.

His father blustered. "You're right - I was taken off guard. Old habits. Ah, but this is the future, and just in time. I find myself grown old, my son, and what old man wants to see a legacy of daughters?"

"I have sisters?" Loren murmured in astonishment. "I was raised alone. Having sisters seems like wealth to me."

His father gave a short laugh. "No wealth with this many girls," he said. "But what do they matter? We'll keep them if you like," he said, laughing and slapping his son on the back.

"Dear sisters," the boy said, as the sisters swept in at suppertime. He had a faint flush on his cheeks, "let me first say how pleased I am to meet you, how much I've dreamed of sisters in my barren life. And a father," he added hastily, raising a glass. "To father!" he cried and they all raised their glasses and cried out cheerfully: "To father!"

At first the old man found a renewed vigor at the arrival of his son, and rode and walked and ate and drank exclusively with him. He noted a bodily modesty about the boy, and thought it a shame he had been raised by women, because he had a natural quickness and spirit that a father might have shaped into something fine.

After a week, he felt tired again, and went to bed early, his great eyes sunken, his great head weak. Loren waited until he was sure the old man was asleep, then he sped out to the lake, tore off his male clothes and plunged into the water after his sisters.

Her heart soared as she neared the ball and caught up with the others. "Wait!" she cried. "I hate being a boy! It's an awfully dull life, with no one to talk to, and father watching over me relentlessly, and shooting at small things unfairly. I'm bound to make a slip, he watches me too closely."

The sisters conferred and agreed that another brother would keep Loren from loneliness, an older brother from a previous wife - and so it was decided that Doloreen - who always complained she was overlooked, anyway - would join Lotte - or Loren, they corrected themselves.

The next morning the sisters reported that Doloreen was ill, and the day after that no better. On the third day the sisters begged to send her to her mother, a noted herbalist, and her father consented. His son, in fact, had insisted, and what did he care, really, if the house had one less girl?

Within a week, the carriage returned with the news of Doloreen's death - and more to the point, a young man with a happy stride gave him the news in a mournful voice that ended with the phrase, "Imagine my sorrow to see her, sir, my sister."

"Sister," the king said thoughtfully. "So your mother re-wed?"

"Ah no sir, never. She said her happiness was complete as long as she could keep one of her children by her side, and that was me. It is only by this carriage and my sister's death that I learned how to find my father. Sir, my name is Nicholas." He bowed, his hand nearly touching the floor.

"Another son!" the old man cried in wonder. "How awful these women are and what a good thing I didn't kill them all. Come closer, let me look at you." He held him and searched him with his eyes. "Yes, the face says it all. So like your sister, you could be twins! Though she wasn't quite so tall, of course, and her eyes were blue -"

"Her eyes were brown."

"No doubt that was the illness. Come, let's not quarrel over trifles the first time we meet. You have a brother, you know, a younger brother."

"And sisters, I understand."

"That too," the father agreed, and took him off to meet Loren. "Two sons," their father said, marveling.

"Who knows," Nicholas said, winking to Loren. "Who knows - there may be more."

"I will have to change my will. It will all go, of course, to the first born son." He waved his hand around the estate.

"That's right," Loren said, startled. He looked at Nicholas, who grinned to himself, his eyes wandering around the house and the grounds, his eyebrows arching. He took in enough air to make his chest swell. He wet his lips.

"What difference does it make?" Artemis asked Loren later on. "You or Nicholas - it's all the same."

"It's not the same," Loren answered. "He's not like me, I saw his eyes. He's greedy."

For Nicholas was quick to claim things, going around with his father and discussing changes. He wanted trees to come down so he had a better view from his window; he wanted a new stable built for horses, which he rode until they foamed. He had neighbors to dinner and foreigners came to tour the house, and he was invited to other estates for weekends and came back boasting of his popularity. And he intended to marry.

"Marry?" Artemis gasped.

"Oh only in name," he assured her. "Some pretty young thing without a clue in her head but with a good pedigree." He glanced at his shocked sisters. "What's the point if I don't marry?" he asked. "That was the plan, wasn't it? What's the point without it?"

"But," Bethamis said carefully, "if you marry and you die, the place goes to your wife. We'd be out on our ears."

"Oh don't worry," he said indifferently. "If I married without issue, the place would go to Loren."

At which Loren's teeth began to show, and a plan fell in place in his heart.

Nicholas ordered a party upon the water, with boats and lights and musicians and singers. People leaned over the edge of the boats and pointed below them, where other lights and dancers appeared.

"Reflections," Nicholas said lazily. "Just reflections. Look," he said, and tossed a stone into the water. Everything broke apart and his guests laughed.

Bethamis leaned over the side of a small boat, which she'd taken out herself, and she peered down below, where she could see that the rock had landed on a dancer, who was stumbling back inside the house. She rowed along the shoreline of the lake, keeping as much as she could to the shadows, trying to hear what her brother was saying.

"See that?" her brother said, pointing to a rocky area. "I intend to build a pavilion there, with gondolas and floating beds." He laughed and drank another draught of port, which he had grown to love and which his father spoiled him with. His voice was loud and booming; he plucked fish from the lake and pulled reeds from the shore, and then tossed them when he grew tired of them.

The party lasted for days, during which Artemis limped, during which Ellerence and Fiorence faced each other without remission, and the other sisters, too, chafed at being kept from the lake. Nicholas had the house overflowing with guests; they couldn't take the chance on being seen.

But the angriest was Loren, who saw how arrogant and profligate his brother was. Nicholas frequently forgot to introduce him, even, as if he were one of the sisters, and not a boy. Loren grew angrier and angrier, and went to his father.

"He's not your son, sir," he said. "I have seen him naked, and he has a tail, I've seen it, he's the devil himself. I'm sorry to grieve you."

"A tail!" the king said, astonished. He had heard of beings with tails, there were stories everywhere about it, and he sent for Nicholas at once. "Disrobe," he demanded. "I know what you are!"

Nicholas was alarmed. Disrobe and expose himself to be a woman after all? How had his father heard this? He cast his eyes around the room, which contained his father's courtiers and lawyers. "I am too modest," he said finally. "Raised as I was by women."

"Strip him," his father ordered, but Nicholas ran away and was gone.

The king turned his attention to Loren, who stood near him. "And you?" he asked. "What are you?" His eyes were sharp and unloving

"I am only your son," Loren said weakly, his heart pounding. He took a step closer to the door - a movement his father noted with an intelligent eye.

"You have the choice - leave without question now or be subject to the test," the king said.

And Loren fled.

"Call my daughters," the kind said, "however many there may be."

"Father," said Artemis, entering quickly, "father, we're here."

"I know who you are," their father said. "Known you since you were born, and only lately have I discovered the value of a girl grown at home. Never before has a king left his worth to a girl; it has ever been sons. But I am king, and I decree: from this time forward, it all goes to daughters, who shall rule it together. Sons are the very devil," he said.

When their father began to weaken from his final illness, the servants were released with gold coins filling their hands and the oldest girls went off to return as men and wed their sisters. A great ceremony was held, with tables of food and wine, and neighbors from high and low called in to rejoice. The sisters and their husband-brothers danced all night and into the next day. Occasionally, a tradesman would murmur, "That one there - do you see it? Bent over like that, like the eldest that was. Do you see it?" but people were inclined to fill their glasses up again and join the merrymaking. And after that, the blissful couples shut the door on all outsiders and ran their lives as husbands and wives for the sake of the servants, who all went to bed early and never saw the sisters stepping into the waters or returning at dawn, happily spent.

Deus Ex Machina

Caren Gussoff

Once upon a time, the Wicked Witch stood in an alleyway trying to remember how to slit her wrists. She'd read something about it just recently; whether one should slice horizontally or vertically. One direction just hurt really badly while the other would get her badly hurt.

The Wicked Witch doesn't want to kill herself. She needs to inflict pain on herself. And while this night is not the first time the Wicked Witch will hurt herself, she doesn't tremble any less, Wicked Witch or not.

There are conventions to fairy tales. Fairy tales usually begin: "Once upon a time," just like this one. They usually follow up with, "in a land far, far away," the connotation being of course lands of green and blue, mysterious and fragrant forests, lands of beauty. This fairy tale, however, breaks this convention. It takes place in Seattle's Capitol Hill neighborhood, in a pitch-black alley, running parallel to Bellevue Avenue, connecting John and Republican Street.

In addition, fairy tales do not tend to begin with the Wicked Witch at all, much less the Wicked Witch about to carve open her arm with a bit of aluminum siding.

While this fairy tale will continue to break some conventions, there are many others that it will adhere to, besides the beginning. Here is one: a fair maiden is involved. Here's a second convention: this fair maiden is in danger and someone, something, has to rescue her.

Here is, even, a third: the maiden has disregarded all counsels and cautions, and thusly, she's in terrible danger. This is typical of fair maidens - and princes and heroes and the children of peasants - someone, something, along the way warns them of some peril, and by such warning, they seem compelled to taunt that very peril. In this case, someone, somewhere, must have warned the Fair Maiden about the perils inherent in walking alone at night, the grievous harm of which the darkness is capable. Certainly, someone, something, must have instructed her against veering off the pathway, off the sidewalks, away from gentle glow of the streetlights. All of these warnings went predictably unheeded, and this night, the Fair Maiden teetered in her platform shoes at 3am in this alley.

The Wicked Witch stared down at her wrists, all the tendons and nerves and her pulse beating under the skin. Beside her, raccoons rummaged through dumpsters, headlights shone down the alley from passing cars, then blackness.

Here is how this fairy tale will break convention (again): the grievous harm of which the darkness is capable is not the Wicked Witch, standing poised with a shard of rusty metal. It could have been, as the Wicked Witch had been hunting fair maidens all evening, looking for one about her height, about her weight, about her coloring (*that one is too big*, the Wicked Witch thought, *and that one is too ethnic*, until she saw this particular fair maiden leaving the club alone, *but this one is just right*). No, the grievous harm of which the darkness is capable began hunting the Fair Maiden just a block or two back. He ducks in and out of sight, a shadow, the Ogre, the Giant, the Big Bad Wolf... The Fair Maiden hums along with the music in her earphones, carelessly swinging her little glittery purse between her fingers. She is totally unaware that she is being hunted, much less by both the Wicked Witch and the grievous harm of which the darkness is capable.

The darkness follows the maiden and the Wicked Witch follows him. He is stupidly single-minded, and the Wicked Witch could move up on him easily, if she could only remember which way to slash her wrists.

Here is another convention: the Wicked Witch does not save the maiden for any pure, altruistic motive, to protect her from the darkness because it is the darkness. She's a wicked witch, not an ambivalent witch. There may or may not be enough human left in her to feel something about the Fair Maiden's predicament, but the Wicked Witch spent all evening looking for someone that would be a good match for her, and she isn't about to let the Shadow, the Ogre, the Giant, the Big Bad Wolf feast on her hard work.

Outside of convention, but worthy of note: whatever the darkness has planned for the Fair Maiden is worse than the Wicked Witch. All the

Wicked Witch wants is the maiden's ID and health insurance card. And some lip balm, if she has any. The Wicked Witch's lips peel off like tissue. She chews them a lot. It's a nervous habit.

So, the Wicked Witch really has to step in here.

She knows this is a conundrum. If she saves the Fair Maiden and the Fair Maiden has any brains, she'll run away.

She looks at her wrist, tries to remember which way to slit. Vertical? Horizontal? Diagonal? One direction will draw blood, the other she'll bleed out. She decides to slash horizontally, across her forearm. The Wicked Witch wonders briefly when she'd last had a tetanus shot, but decision made, she counts to three and cuts. It stings, but just for a moment, then her magic rises up behind her eyes like a sneeze.

Enchantment, my ass, the witch has often said and thinks again at this moment. There is nothing enchanting about this. She commands: "Up, over the roof."

The Shadow, the Ogre, the Giant, the Big Bad Wolf is flung into the air, without grace, over the roof of the apartment building. He dangles there, kicking his feet.

Then she says: "Plummet to your death, motherfucker." There is a crash and a scream and it is over.

There is no time to savor the moment. Heat, blackness, nausea, release, collapse. *Fuck*, the Wicked Witch thinks as her head smacks the pavement and everything shuts off. *Fuck*.

The first time the Wicked Witch realized she was the Wicked Witch, it was because she'd eaten bad Tandoori chicken. It looked perfectly innocent and dazzlingly orange, but she woke up distended and sick. Being young, she popped a few Rolaids, smelled the clothes piled on the floor, and then rushed over to her day shift, cashiering at the mall Barnes and Noble.

Her good, kind parents told her she was special, but good, kind parents say that to children all the time, who aren't wicked witches. Her good, kind parents told the same thing to her sister.

The Wicked Witch liked working in a bookstore. She was poorly paid, but being young, she neither cared nor expected more. The only thing she didn't like about the bookstore was their regional manager, Mikhail.

When the food poisoning hit, it was vicious and instant. Her heart rate doubled and she tried to cling to the cash register. She fell. *Fuck*, she thought as her head smacked the carpet. *Fuck*.

Customers called for help and ambulance, and someone paged Mikhail on the intercom. The Wicked Witch vomited into a plastic bag. Then, Mikhail appeared behind the counter.

"What the hell is going on?" he hissed.

"She's sick," someone said.

"She isn't sick," he said, grabbing the Wicked Witch's arm, pulling her. "Get up. Get up now."

"I think I have food poisoning," The Wicked Witch said.

"What you have is a line of customers," he told her. "You can have food poisoning on your break."

Then it happened - not the magic, yet, but the diarrhea. The Wicked Witch shit her pants and it burned like acid. The customers stared at her.

And Mikhail began to laugh.

It was just a thought: *You asshole. You are an ASSHOLE.* She didn't mean to do it. She thought: *You are an asshole.*

And then, he was.

Someone screamed. It might have been the Wicked Witch. Where Mikhail had stood was a two-sided torso, two buttocks on either side, both with extremely prominent, red anuses.

An asshole.

And the Wicked Witch realized she was special.

The Wicked Witch doesn't know where she is. She feels sunlight, she smells bergamot. It's pleasant. Then she opens her eyes slowly against the brightness. Morning sounds through the window; busses, honking, birds... Things begin to focus. She is lying on a futon in a clean, white living room and her forearms are dead, heavy, and wrapped in gauze. She makes a fist and tears up from the pain.

She also realizes she is naked.

The Fair Maiden stands above her:

"Do you take sugar or cream with tea?" she asks the witch. She holds a cup and saucer. "Earl Grey."

The Wicked Witch doesn't know what is going on, so she tries not to sound too wicked:

"Both," she answers. "Lots of both."

"I washed your pants and stuff," the Fair Maiden says. "But I threw out your shirt. It was all bloody." She places a faded blue t-shirt on the arm of the futon. "You can have this one. You'll have to sit up. Do it slowly. You're probably hurting badly."

The Wicked Witch's head is tender where it struck the concrete. She turns away and pulls on the shirt. The Fair Maiden looks at the cuts, marks, scars on the Wicked Witch's body as she dresses.

The Fair Maiden and the Wicked Witch look almost nothing alike in the light, but the Wicked Witch still thinks she could pass with a little doing. Then she could go to a real doctor after she hurt herself. It wasn't the Wicked Witch's fault that the only time she could do magic was when she was hurt, but her health plan had dropped her long ago and she was living scared.

The Fair Maiden unfolds an old tin tray over the witch's lap, and serves her a cup and a plate of cinnamon toast. Her arms are thin, translucent and damp. They remind the Wicked Witch of raw fish filets. *I could pass for her*, the witch thinks, *but maybe just barely.*

"How are you feeling?" the maiden asks.

"I don't know yet," the witch answers.

"Eat something," the maiden says. "Last night..." she starts, then stops. She watches the witch try to drink her tea with aching wrists.

"Didn't anyone warn you about walking home alone at night?" the witch asks, looking at her. "In an alley?"

The maiden doesn't answer. Instead she says, "Let me help." She blows at the steam, puts the cup to the witch's lips. She holds the toast out for the witch to nibble, but leans back, like she is feeding a wild animal.

"It's lovely," the witch says. "Thank you."

"Thank *you*," the Fair Maiden says. "You saved my life." She twists her yellow hair into a nervous, flimsy knot.

The witch eats her toast and sips her tea: it has a strange, but definite curative effect. Her wrists hurt less. She can hold the cup with only a little tremble and almost no twinge. "The last thing I remember is passing out."

"You lost an awful lot of blood," the Fair Maiden says. "But look." She begins to unwrap the bandages around the Wicked Witch's wrists.

The cuts are angry, but sewn with tidy little stitches.

"Did you do this?" the witch asks.

"My real mother taught me embroidery before she died." The maiden looks at her wrists. "That's called the herringbone stitch."

The witch nods, admiring the handiwork. "It's lovely."

"You think?"

"Yes."

"Really?"

"Definitely," the witch says.

"Thank you," the Fair Maiden says. "My stepmother always said I had no talent for it. Or anything else, for that matter."

Here is another convention: an unkind stepparent raised the motherless fair maiden. We can assume her father was meek and compliant, a peasant, a sheepherder, or maybe a bank clerk.

As the Fair Maiden and the Wicked Witch drinks tea, the witch's wrists hurts less and less.

"It's so nice to have company," the Fair Maiden says. "This apartment's lonely. Like I'm stuck in a tower or something."

"How did I get here?" the witch asks, draining her fourth cup. She no longer feels any pain.

"I carried you," the maiden says. "I'm stronger than I look." The Fair Maiden makes a muscle. The witch squeezes the maiden's bicep. It feels like two apples under her skin. It's impressive. The witch says so and the maiden smiles. She is relaxed and happy.

"So," the Fair Maiden says. "How did you throw that guy over that building?"

The Wicked Witch tries to think of a good lie. Nothing comes to mind.

The Fair Maiden waits for the witch's answer.

"I'm the Wicked Witch," she says.

After the Barnes and Noble incident, the Wicked Witch tried for weeks to do magic again. She squinted at objects and thought as hard as she could. Nothing changed into anything else and the only objects that moved were the ones she threw against the wall.

One day the Wicked Witch spent the day squinting at her sister.

"What are you staring at?" her sister asked.

"Nothing at all," the witch answered and continued to squint.

"Stop it," her sister hissed.

The witch just squinted.

"Mom and Dad just feel sorry for you. They think you're crazy," her sister said. "Just quit it already."

"I'm the Wicked Witch," the witch said.

"You're crazy," her sister answered. "You're not a witch." She reached over and pinched her. "Quit staring at me."

"Ow," the witch said. "I am a wicked witch. You're just being mean and catty."

"Whatever," her sister said, and pinched her again. Then she imitated the Wicked Witch: "You're just being mean and catty."

"Stop it," the witch said. "I mean it."

"You're not a witch. You're a loser." Her sister stood up and shoved her.

"Shut up," the witch said, pushing back. "You never shut up."

"It's true. You're no witch. You're a loser," her sister said, and jumped on the witch, wrestling her to the ground.

Part of this was sisterly. These two sisters had a history of rolling around like puppies, nipping at one another. They had unresolved issues, like all sisters do.

But the witch's sister pinned her on this day, pushed the witch's arm behind her back, and sat down.

"You're not the Wicked Witch." She said, tugging the witch's arm. "Say it."

The Wicked Witch wriggled to get free, but her sister pulled her arm tighter.

"Say it."

"No," she said. The Wicked Witch was exhausted and went limp under her sister, but her she just pulled and pulled. *Shut up. Let me go, you bitch*, thought the Witch. *You fucking bitch.*

And then she was. And the witch was free. Her sister leapt off her and onto the sofa, barking. Her tail thumping the cushions.

Then the Wicked Witch understood.

Here are other conventions: magic is literal. And it carries a price.

The dryer buzzes, and the Fair Maiden retrieves the Wicked Witch's jeans, underwear, and socks. They are warm and have the fresh, chemical smell of dryer sheets.

As the Wicked Witch buttons her fly, the maiden says:

"You don't seem like a Wicked Witch. You don't look like one, either."

"What do Wicked Witches look like?" she asks, lacing up a boot.

"Not like you," the Fair Maiden says. "You're kind of pretty." Then a pause, and, "aside from, maybe, the scars."

"Well," the Wicked Witch says, looking under the futon for the other boot. "I am."

"Maybe you're not wicked."

Dressed, she faces the Fair Maiden. "All witches are wicked," the Wicked Witch says. "Haven't you read any fairy tales?"

"Of course," the Fair Maiden answers, defensively. "There's plenty of stories with good witches."

"Ok. Name one."

She thinks for a second. "Glinda. Glinda was a good witch."

"Not really," the witch says. "She didn't do much to help Dorothy, did she? In fact, Glinda gave her the shoes that began the whole thing with the Witch of the West, then sat back and watched the shit rain down."

The Fair Maiden winces at that. "The Little Mermaid?"

The Wicked Witch shakes her head. "No way. The Sea Witch took the mermaid's voice and gave her legs that were torture to stand on. And," she adds, ". . .remember, the mermaid had only thirty days to land the prince or she would become, what, sea foam?"

"Ok, Cinderella."

"That was a fairy godmother. Fairy godmothers are very different from Wicked Witches."

"Like how?" the Fair Maiden asks.

"Well," the witch says. "Fairy godmothers are the ultimate deus ex machina."

The maiden blinks at her.

Here is yet another convention: the Fair Maiden is not a literature major.

"A deus ex machina is actually from Greek tragedy," the Wicked Witch explains. "It's like when there's nothing else that can save the Fair Maiden, the Fairy Godmother appears."

"Uh-huh," the Fair Maiden nods. She looks expectant, excited. "And then?"

"And whether or not she has any place in the story, she fixes things for the maiden, resolving the plot."

"Then what?" the maiden asks.

"I don't know," the witch says. "The story is over."

"Well," the maiden starts, pointing her finger. "Isn't that what you did, like a fairy godmother? How you acted? Last night? You aren't wicked at all." She looks pleased.

"No, no, no," the witch says. "That's not exactly what happened."

"It was exactly what happened," the Fair Maiden insists. She folds her hands in her lap like a child trying to behave. "I was in trouble and you were the deuce ex macarina. You saved me. And that's not wicked."

"Deus ex machina," the witch says. "But, I killed that guy. I can only do wicked magic."

"But, you saved my life."

"I did." The witch nods. "But, why do you think I was there? In that alley? I was following you."

The Fair Maiden isn't listening. "What happens to the Fairy Godmother in-between stories, do you think?"

"I can only do wicked things," the witch says again. "I hurt myself and do wicked magic. That's how it works."

"That's how it works," the Fair Maiden repeats. She is thinking of something else. "What happens to the Fairy Godmother in-between stories, do you think?" she asks again.

The Wicked Witch is done with this conversation. She wills the maiden to go into the other room so she can steal her wallet and leave. "I don't know," she says.

"Do you suppose the Fairy Godmother waits around until the Fair Maiden needs her again?" she asks.

The Wicked Witch doesn't answer.

But then the Fair Maiden pats her leg. "Why don't I make us up some more tea?"

The day the Wicked Witch turned her own sister into a dog, she said to her sister sadly: "I told you I was a wicked witch."

Her sister barked and howled. She tore into the upholstery.

"I didn't mean to do it. Do you understand?" the Wicked Witch asked.

Her sister seemed to; she slumped onto the cushions but wagged her tail a few times.

"I understand how it works now. Listen to me carefully. You're going to have to attack me," the Wicked Witch said.

Her sister's tail thumped the sofa with a hollow noise.

"I can only do magic if I'm hurt," the Wicked Witch said. "You're going to have to attack me."

Her sister didn't move. The Wicked Witch grabbed the dog's head and held it, looked for her sister inside the strange eyes.

"God damn it," she said. "Bite me."

The dog wriggled from her grasp and jumped from the couch to the bookshelf, then ran into their parents' bedroom, hiding under the bed. The Wicked Witch followed her and banged on the mattress.

"Come out here. Hurt me."

Enchantment, my ass. There is nothing enchanting about this, she thought, head down, full speed into the bricks around the fireplace. Blood filled her eyes. Someone screamed. *Undo this,* she thought.

Here is another convention: wicked witches can only do wicked things. It didn't work.

Her sister licked the blood from her face. The Wicked Witch patted and stroked her until she fell asleep.

"How are you feeling?" the Fair Maiden asks.

"Better," the Wicked Witch says. "Hungry."

"Good," the Fair Maiden says. "Do you like tuna fish? I have some tuna fish. I can make us tuna fish sandwiches." She goes into the kitchen. "This is great," she calls. "I like taking care of you. It makes me feel good." She waits for an answer.

"Yeah," the Wicked Witch says.

"It's so lonely here, so isolated."

"Yeah," the Wicked Witch says again.

"I love to cook," the Fair Maiden calls again. "My stepmother always said I had no talent for it."

There's banging and busy noises from the kitchen. This is the cue she's been waiting for.

The Fair Maiden's keys and wallet are, predictably, in a carved wooden bowl on a stand in the hallway. The Wicked Witch takes the wallet and turns to leave.

But she feels dizzy. Maybe she stood up too quickly. *I lost a lot of blood,* the witch thinks. She feels weak and tired and full of air. She leans against the wall and slides down as the room starts to swivel.

The Fair Maiden stands above the Wicked Witch. It is hard for the witch to focus on her.

"How are you feeling?" she asks.

"Woozy," the Wicked Witch answers.

"Any pain?"

"None," the Wicked Witch says, holding onto the floor so she doesn't slide off. "None at all."

"No pain?" the Fair Maiden asks. "Good." She reaches for the Wicked Witch's hand and takes her wallet back. "That's the Xanax," the Fair Maiden says from far away. "In your tea."

The Wicked Witch can barely hear her.

"I ground them up," the Fair Maiden says. "Xanax, a fistful of Oxys, some Klonopin." Her voice echoes, like across a canyon. "You couldn't even taste them."

Here is the last convention: nothing is ever as it seems.

"You won't be going anywhere today, Fairy Godmother." The Fair Maiden pulls the Wicked Witch up and walks her back to the futon. She is stronger than she looks. Her muscles move like apples under the skin. "It's so nice to have company." She sits the Wicked Witch down. "I made us tuna fish sandwiches." She starts to unlace the Wicked Witch's boots. "We'll have some sandwiches now, and someday, I'll need your help again, Fairy Godmother." She takes a step back and watches the Wicked Witch slide off onto the floor.

Fuck, the Wicked Witch thinks, as her head thumps into the leg of the futon. *Fuck*.

Bluebeard's Child

Alison Littlewood

There were so many hearts on my bedroom wall, all tied around with gold and silver bows. Small candy pink ones; deep blood red ones; fat crimson ones; others with chambers and ventricles and valves, gleaming in shades of ruby. So many. I could remember when it was just one. My father drew it on the wall, and then carefully stenciled it in with a brush. The white plaster showed through the pink, as if it was already fading away. He glanced at me as he left the room, but never really caught my eye.

That one was for my mother. My real mother, I mean, before the others came.

The hearts glowed. There was a rhythm to it, a pulse all their own. Sometimes I could hear them beating; the throb of it found its way into my dreams. I could still see them when my eyes were closed, and it was like sunlight shining through my eyelids. I stayed awake sometimes and listened, feeling the beat like a warm red tide, flowing in and out.

Dad shook cornflakes into two bowls and poured in the milk. There hadn't been a housekeeper in a long while, before I was born. That time was lost, along with so many memories. Sometimes I thought he'd even forgotten my mother, the first of them, the queen of them all; then I would see a certain expression in his eyes - especially when he looked at me - and I knew that he had not.

"Where's Mum?" I asked now. I didn't mean my real mother, but the new one; she was usually up before us, toasting bread and boiling eggs. He passed me a bowl.

"She left."

"Left? What do you mean? She never said she was going anywhere. She didn't say goodbye."

She wasn't my real Mum, but I had liked her more than the others. She had been nice to me.

"She left," he insisted. "They all leave." He stared at the polished mahogany table and spooned cornflakes into his mouth. Milk dripped onto his beard and shone there, white drops against the bristles that were more grey these days than blue.

I believed what Dad had told me, and the next time I had a mother I followed her around like a puppy. I brought her flowers from the rose garden. I read my books to her until she was sick of them. I went with her to the shops, all around the grounds and down to the village. I tied ribbons in her hair, as if I could lash her to me somehow. It didn't make any difference; after a time, she left anyway.

In those days, Dad would comfort me. He'd pat his lap and I'd climb into it. Sometimes he'd get his pipe and take deep drags, making the bowl glow orange. I'd tamp it for him, pushing the greasy substance down before he set a match to it.

I'd snuggle in and he'd breathe soft blue smoke into my face, calming me to sleep.

The new mother was pale and sort of shiny. She had platinum blonde hair and a big smile. Her lips were painted shell pink and her eyes were blue and wide. She wore a pink tank top, tight black jeans, and a glittery chain-link belt slung low around her hips. She wasn't much older than me. I scowled.

"Meet your new mother," Dad said.

"Hello, sweetheart. I'm thrilled to meet you. I know we'll be great friends."

I snorted and walked out of the room. I gave her a week; just another fool who thought she was secure for life, who thought she had it made by snagging my dad.

I lay down on my bed and stared into the canopy. I wished I could remember what my real mother looked like. I thought she must have been dark, like me; my hair is almost black and starting to curl. I couldn't tell what sort of shape she might have been, yet. My figure was just forming, my breasts starting to push at my blouse. I needed a bra, but didn't know who to ask about it. Maybe I should ask my new mother; I bet she'd be the more embarrassed.

Through the door, I could hear the usual speech. Here is the kitchen, here the pantries, here the library. Here is the oven and here is the sink. And then: here are your keys. Yours, now. Lady of the manor, blah blah blah. Oh, yes - just one other thing. That black key - for the little door in the attic - yes, that one. My study: it's mine. You can't go in. You mustn't. Promise me.

Did he ever really believe that she wouldn't look, that this one was for keeps?

I heard them later. They played some sort of wailing music, really loud, on and on. I peeked into their room.

They were dancing. She snaked her hips against his round belly, which he waggled at her. He'd dyed his beard again and it was a bright vivid blue. She'd put blue streaks in her hair to match, as if he had rubbed off on her.

They fell back onto the bed, laughing, their eyes glazed. He leaned over and picked up the pipe, took a hit, then passed it to her. She raised her eyebrows but took it anyway. I could smell the sharp herbal tang from the doorway. They tilted their heads to the ceiling and breathed out blue smoke. They laughed.

The next day, her eyes were dull and her hair lank. She grunted something at me, pointed towards a pot of coffee. She cradled a mug of it in her hands. Her face looked darker without the make-up, but her lips were still pale. She looked older, like her skin was drying out.

It'd be the heavier stuff soon. It was happening quickly this time. He'd drag her in, wear her down, get her to smoke, drink, inject. He'd get her to wear the leather he kept under the floorboards; the things he thought I didn't know about. After that, the whip. He'd make her crawl, tell her when she could eat or drink or shit. When he thought I was out, he'd give her the collar with the silver spikes and drag her about on a lead.

Why did he want her to stop at the key? Why that? It was as if he needed her to keep a little piece of herself that was good and pure, a little room locked up in her heart that he could not touch.

I was nine, I think, when I found out what was in the study. Or at least, what happened when my mothers found out what was in it.

I woke up late one night. The hearts on my wall were unusually quiet and still. There was something poised about them that I could sense, and it was cold, although it was summer.

There came a heavy dragging sound from the corridor. I didn't move, only listened. After a moment, I heard it again.

I bit my lip. Then, as the sound passed away down the hall, curiosity took over. It was like something gleaming, like something new. I padded to my door. As I did, I felt something at my back and turned. Behind me, one after the next, the hearts began to glow. They looked like eyes opening one by one.

I opened the door.

The corridor appeared grey in the dim light that crept through the curtains, but halfway along it, a darker shape hunched. It was bent over something on the floor. It leaned in and there was a sucking sound, then a licking sound, and then a moan.

I stepped into the hall.

The thing was wearing my father's vest. Grey hair tumbled down its back. It hulked in the dark, plucking at what lay on the floor, dragging it along. Suddenly, like a door opening in my mind, I knew what it was. I let the real door fall closed behind me with a bang and the thing turned. I saw its eyes first, shining coldly in the darkness. Then its beard caught a beam of moonlight; it shone a blue that was a little too bright. Below his lips the bristles were dark and matted damply together; for a moment they shone crimson.

It held out its hands towards me. Something dripped onto the carpet from the thing it held between his fingers; something soft and pliant and wet.

My father let out a sob. "Please," he said. "Please."

I opened my mouth but no sound came out.

"She looked," he said. "I told her. It's mine, my study. I told her not to look."

I stared.

"She wasn't worthy of you," he said.

The next day, he came into my room. He found a space on the wall and began to paint. This time the heart had substance, solidity, depth. Torn veins surrounded it like hair blowing in the wind. It ranged from the palest pink to the deepest purple. He never looked at me, all the time he did it.

Their friends would come to the door, or fathers, or sisters, trying to find out where their girls had gone. Dad threatened to set the dogs on them. Sometimes he'd say she left with his candlesticks, or tankards, or his watch. Sometimes he said she slept with someone else and had finally run away with them, the gardener or the handyman, though we had neither of those things.

After the time I saw him in the hallway (those hands; those eyes), he answered the door, but then just stood and stared. I could hear someone asking questions about why their daughter hadn't contacted them, but my father didn't answer. His bulk almost filled the doorway but I squeezed my head under his arm.

The man on the steps was old and thin and grey. His hair clung to his head in tufts. His eyes looked red, as if he'd been rubbing them.

I felt my father's gaze fall to the back of my head.

"We don't know why she left," I said. "She didn't tell us. She didn't even say goodbye, did she, Dad?" I twisted my neck to glance up at him. Slowly, he shook his head.

"I think I did something wrong." Tears sprang into my eyes. "I think it was because of me."

I looked at the old man, but he was already backing away.

I told him not to take a wife again and he didn't, not for a long time. I said it was better, just the two of us. We'd drink lemonade and play games and go for walks. It lasted for ages.

Then one day I came home and found her there, a new one. Her face was smooth and her eyes were blank.

"Sweetheart," he said, forcing a jolly tone, "meet your new mother."

I stared at her. After a long moment I went and buried my face in his chest, holding on to him, showing her that he was mine. I was glad when she went. There's nothing left of her now, just a grey smudge on my wall where her heart used to be.

The latest mother, the shiny pink one, came into my room and sat down on my bed.

"This is pretty," she said. Then she saw the hearts - really saw them - and she started. She shook herself, then looked back at me. "I thought we could go shopping. I noticed - well, that some of your clothes are a bit small. We could pick out something new."

She had drawn rings around her eyes with something black and chalky. Her lips were thin and shiny and her cheeks had spots of pink blusher on them.

"You're growing up," she said. "I thought you might like more grown-up things."

I shrugged. Then I said, "I like your belt." It was the silver chain-link one she'd been wearing when she arrived.

She slipped it off and handed it to me. "You can have it."

Maybe she was all right, after all. Maybe she wouldn't look; she might be the one that was for keeps. Perhaps she was really going to be my mother.

As she turned to leave, I had an idea.

"You know that door in the attic?" I said.

Dad came into my room early in the morning. I sat up in bed and rubbed sleep from my eyes. The hearts on the wall were silent. He walked over to it, found a blank space and bent down.

"Dad?"

He was scrawling something, hard, into the wall, a pearlescent pink scribble. He added two simple child's-drawing arches at the top, then a point at the bottom. It was the colour of the inside of seashells, and it whispered as he scraped with the crayon. Then I saw what he was drawing it with - her lipstick - and I put my hand over my mouth.

When he'd finished he put a hand on my shoulder and pushed me aside. "I'll get another," he said, as he walked from the room.

I stared at myself in the mirror. My hair was in bunches and I saw how ridiculous it looked. I pulled it free, not caring how it hurt. My face, framed in straight brown lines, looked older at once.

My t-shirt was small and my skirt too short. It was yellow, with crisscross stripes, and my thighs were squeezed into it.

I pulled open my drawers. More t-shirts, candy-shaded, with cartoon characters on the front. Skirts in all colours, shorts in yellow and orange. I threw them all onto the floor.

I heard the hearts, each adding to the rhythm they made one by one, as though they were waking. The rhythm wouldn't stop now it had begun; it was the blood-red sound of something set in motion.

From my wardrobe I threw out plastic shoes, furry slippers like teddy bears, a pair of boots shaped like frogs. From the bottom I pulled out a battered suitcase. I clicked it open and found something I had forgotten ever existed.

It was a photograph, old and creased. It showed a serious looking woman, her hair almost black and falling over her shoulders in curls. She had a pale, clear forehead, a straight nose, a wide mouth. I looked in the mirror again. It was me; or rather, it was like me, someone I could possibly be one day. I slipped it into the pocket of my skirt.

"Are you there?" It was Dad's voice.

I looked around. My room was a wreck. I shut the wardrobe door on the suitcase and kicked it closed. I took a deep breath.

"Hello?" He was outside the door.

"I'm busy."

"I wanted to talk to you."

"I'm not dressed."

There was a pause.

"I have a present for you. To make up for - well, things. I thought you might like it. You're ready."

I didn't speak.

"I'll leave it here, outside your door. Only - you know the rules."

I waited until his footsteps had faded away before I looked.

Lying on the carpet was a large, spindly bunch of keys. There were keys for everything: all shapes and sizes, some rusted, some bright silver, some made of brass. Some had big, uneven teeth. Some had wobbly edges while others were shiny silver with grooves along the side. Only one of them was black.

My father's bedroom was dark, the heavy red curtains still drawn, but it was empty. I slipped in and closed the door behind me. I thought about locking it, but I wasn't going to be long. I only wanted to look.

The wardrobe was sleek and black and set into the wall. I ran my hand over the surface until I found the keyhole, then flipped through the keys. I tried one but it wouldn't work. Then another. The third turned easily under my hand.

The door slid open with a loud grinding noise. I paused but nobody came. There were shirts, jackets, trousers. His clothes. As quietly as I could, I tried the other door.

I had expected it to be empty, but they were still here, her things: the black jeans that had made her legs look so long, a tight red dress, sequined tops that shone even in the dim light.

I pulled out a black skirt and a silky grey top. Elegant, I thought. They looked elegant: a woman's clothes.

I tried the box on her dressing table. It was full of powders, paints, brushes. I sat down.

The suitcase was still in my wardrobe. I thought of it as I went around the house, locking doors that had been unlocked, unlocking doors that were locked. I found a cellar I had never seen before, full of musty-smelling ampoules and old glass bottles stoppered by cobwebs. There was a whole network of pantries beyond the kitchen. It was as if I were seeing the house anew, and my place within it.

Lots of people envied my father. He had lands from here to the mountains and down to the sea. He had a garden it took all day to walk around. He had more rooms than I had ever counted. For the first time, I realised people must envy me.

I went back to my room and sat down on the bed. I ran my hand over my silky top. Around me were the pink hearts, red hearts, purple and ruby hearts. There was a faint beating sound, as though it came from a room far away. There was a soft hushing, too, as if they were whispering to each other. I didn't look at them.

I held a key in my hand. Only one key, a small key, a black key. The one place I hadn't looked.

I'm his daughter, I thought. *It's different.*

The hearts whispered louder. As the beat grew, echoing through my body, I got to my feet.

The attic was past the old, empty servants' quarters, along the gallery. I moved quickly, though there was no need to hurry. He would be downstairs somewhere, or out in the garden. And what if he knew? I was the lady of the house. It was mine too.

The gallery ended in a narrow wooden staircase. The staircase ended in a small black door.

I glanced around, although I had already made up my mind. I pushed the key into the lock. The suitcase was still there, I reminded myself, and I turned the key.

The door creaked as I pushed. As it opened the light fell across the floor, glinting upon row upon row of jars, throwing back shades of ruby, and purple, and pink, and red. As the door opened wider a rank meat smell came out, followed by rustling, the sound of something moving across the floor.

There was a shape in there. It was like my father, and yet unlike him too. It had his face and hands and eyes; and yet it had a hunger too, and a coldness, and a grin that could stretch wide enough to swallow the world. As I looked, the shape reached for me with its long, long hands, and it began to laugh.

"I'll get another," it said.

Sickly Sweet

Ephiny Gale

One fine day behind the mill, my father chops off my hands.
He does it with an axe, on a tree stump. He says the devil is coming. That he promised the devil my hands, in exchange for his life.

I do not believe in the devil. My father has been hearing voices for some time.

There is a lot of blood, but no pain. I have heard stories of soldiers, those with their arms sliced off who screamed, not because it hurt but because of the shock of seeing their shoulder and limb separated. The pain is so great that your body snuffs it out. For a little while.

I yell, too. I shriek. I clutch my bloody wrists to my dress and back away, sprinting, stumbling into the forest. My father does not pursue me; the devil can find me anywhere, if I am still wanted.

I curl up at the base of a tree, nesting in its roots. The pain arrives like a delayed traveller. I think I am going to die.

I do not die. I wake with my wrists attached to my dress, the brown of dried blood mixing with the brown of the fabric. They stick, knitting with the cotton, where I'd pressed them tightly to stem the blood flow.

I shift my torso and feel the dried blood cracking on my stomach.

My wrists are swollen, ballooning, fiery things, far more vicious than the worst burn I have experienced. I am loath to upset them further. With effort, I push myself up the tree trunk by my feet, and the bark scrapes sharp against my back.

I begin to walk.

It is a long walk. Several seasons change. My wrists heal, as much could be expected, turning into knots of scar like the knots on an old tree. I take pleasure in small, animalistic activities; biting into a sun-warmed peach and letting the juice run down my chin, diving to the muddy bottom of a river and propelling myself up with jack-knifed legs.

In spring, blood appears between my legs and again, I think I will die.

I do not die.

Later, it comes again, many times.

I don't die then, either.

In the heart of the second autumn, I stumble through a pile of leaves into a clearing. Low, golden sunshine illuminates the charred ruins of a house. And within the ruins, beneath the powdery ash and grey, brittle wood and occasional brick, something glints, metallic and inviting.

I step gingerly over the rubble and peer at my treasure. Nestled safely and perfectly, impossibly intact: a pair of silver hands.

I drop to my knees.

With infinite care and precision, I wipe each hand along my tired, tattered brown dress until the dirt disappears. The joints in the fingers swing back and forth, more or less like a real hand. There is no rust, no squeaking. When I slip the metal cuffs of the hands onto my wrists, they fit exactly, as if they have been made especially for me.

I have avoided people, for the most part, since my hands were stolen. Now I feel buoyed, lighter; I jog to the nearest town, contented simply by the burbles of conversation, the currents of humans flowing past each other in the shopping district.

So many man-made shapes and colours make my head spin. I wander past shops selling thick, salty-looking ink in glass flasks; stalls with glazed, salmon-coloured hams suspended from ceilings; doorways with silk jackets, the colour of morning dew and encrusted with dozens of precious stones.

"You!" A booming masculine voice hits me in the ear, not three paces away. I stop, glance around. He is looking directly at me. "Are you going to pay for that?"

My heart hammers in my chest. I look down, and see a large bag of flour, and a slightly smaller bag of brown sugar clutched in a silver hand.

Adrenaline pours into my veins. I am a criminal. I am mortified. I feel about to faint.

The other silver hand curls, reaches into my pocket and pulls out three gold coins. I stare. I have never had any money of my own, and this does not feel like mine, either.

The merchant huffs and holds out his own sweaty hand.

"I'm sorry," I whisper in my rusty voice, dropping the coins down into his palm. He nods like he doesn't believe me.

I take off along the cobblestones, down the streets into the forest. I make a nest in some tree roots, place down the flour and the sweet, caramel-smelling sugar and examine the silver hands.

They do not feel like my hands. I cannot move the fingers of my own free will, and yet they have moved. They have curled and grasped and extended without my consent.

I shake, pressing one hand between my knees, pulling back my arm to wrench the hand away like an unwanted glove. I grunt. But no matter how hard I press or pull, the hand stays a part of me. It slips out between my knees like it's melded to my skin.

I try again with the other hand to no avail.

When my tears fall, I let them fall on the silver, and I wish fervently that it will rust.

I take the flour and sugar to the clearing, to the ruins of the house. I remember a formation of low bricks, sticking out amongst the wreckage, which gave me the impression of an oven.

I search through the rubble for any other bricks, stacking them together, interlocking them with the remnants of the old oven. The silver hands grab everything easily, nimbly, more skilled at construction than I was ever with my own flesh. They are clever, these hands. They fit the oven together like an expert puzzle.

At the end, the finished oven sits there, red and swollen, and reminds me of my bleeding wrists.

I am ashamed to say I go back to the town. More than anything - food, love, justice - I feel I am starved of opportunity.

The hands have made me ravenous.

From the stalls they pick jars of cinnamon, towers of sea salt, butter wrapped in golden cloth, cloves and ginger in wooden boxes, eggs in woven baskets... And each time, a silver hand dips into my pocket and fishes out gold coins. I never see the coins fall in, but I learn to recognise the slight weight in my pocket, the almost imperceptible clink as the silver hands pilfer someone else's pockets or bags.

I return to the clearing laden with parcels.

I sit in the rubble and press the cinnamon and ginger to my nose, inhaling deeply. I rub the exquisite, perfectly smooth egg against my arms, face and neck. I tip a little of the salt onto my tongue and revel in it, my eyes sliding shut.

And then the hands really get to work.

Deep in the woods, though not that deep, stands a house made entirely of gingerbread. The walls and roof and floors are gingerbread, as are the chimney and single iced door. If you licked the windows you would know them to be sugar, and if you bit into the windowsills you would know them to be thick, fresh marzipan.

The house does not age, or rot, or melt. Encrusted in the gingerbread are hard candies of every flavour and colour, liquorices which seem to sparkle, candy-covered chocolates in the shapes of hearts and stars and clovers.

Inside the house there lives a woman, though she was only recently a girl. They say idle hands are the devil's work, but how fervently I wish mine would stop.

The silver hands are always moving, like mechanical spiders desperate to get out of the rain. Sometimes they clean and scrub and tidy. Sometimes they play over my body, prying open my mouth and feeling my tongue, the ridges of my teeth. Sometimes they crawl between my legs and play me like an instrument, running their intelligent fingers inside me and warming with my body heat.

Sometimes I don't mind.

Mostly, they like to cook. They like sugar. They like ever more elaborate desserts, which never seem to go off and pile in towers, gathering on most surfaces of the house and in ever-expanding nooks and crannies. They cook shelves and cupboards for more cooked treats.

They cook another room for the house.

Often, at night, I suffocate the hands beneath my mattress and feel them struggle, twisting, beneath my body weight. After a little while they give up. Alone, unmoving, quiet washes over me. Bliss.

There are usually scars from this ritual when the hands break free; long scratch marks across my torso, legs or back, one or two or five in a row, but they're always worth it.

And then, one day, a gap in my wall appears, and on the other side a chewing child.

They freeze when I open the door; a boy with his mouth stuffed with gingerbread, and a girl with her lips wrapped around my windowsill. They are short, sickly pale and bony, their wide blue eyes protruding too far out of their skulls. I suspect they're not much younger than I am.

SICKLY SWEET | 43

The boy swallows hastily, the girl detaches her lips.

"You must be very hungry," I say.

The girl smiles and digs her fingernails into her other arm. "We've walked for three days," she says, "with very little food, and are lost in these woods, and our parents can't feed us anymore."

A dozen competing emotions swim inside me like a school of fish.

Eventually, I say, "If you believe you shall starve if you don't come in... You may."

The children's faces relax with joy. A silver hand pushes the door fully open, and with barely restrained hunger, they dart inside.

I feed the children like they've never eaten in their lives.

I bring them sticky date puddings drenched in hot fudge; towered chocolate cakes with sparkling shards of sugary caramel, raspberry and mint strewn in three layers; macaroons in twelve different flavours; cupcakes containing huge chucks of cookie dough; scones with jams and the fluffiest creams and melted chocolates.

When they've eaten their fill, groaning with pleasure on my wooden benches, I make them a bed of marshmallows in the corner of my living room. They curl up on the soft, rubbery pillows and are asleep within minutes.

I clean for some time to delay my own sleep. The hands have been delighted all evening, practically dancing off my wrists, and the guilt eats me up like acid. I should send the children on their way after breakfast tomorrow.

Later, under my blankets, the hands do not want me to rest. They want to play.

I decide I won't put them under the mattress tonight, won't make them angry with the children in the house.

I will send the children away tomorrow.

I am still half asleep when a third hand appears on my shoulder. I pay it no more attention than my own breathing.

"Are you alright?" asks a female voice.

My eyes snap open. The girl's blonde hair, inches away, is almost iridescent white in such early dawn. Unaccustomed to either company or shame, I throw my arms to either side of me.

"You were making noises."

I try to control my breathing, try to restrict the bile rising up my throat. "Noises?" I whisper.

"Murmurs, mutterings in your sleep... You were having a nightmare?"

I consider the girl's open face. A small glob of melted marshmallow is stuck to the side of her forehead.

"Always," I say.

We pad through the front door and around to my back garden, little more than two fruit trees and a small hill of seeded soil. The girl stares at every fruit and every leaf, cataloguing and greedy.

I hold out my arms. "You're very welcome."

She falls to her knees before a dozen strawberries, shoveling them into her mouth with dazzling efficiency. I sit nearby, my hands drawing meaningless patterns in the damp dirt. In the end she leaves three on their stems, wiping the crimson juice from her lips. Her hunger seems to still.

I suspect it's rude to ask, but the children will be gone in a matter of mouthfuls. I ask, "Do you despise your parents, for letting you down?"

The girl's eyes widen. "Why would I despise them? They did their best."

"They almost killed you."

"They sent us away because they couldn't bear to see us starve before their eyes. I can't hate them for that." She picks a fat lemon from the tree and peels the skin with a combination of fingernails and teeth. "We aren't starving anymore, thanks to you."

She comes and sits next to me, too close; my hands may damage her. I scoot back. In the dull light I'm uncertain, but I think her face falls.

"It's not personal," I say. "I lost my hands a long time ago."

She studies the patterns on the ground. "They seem to work well enough."

"They're not..." I'm afraid, suddenly, that the hands can hear me. "They're not really mine." The last word morphs into a gasp as a sharp silver finger digs into the flesh of my side. A tiny darker patch appears on my brown dress.

Perhaps the hands can hear; perhaps they simply sense intention.

The girl is up on her feet. She hesitates for a moment, rocking back on her heels, and then kicks the offending hand away from my side. With her right knee, she pushes my shoulder to the ground and pins the hand with her left boot. It convulses like a dying spider.

My other hand is blessedly still.

The wind has been knocked out of me. I lie with my head in the dewy grass, staring up at the frightened girl. Her shin is warm along the side of my torso. I can't remember the last time I touched someone.

"Do you need bandages?" she asks. "Something else?"

I shake my head against the grass. "I don't think it's deep. It will heal like the others."

"Others?"

The hand stops its convulsions after one last spasm, but the girl doesn't move away.

"There's a town to the east of here," I say. "A bit less than half a day's walk away. You should head there. Take as much food as you want, I insist."

She doesn't respond. Instead, she looks over her shoulder at an empty wire cage. "Is that for meat?"

"Chickens," I confirm. "But years ago." I'm hit with old memories of the hands snapping their necks.

She nods. "Are we safe to go to breakfast?"

I take several moments considering the frozen hands. They are playacting, surely, but I suspect they'll behave until their next calculated moment of rebellion. "If we behave," I say. "Though they shan't like you leaving."

"I'm not planning to leave," says the girl.

Breakfast passes in relative silence. At one point the boy reaches over and scratches the marshmallow off the girl's forehead. She smiles at him and crinkles her nose, and I feel a stab of jealousy for that kind of easy companionship. This morning, the hands have refused me any liquid but melted chocolate in a mug. I take tiny sips; sickly sweet.

With a couple of short, insistent gestures the girl directs the boy to my back garden. She follows, announcing she'll be back in a minute, and either I believe her or the silver hands do, because they make no move to cease scratching patterns into the wooden sides of my mug.

The girl does return shortly, without her brother but with a strange sort of smile. She tosses a second lemon in the air between alternating palms. "We should do it," she says. "What you were talking about in your sleep."

I feel instantly naked.

"We should eat the boy," she says. "Cook him."

The only sound is the lemon thumping in her hands.

She presses on: "I mean, not even chicken for years. You must be starved for meat. I've locked him in the cage." She points needlessly to the garden. "Go and see."

I hear the blood beating in my ears. I step outside; the cage has not moved. The boy is curled against the far corner, one blue eye open and fixed warily on me.

I take another step and he cries out. I am speechless.

"Not any closer!" he yells. "I know what those hands can do!"

I hold them up, clear in front of me. The silver fingers wriggle.

"You put them away!"

The venom in his voice makes my throat constrict. I tuck my hands tight behind my back, which is the best I can do. I venture another step.

Like a well-practiced magic trick, he reveals a rusty key - the key to the cage - and winks. It disappears again.

I take out the silver hands.

"Are you going to eat me?"

I realise with relief that the hands can't reach him while he's caged.

"Not now," I say, to buy some time. "I have to fatten you up first.

You're so thin; it would hardly be worth cooking you now."

His tears come right on cue, and when I return inside to his sister, she's sitting cross-legged on my dining table and squeezing lemon juice onto her tongue.

"Do you have an axe?"

My hands pause in the middle of kneading lemon-scented cookie dough. "No," I tell her, and the hands start up again.

"How do you chop firewood, then?"

"No firewood." I push a lock of hair out of my face with my shoulder. "I use oil."

The girl's mouth cracks open.

"It never seems to run out," I confess, and find I can't meet her eyes any longer.

Her footsteps retreat towards the front door. "It's just - I've been looking at your knives. We'll need something hardier to chop up a boy. A cleaver? I'll go to the town you talked about. Be back just after nightfall if I leave now."

I nod, not entirely sure what I'm agreeing to. "There's some money in the cupboard to your left, the one with..."

The silver hands have raced across the table and are climbing up my torso, digging painfully into my flesh as they crawl. I try and wrench them away, but my arm muscles are weak from this angle and the fingers sink into my stomach and breasts too deep.

Within two seconds the cold metal is wrapped around my neck, still covered in traces of cookie dough.

The thumbs are pressed tight into my oesophagus. My lips open in a continuous gasp. I struggle, bashing the hands against the edge of the table, but they hold fast. My vision blurs.

The last thing I see is the girl, her arms prying at my wrists. She calls my name like she means it.

When I wake, it is surreal. Under any other circumstances I would freeze completely. At this very moment I am too wrung out to care.

I am lying on top of the bed, the woolen blanket scratching against my naked back. My arms are wrenched to either side of the mattress. The silver hands are out of sight, and tugging confirms that they are both tied securely under the bed.

The girl has removed my dress and is straddling my hips, wiping my cuts with a rag soaked in green liquid. The rag stings like being sliced up all over again.

Absinthe, then.

There are perhaps two dozen cuts staggered over my torso. The girl attends to one just next to my nipple and my chest shudders. She glances up, registers I'm awake and immediately averts her gaze.

"Apologies. There was…"

"You don't have to apologise." My voice comes out hoarse and scratchy, followed by a minor coughing fit.

The girl leaves to fetch a glass of water. As she goes, her thigh brushes over my hip. My mind feels ill and unanchored, like I've come down with a fever, but I don't think I have. Thoughts arrive as if through a fog.

Sipping is awkward, with her hand behind my head and the cup at my lips. I take tiny, restricted swallows and trails of water runs down the sides of my mouth. She wipes them aside with her thumb.

"What did you tie them up with?"

"I found rope in a kitchen cupboard," she says.

"It won't hold them for much longer. An hour or two, maybe. They'll slice through it. They've hollowed out chunks of my mattress."

Her face falls, her hand holding the cup shakes. A couple of drops escape, falling onto my skin and running down the cleft between my breasts. She turns away to gather her composure.

Three long, fresh scabs run down her forearm.

Eventually, she says, "Well, what else will hold them? Anything here?"

"Chains would," I say. "I have none. The mattress might for another hour, longer if they thought that wasn't going to be permanent."

She plays with her fingernails while she considers this. Glances under the bed, then climbs on and reclaims her position over my hips. "I was going to…" She leans forward, biting her lip and touches my elbows, making a sawing motion with her fingers. "But there's no time."

I nod. The axe. The cleaver. "How did you tie them up at all?"

"Oh. I wasn't planning to. But once you passed out, they went limp for a while. I don't think they want you dead." Her blue eyes bore into mine. "Really dead."

When she doesn't get a response, the girl picks up the rag and the absinthe again. "I know it seems a bit redundant. But may I?"

My mouth feels too dry. "Alright."

Her wipes with the rag are gentle and precise. She rests her other hand on my arm, my shoulder, my ribs for balance. Her skin feels twice as soft and warm as my own. Sometimes, she traces my many scars with an absent fingertip.

Despite myself, my tears start to fall.

She kisses them from the sides of my face, her lips like velvet. The light fabric of her dress grazes my stomach, my breasts, my nipples. My skin breaks out in goosebumps. My breath comes out in tiny sighs and shudders.

She kisses my forehead, my cheeks, my lips. I feel like I'm floating up out of my body, and the stinging fades to background noise. There is no mattress, no rope, no silver hands.

Then her own tears fall onto my collarbone.

"Is there anything we can do for you?" she whispers. "Anything at all?"

When the words finally come, my voice is cold and composed. Not quite my own.

"We have to cook the boy," I say.

Inside the oven, the fire blazes. Flames of a million different yellows and oranges lick at the bricks. The boy has been fed and watered. The girl has prepared the lemon-scented cookie dough for baking.

The hands are largely behaving themselves, almost humming in anticipation.

I will my pulse to slow and turn to the girl. "It's time."

She looks me straight in the eyes, so blatantly that I'm worried a silver finger will impale me. "Are you sure?"

"Yes. Check that the oven is hot enough, will you?"

She tugs open the oven door. The heat is noticeable even from here. The girl peers inside, the flames playing over her lovely face. "I don't know how to," she lies.

I blurt out the first curse I can think of. "Let me, then." I shuffle over and take her place, my heart inside my mouth.

I stick my head clear inside the oven. Farther than necessary. So close that the fire sparks in my hair and I can feel my face beginning to burn.

"It's ready," I call.

And she shoves me inside, where the world is white hot.

My last thoughts are a series of cluttered imaginings: that the girl and her brother run home, their arms full of candies and treasures and coins.

That they leave the remains of the gingerbread house behind them, a smoking pile of powdery ash.

That they arrive, safe, to loving parents.

And that somewhere, the devil appears to a father who bargains a daughter he forgets could be, behind his mill.

It's a small comfort. To know I'm not the only one.

And the silver hands don't burn at all.

Bunny's Lucky Slipper

Pat R Steiner

Carolyn Rosenbaum came across *Bunny's Lucky Slipper* while on her lunch break. The anonymously written book looked smaller than she remembered. Resting easily in her palm, its cloth board cover pulled away from the stitched pages. Half the cover's spine was missing. She rubbed her fingers against the scratchy hardened glue that bound the pages together and the few loose tickly-threads sticking out, then brought the book up to her nose and sniffed.

She had to have it, damaged or not.

Without a thought, she slipped *Bunny* into her coat pocket. Retracing her steps down the thrift store's dim aisle, she approached the elderly man behind the counter, nodded her head as he smiled at her and walked out the door while an old-fashioned bell rang above her head.

She wouldn't think of the book again until later that evening.

When she got to the rectory, Rabbi Liss asked her to stay late, wanting her to prepare for next week's audit. Carolyn assured him it wouldn't be a problem, and from one o'clock until six-fifteen she sat in the tiny office, seated behind her tiny desk while she stared at the wood-paneled walls. At six-sixteen, Liss poked his head inside and informed her that any remaining discrepancies in the temple books would have to wait until after Shabbat. He chuckled when he said this, winking a second later.

After saying her goodnights, Carolyn walked the four blocks home to her sub-floor apartment. Inside, she triple-locked the door and hung up her coat. Moving to the bathroom, she undressed, folded her clothes neatly, placed them inside the laundry basket and went to fill the tub. Minutes later, wine glass in hand, candles lit around her on the bathtub rim, she contemplated her options.

The Internal Revenue Service, unlike Rabbi Liss, wouldn't be fooled. She would go to prison. How much time? She hadn't a clue. She would become a family embarrassment though. She could hear her mother's denials, *Stealing from the Temple? Never. Not my daughter. Not my little bunny.*

"Yes, Mama, it's true." Her voice echoed off the bathroom tiles. "You gave birth to a felon. What do you think of that?"

The wine, when she gulped it, tasted bitter in her mouth and burned as it trickled down her throat. She set the empty glass next to a candle, tipping it over. The flame snuffed out with a wet hiss.

She knew she should feel guilty - she desperately wanted to - but she didn't. Months ago, when this all started, she had felt *something*, if not exactly guilt then a close relative of remorse, a twinge of uneasiness deep within her core. She had done wrong, broken the laws of Man, and of God. *Thou shall not steal.*

Yet that twinge had also felt good. Carolyn tingled all over remembering that first time. *Taking the forged check to the bank, the teller never hesitating - handing the cash over to Carolyn ...*

It had been so easy, too easy, the money just waiting for her to take it, begging her to take it. And she had. Week after week. No one the wiser, until the IRS sent their damned official notice. A random audit. Sorry for any inconvenience. Have pertinent records available by -

After all, it wasn't as if she'd killed anyone.

She glanced up at the razor dangling from the nearby shower rack like a hangman from a noose.

Unless she killed herself.

Yet who would find her body? Rabbi Liss? Come to see why she hadn't appeared for the audit. She didn't want to embarrass him with her nudity. Her mother then? She snorted. It would be too much for Mama. Not the fact that her daughter had made blood-soup of herself, but that someone would have to clean up the mess left behind. That *she* would have to do it, Mama not allowing anyone else the responsibility of dealing with her daughter's disgrace.

No, suicide was out of the question.

Using a big toe, Carolyn pressed the drain lever. The water lowered in slow increments, the vulgar gurgle-suck of its whirlpool departure a prolonged raspberry.

A short time later, wrapped in her bathrobe and seated at the tiny kitchenette table, she took a bite of toast topped with the last of the sardines, *chewing over* her situation some more.

Yes, she'd been caught - or would be come early Monday - but it wasn't her fault, not really, she'd just been unlucky, that was all: bad luck.

The toast scratched her throat when she swallowed. She'd forgotten the milk. Rising from the chair, she went to the sink, grabbed that morning's coffee cup and turned toward the fridge. Bent over the opened door, she reached for the half-gallon milk container, and -

One particularly terrible rotten day, Bad Luck Badger chased Bunny from her hidey-hole-in-the-ground home.

- her hand paused.

Bunny's Lucky Slipper.

She stood upright. She'd completely forgotten the stolen book. Yet another sin to add to the growing list. Somehow, without even realizing it, she'd become a hardened career criminal. Shivering, she glanced down. Her bathrobe had slipped open. Fingers of cold air from the light-filled refrigerator caressed an exposed breast. Re-cinching the robe's sash first, Carolyn shut the fridge door and went in search of her coat.

Sitting on the couch, she grabbed the nearest accent pillow, placed it upon her lap, and then propped the book onto the pillow so she could examine it more closely.

As in the store, the thin volume looked smaller than she remembered. A ghost child's finger traced the words on the cover while Carolyn did likewise, her fingers rubbing across the hand painted letters.

Hand painted?

That was wrong. Her Bunny had had slightly engraved gold letters, all in bright precise capitals.

Carolyn lifted the cover. Inside, were the title page and the title illustration - an ink and watercolor painting of Bunny wearing her solitary lucky slipper. These looked about the same as she remembered but with minor differences. The title now arched like a rainbow where before it had always been as straight as any ruler edge. And Bunny... Carolyn's only childhood friend had had blue eyes. This Bunny's were emerald green.

She moved to turn the page, but hesitated. There was something else...

Biting her lower lip, she realized what she'd missed, what was literally missing from the page - the boring stuff she'd always skipped over as a child: *Omar and Kettering, Publishers, New York, 1968.*

Skipped over, except for the copyright. The same year as her birth. Because of that coincidence, a younger Carolyn had believed Bunny's anonymous author had written the book specifically for her. Moreover, there'd been the inscription on the following page: *For C, along with my unending love.*

Who else could C be but young Carolyn herself?

Carolyn turned the page, and sure enough, there was the same dedication. Like the cover, the lettering looked hand written, not the usual typeset she'd poured over countless times.

An idea struck. She flipped through the pages, pausing here and there when she spied something changed, something slightly off.

Yes, it had to be. What she held in her hands.

Carolyn realized she mostly likely possessed, had in fact stolen, the original *Bunny's Lucky Slipper*.

... Bunny and Badger sat together at the kitchen table sipping rutabaga soup while outside the sky turned from red to purple to deepest blue to black. The End.

Carolyn, coming back into her own body, her cheeks wet with warm tears, started to close the book but then noticed yet another difference.

An additional page.

"What's this?"

Fingers shaking, she read: *H. Hogarth 2 Summerfield Ln.*

Bunny's anonymous author had signed *his? her?* name.

It had to be - the handwriting was the same as in the rest of the book, the same precise letters like a child's toy blocks laid out all in a row.

She blinked and saw there was one more word: *Skaneateles.*

When Carolyn tried to pronounce the name, her tongue tied itself into knots. After her laughter stopped, she leaned back and sighed. "Well, H. Hogarth of Two Summerfield Lane, we'll just have to see where you once lived, won't we?"

Leaving *Bunny* propped upon the pillow, Carolyn skip-hopped into the guestroom her mother used on the rare visit, skirted the bed and plopped down at the small desk that shared the cramped space. The computer, bought with stolen funds, was top-of-the-line and booted up in a flash.

She Googled the strange sounding word.

Skaneateles, a tiny upstate village nestled snugly along the northern shore of a finger lake with the same name. She clicked *earth view* and a wave of vertigo overtook her when a green patchwork quilt of farm fields and woods replaced the sterile map. She added the address, resent the search, and a red pushpin arrow magically appeared far down along the lake's southwestern shore. She zoomed in. Located along a peninsula that jutted out into the lake like a distended belly button, Summerfield Lane and its surroundings possessed one massive building - a mansion? - and a half dozen smaller out-buildings, structures which looked more like suggestions of buildings than real ones.

Carolyn grinned. "I've got you now, H. Hogarth."

She zoomed in until the larger building turned into unrecognizable pixels then reversed herself, rising into the air until the screen birthed a giant-sized blue body.

Returning to map view, she read *Lake Ontario.*

Skaneateles, so close to the Canadian border...

An idea seized her, a way to solve her problems and have a bit of fun in the process. She would make a run for it, become a fugitive, a criminal on the lam. But first... first she would visit Skaneateles. More specifically, Two Summerfield Lane. Grinning, she printed the map and the directions.

She almost shut down the computer then, thinking already of what she should pack, when - on a whim - she backed up a screen and added *Hogarth* to the search engine's parameters. A slew of hits came up but none of them seemed connected to Bunny. One mentioned a missing child, another, a soup recipe. She frowned, but then brightened. What did she expect? H. Hogarth had remained anonymous for decades. Why would her name - Bunny's author had to be a woman - pop up on a search?

H. Hogarth.

What would the H reveal itself to be? Helena? Hillary? Hester? Carolyn hugged herself. Bad Luck Badger had barged his way into her life in the form of the IRS, and now, just like Bunny, Carolyn would make her way out into the world to find her own good fortune.

Bunny didn't see Maurice Mole until she bumped into his wagon. The red wagon tottered and teetered before it tipped. The waxy and white-bodied grubs he had collected all that morning long tumbled out onto the sun-warmed soil. They squiggle-wiggled about trying to get away while Mole fretted and prattled on.

"Oh dear," he cried. "Oh my. Oh, gosh-golly gone it. There goes my breakfast... there's my lunch. Oh, what cursed luck." Picking up a grub, he pointed it at Bunny. "Gee-golly-gosh, Bunny, whyever don't you watch where you run?"

"I'm so sorry, Mr. Mole," Bunny said, sniffling, "but I'm in a fateful fix. I do hope you'll forgive me."

Before he could reply, she dashed off, hip-hopping away willy-nilly.

Early the next morning, Carolyn went to borrow her mother's ancient station wagon. Not that she expected to return it. Bunny may have eventually returned home, but that wasn't how Carolyn planned to end her story. She asked the taxi driver to wait with her luggage while she went to get the key.

The driver, an emaciated elderly man with scraggly whiskers, a long thin nose and close-set eyes that seemed to stare perpetually at the bridge of his nose, glanced at her in the rearview mirror. "It's your money, lady."

She almost blurted out, *No, it isn't*, but nodded her head and said, "I'll just be a few minutes."

Their first stop had been the bank where she'd closed out the temple's building fund account.

The driver shrugged. "Meter's run'n."

She couldn't get over how similar the driver looked to Mr. Mole. Chuckling at herself, she opened the door and climbed out.

She patted the taxi's trunk as she passed. Within were the deluxe five-piece luggage set she'd bought online a couple months earlier. Last night she'd filled them with the essentials for her new life. Reaching the building's steps, she stopped to look back at the taxicab. She wondered. Had her subconscious known when she'd ordered the luggage she'd go *rabbit* someday? Shaking her head, she giggled at her witticism then dashed up the Brownstone's steps two at a time.

Inside, she followed the sound of snoring down the hallway to her mother's closed bedroom door. She turned the knob and pushed the door open. Her mother, her mouth agape, lay under a green-patterned comforter.

Cold, so cold, Mama had complained for weeks straight. *I tell you, I feel death's cruel fingers on me all the time now. Just you wait and see, little bunny, I be joining Papa soon enough.*

Like the luggage set, Carolyn had bought the comforter online, shipping it directly to her mother's address. Seeing it now firsthand, the similarity of its pattern to the aerial view of Skaneateles shocked her. Was this just another coincidence? Her mind making loose connections where none existed, or was fate leading her down this particular path?

From outside a horn honked, and she realized she hadn't heard a snore for some time. Her eyes fixated onto her mother's creased upper lip, but she saw no movement there. The chest beneath the comforter was still as well. Carolyn counted in her mind. *One Skaneateles. Two Skaneateles. Three Skaneateles. Four …*

She was up to seven - her lucky number and a good omen for sure - when her mother's chest heaved upwards and the loudest sucking gasp yet shattered the bedroom's silence, ending the count.

No, not dead.

The comforter had slipped down revealing the top of her mother's nightdress. The chest beneath the fabric looked time-flattened, Mama's breasts, twin deflated birthday balloons.

Another blast from the horn.

Carolyn let out her own breath, the moist air slipping from her pursed lips as a slow hiss. "Hold on, Mr. Mole," she whispered.

A last look at Mama and Carolyn slowly re-closed the door.

Moving quickly, she went to the kitchen where she spied her mother's purse on the table. She rummaged inside until she felt - and heard - the singing keys. Pulling out the familiar key ring, she used a thumbnail to ease out the station wagon key before replacing the other keys.

Seconds later, back at the front door, her heart beating madly inside her chest, she hesitated once more.

She couldn't just leave like this. Just vanish. *Poof.*

Pocketing the key, she turned and hustled back into the kitchen. By the phone were a pen and a notepad. She picked up the pen.

Dearest Mama,

I've decided to start a new life far away from here. Don't worry about me, I'm a big girl and can take care of myself. If in the coming days, you hear anything bad about me, just know I am terribly sorry and that my actions had nothing to do with you.

With all my love,

Carolyn

She tore the note from the pad, reread it - and after sucking on her inner cheek - crumpled the paper and jammed it into the same pocket beside the key.

She snatched up the pen again and scribbled.

Mama,

I took the wagon.

Bunny

Carolyn's luck grew all day long. It started the moment she sat down behind the station wagon's steering wheel and noticed the fuel gauge.

F is for fortune. F is for freedom. F is for fun.

The feeling grew as the miles dialed up on the odometer, while outside the windshield, the scenery changed from cityscape to suburb to countryside. At one point, she thought she might be deluding herself when a flat tire forced her onto the interstate shoulder, but this brief moment of self-doubt evaporated, when - not more than a minute after having put on the hazard lights - a trucker pulled his eighteen-wheeler up behind her hobbled ride. As burly and as uncommunicative as Big Bear from Bunny, the man replaced the blown tire lickety-split. Then, before she could so much as offer him some cash for his help, he grunted, *No thanks, Ma'am. You're welcome, Ma'am,* and ambled back to his rig and drove off leaving her tingling all over, and not more than a little bit dizzy.

Mother Fox insisted Bunny come live with her and her family.

"The children will just love you, Bunny," Fox said. Her wide pointy-tooth smile spread from ear to ear. "They'll just eat you up. So please, stay."

"Thank you so much, Mrs. Fox," Bunny replied, "but I do have a home ... or I had one once upon a time. And I'd really like to have it back." She kicked at a pebble underfoot. "I just need to find my luck is all, and everything will be hunky-dory. I'm sure of it, you'll see."

Fox's grin soured. "For one night, Bunny dear. Pretty-please, stay. Come for supper at the least." She placed a clawed paw upon either of Bunny's shoulders. "Please dearest-dear, I insist."

Skaneateles.

With growing delight, Carolyn drove by gingerbread Victorian ladies one after another. Set far back in their shaded lots, they nodded demurely at her passing, their faces painted ever so brightly, as if they had come into existence that very moment just for Carolyn's enjoyment.

She nodded her own head at one particularly exquisite pink and lime-green structure. "How do you do?" And quickly added, "Why, I'm ever so pleased to make your acquaintance." She giggled. "Perfect."

At the next stop sign, the sparkle of countless diamonds caught her eye. It was the town's namesake lake. She directed the wagon toward it, spotting many happy white sails dancing across the lake's surface. Beyond the boats jutted a long pier. Weekend strollers walked its surface, no doubt enjoying the day as much as she was. She slowed the wagon and passed a lakeside park where a picturesque gazebo squatted amidst the greenery.

"Just perfect."

She reached downtown Main Street, and spotting an open parking space beside an ice cream parlor, she decided that a single scoop vanilla cone sounded just about... well, perfect.

The proprietor handed Carolyn her change. "Hogarth, eh? Never heard of 'em." He closed the drawer on the old-fashioned cash register.

Taped to the register's back was a flyer with a grainy black and white photo of a young girl. Beneath her smiling face was written: HAVE YOU SEEN ME?

"But that don't mean much. Lots of new folks buying up the old family places round about the lake."

"Really? I'd have thought she was from one of the old families." Carolyn stuffed the coins into her pant pocket, feeling the roughness of crumpled paper against her fingers.

The man, a dead-ringer for Timothy Turtle, scratched the inside of an ear. After a few thoughtful moments, he removed the index, examined the nail and flicked off whatever he'd found there. "Nope, doesn't ring a bell."

"Are you sure? *H. Hogarth.*"

"A-huh. Sure as sure can be."

Melted ice cream dribbled onto her hand. She licked it off before she spotted the nearby napkin dispenser. Pulling one free she wrapped it around the cone. "Positive? No Hilary Hogarth? Or maybe a Hester?"

Twin cherries popped into existence upon either of Mister Turtle's cheeks. "Thank you for your business, Ma'am. You have a nice day now."

From the parking lot, the Public Library looked like a castle. Carolyn locked the door on the wagon and turned to admire the building's brick-work.

Mr. Turtle had lied. She just knew it. Her lucky feeling told her so. Yet why would he do that?

A slight lake-smelling wind ruffled her hair. The sun, well past its ze-nith, still beat warmly upon her hair and shoulders.

Unless, the locals wanted to protect their famous author. Maybe fans came to visit H. Hogarth all the time. Bothering the reclusive author. Not that that was what she was doing. After all, wasn't she C from the dedication?

The buzz of a bumblebee filled her ears. She glanced up at the library's turreted gable. If any local information existed about H. Hogarth, she would find it here.

The buzzing became louder when she took a step toward the sidewalk. Annoying and a bit discomforting, the sound grew, filled her head until her teeth vibrated. She managed to utter, "Oh, dear," before she stum-bled and fell.

"Are you okay?"

Still dizzy, Carolyn turned her head sideways. A sharp pain shot through her forehead behind her eyes. Everything had turned red. Even the woman who'd just questioned was a brilliant crimson.

"Ma'am," the fox said. "Should I call for help?"

Carolyn's head felt too heavy when she shook it. Her voice warbled. "No, no. I'm fine. I just ate some ice cream." She pressed a palm to her brow. "I guess I ate it too fast. Got that whatchamacallit?"

"Brain freeze?"

Carolyn removed the hand and looked again at the speaker. Not ex-actly Mrs. Fox, but a woman near Carolyn's own age with carrot-orange hair. *Ms. Fox? She'll have freckles too*, Carolyn thought and confirmed the fact when her eyes once more could focus. "Yes, brain freeze."

She moved to stand, but the woman quickly stepped off the sidewalk and said, "Here, let me help."

"Why, thank you." Carolyn took the offered hand and stood. A shorter wave of dizziness passed through her but the woman steadied her, grip-ping her arm. Her left thigh felt numb. She reached down and rubbed it.

"Hey, we'd better get you inside."

That sounded like a good idea to Carolyn and she said so.

"It is a hot day," the woman said. "Maybe you've gotten too much sun?"

Carolyn didn't tell her she'd been driving in a car all day long, she didn't want to disappoint her savior. She patted the redhead's arm. "Perhaps. And I was heading inside anyways."

Without releasing her grip on Carolyn's arm, the woman grinned.

"Well, lucky that."

Yes, luck. This was her lucky day after all.

Taking short baby steps, the woman led Carolyn toward the library entrance. When they reached the door, the woman paused. "By the way, I'm Cynthia Fox. But please, call me Cindy."

It turned out her new best friend Cindy - besides the wondrous coincidence of her last name - also worked part-time at the library as an aide.

"Really?" Cindy said. "I'd love to see it."

Carolyn had just spoken of *Bunny* waiting in the wagon. "Yes, the one and only original. Isn't that ever so exciting?"

They sat side-by-side in matched reading chairs plunked down before an enormous unlit fireplace. Various portraits hung above the large mantle. Carolyn was tempted to stick out her tongue at one thickly mustachioed man, what with him and his dark and brooding eyes.

"Carolyn?"

Carolyn turned to Cindy. "Yes?"

"I asked *wherever* did you find it?"

She waved her hands in shooing gesture. "Oh... in a bookstore." She didn't want to admit she'd stolen it.

Cindy cocked her head sideways and the woman's fox-like resemblance returned. "What are you thinking?"

"I was thinking ... that you should call me, Bunny."

The fox leaned back in her chair and raised an eyebrow. "As in the *book?*"

What she'd really been about to say was that she thought she'd forgotten to open the wagon's window just a tiny little bit for Bunny. However, since she was Bunny too, it really didn't matter then. Did it?

"Yes. All my friends call me so."

There. She'd said it. *Friend.*

Cindy laughed. "Well, of course then. Bunny it is."

"Now you be careful, Ms. Bunny," Cindy Fox said closing the wagon door for Bunny. She leaned down into the open window. "It'll be pretty dark by the time you get there."

There, was the Hogarth family farmstead. Cindy, a treasure trove of local knowledge, had verified all of the scant evidence regarding Bunny's authorship. She'd made Bunny promise not to tell anyone else.

Bunny attached the seatbelt. "You think so?"

"Oh, I know so," Cindy Fox said. "But don't you worry, just follow the directions I gave you and you'll be fine. Henrietta will be thrilled to meet you."

H is for Henrietta.

Perfect. Just wonderfully absolutely utterly perfect. Bunny tingled all over. "Oh, I'm so very lucky to have met you."

Cindy Fox stood back up. "Yes. That you are."

Bunny turned the key and started the engine. "Cindy?"

"What is it, Bunny?"

She thrilled every time Cindy Fox called her Bunny. "I want to thank you, again. You've been ever so kind to me."

She was even more thrilled when Cindy – unexpectedly - leaned forward, and kissed her sweetly upon the lips.

Cindy's eyes gleamed when she pulled back and smiled. "Not a problem at all, Bunny dear."

Before Bunny could hop away to the safety of the blackberry patch, Farmer Fritz snatched her by the ears and yanked her clear off the ground.

"A-ha," Fritz cried in triumph. "Here's the naughty rapscallion that's been nibbling at my onions and shallots!"

The gate was unlocked just as Cindy Fox said it would be. Bunny re-closed it behind the idling wagon and hopped back behind the wheel. The wagon crept up the drive. She hadn't gone more than a dozen yards when the moon leapt from the tallest tree. Milky-blue light poured across the graveled drive, the surrounding land, and the various outbuildings she vaguely recalled from the previous day's so-very-far-away computer search. The concrete-block structures looked like scattered teeth popping up from the ground. Each appeared to have a wired pen area.

Animal pens.

Cindy Fox had mentioned a petting zoo of some sort. Bunny briefly wondered how Henrietta could stay in the black way out here in the middle of nowhere, but thinking that way reminded her of someone else. Someone who she knew used to be her. Someone she didn't really like.

Someone unlucky.

She passed the closest of the small outbuildings. Moonlight glinted off a tiny cracked window, and for the briefest moment, she thought she glimpsed the haunted face of a little girl peeking out at her just beyond the glass.

Her own reflection?

When she blinked, the *illusion* vanished.

Ahead, the main building loomed and she quickly forgot herself once more.

"Three-two-one. Ready or not Henrietta Hogarth, here I come."

"This soup is so very delicious," Bunny said savoring the steaming-hot goodness as it spread outwards from her stomach. "What kind did you say it was?"

She knew the answer before the elderly woman turned from the stove-top - a soup bowl in her gnarled hands - and replied, "Why, Bunny dear, it's rutabaga."

The cheery-warmness inside Bunny stretched out until her toes tin-gled. She laughed before she helped herself to another spoonful.

Henrietta set her bowl down upon the table, pulled out a chair, and sat. Bunny marveled at her creator.

Please, I insist, Bunny. Call me Henrietta.

This friendly informality had come soon after Bunny introduced her-self. Bunny smiled remembering:

The farmhouse door creaking open before she even had a chance to knock. Being in-vited inside without even an exchanged hello-how-do-you-do? The door, just as quickly, shut behind her by the old woman in the flower-print housecoat and quilted slippers.

It was as if Henrietta had anticipated Bunny's arrival.

"What is it, dear?" Henrietta asked.

Bunny grinned. "I was just thinking that this is the nicest day of my life."

"Well, isn't that splendid."

"Yes. It is. I feel so very ... very lucky to have finally met you. I feel like I've known you all my life. That you've always been there for me - in the background and such - watching out for me, guiding me here as it were, to this very moment."

"Oh, isn't that such a sweet thing to say. Why thank you, Bunny dear."

"No, really. I feel so... so honored. I don't know what else to say."

Henrietta smiled. Her teeth were two rows of children's toy blocks, one laid atop the other. "That's quite all right, dear. Most times words just befuddle things. Make situations more complex than they need to be. Life is a simple matter."

Bunny's eyes moved to the small book lying upon the table. She'd set it there not that long ago. "Like in a children's book."

Henrietta's eye flickered to the book. "Yes, there's that, isn't there. Well done, Bunny!"

Bunny glowed at the praise. If only Mother would *just once* have said such kind words.

A moving light played across the grease-stained kitchen wall. Henrietta glanced toward the door and sighed. "Of course, there are no happi-ly-every-afters in real life."

A sudden heaviness filled Bunny's stomach as the soup there soured. She burped up an evil acid-tasting lump and decided rutabagas weren't as tasty as she'd thought.

"But you look tired, dear," Henrietta said. "Such an adventure, you've had getting here."

Bunny yawned. Now that Henrietta mentioned it, she realized she was tired. So very very tired.

"Your bed's all made for you. We'll take you to it presently."

Bunny burped another vile tasting mouthful and thought she might be getting sick.

Standing, she knocked the table with her hip.

The blow felt like a light tap.

She opened her mouth, but her lips and tongue had gone numb. She managed to utter, "Ick," before the room, along with Henrietta Hogarth, turned sideways.

Bunny didn't know where she was. Her last memory was of her eating soup with Bad-Luck Badger. She recalled retiring to her bedroom soon afterwards, where she'd drifted off to a pleasant sleep ...

Gazing about, she twitched her nose.

She stood in a bedroom now. Not her own, although it did look oddly familiar. She supposed one bedroom looked pretty much like any other, it only needing a bed to make it a bed-room. And this room did have one of those, a bulgy green patchwork quilt for its covering.

Had she been sleepwalking? Better yet, perhaps she still slept - as sleep weighed heavily upon her. Yes, of course, that was it: she dreamed... the strangest dream ever.

A creak sounded behind her and Bunny turned toward the door right before a woman slipped into the room.

Her face impassive, her motions slow and deliberate, the woman went straight to the bed; a bed, which Bunny now saw held a sleeping form beneath its patchwork quilt. The woman smiled before she leaned over the sleeper - an elderly woman. Bunny thought the woman might kiss the other, but instead the woman reached behind the sleeper's head, carefully slipped out a fluffy white pillow, and raised it in her hands.

How strange, Bunny thought.

Then the woman did a stranger thing, a terrible horrible thing. First placing the pillow over the old woman's face, she began to count, "One lucky slipper, two lucky slippers, three lucky slippers, four — "

The girl stared at Carolyn with wide dark eyes. "Bunny," she whispered. "You wanna play?"

Just beyond the girl's face, a bright vertical rectangle of light glowed. Carolyn blinked a few times before her mind told her the light came from a gap beneath a door, and that she lay on her side on a cold wooden floor, her cheek pressed into its grain.

Beyond the door, voices argued.

"You shouldn't have sent her here like that."

"She knew who you were Mother. By name. She would have eventually blabbed about it to someone. I didn't have any choice."

Carolyn thought she recognized one of the voices as belonging to the red-haired woman from the library. She recalled the woman helping her to her feet after she swooned.

Cindy Fox?

After that, events became disturbingly fuzzy ...

"And what if she spots one of the girls?"

The girl squatting over her flinched. Her nose twitched. Carolyn noticed she wore old-fashioned pajamas, the kind with built-in slippers. When the girl turned toward the door, a puffy white bobtail came into view above the pajamas' buttoned seat flap. She couldn't be older than six or seven.

"She is one, Mother, or hadn't you noticed? She's like your first - the original Bunny."

"Sure, she's off her rocker, but it's not the same and you know it."

"Then we'll get rid of her like the others."

"Damnations, Cindy. I raised you better. Waste not, want not."

"It's not as if we're letting the fox into the henhouse, Mother. Quite the opposite, I'd say."

"Except'n instead of hens, we got us one great big rabbit."

"Bunny's Lucky Slipper. Whatever were you thinking writing that book? It's a damn road map. I'm surprised we're not overrun with more runaways."

"Anonymous means no one's supposed to know who I am."

"And yet, somehow, they show up year after year."

"So's they do. And who are you to complain, dear? Brings food to our table now, don't it?"

Carolyn heard all this without comprehending. Yes, she'd discovered the original book, but without the name of the town on that extra last page, she never would have found the author's home.

Would she have?

The girl seemed even more agitated. She hopped back and forth as if she had to pee.

Carolyn wanted her to stand still. The movement made her nervous. She opened her mouth to tell the girl this, but her lips didn't work right. In fact, the entire left side of her body felt numb.

It's asleep. I've fallen asleep on a hard wooden floor. What do I expect?

Yet how had she ended up on the floor in the first place?

If she could only remember ...

She tried to rise, but her left arm didn't support her. She flopped back down to the floor.

"What was that?"

"She's awake. I thought you said she'd be out for hours?"

"I'm used to girls, Cindy. Guess I didn't put in enough. Well, at least we know she ain't dead. The way she went down, hard like that, thought for sure she was having a stroke to boot."

Footsteps sounded and moving shadows shattered the bright rectangle.

In a mad dash, the girl hopped over Carolyn's body and disappeared from view.

What was going on? Where was she?

"Might be better if she was dead. Save us the task to do later. Offer us a cover if someone comes snooping after her."

"Oh, Cindy Marion Fox. Quit your belly-aching."

"Yes, Mother."

The door creaked open to admit an intense light that blinded Carolyn.

They were going to kill her. If not now, then soon enough. She had to escape. Get to the car. Get to help. Carolyn struggled, without success, to push herself up from the straw covered ground.

They hadn't bothered to tie her after they dropped her off here.

Yet why should they? Her paralysis made any further restraint redundant. She knew she'd suffered a stroke, most likely more than one. She recalled being dizzy - as early as that morning.

She blew out a long breath and tried to relax.

Get a grip, Carolyn. Think things through logically. She was an accountant after all. Meticulous. Devoted to details. She could think her way out of this.

Just like you did with the stolen money. And speaking of that fiasco, how's that working out for you, Carolyn, bunny dear?

"Stop it."

The words came out as splutters, the T's and P half-formed and slippery. Yet they worked their magic: she stopped her self-recriminations and focused on the present situation.

First things first.

Here was a small concrete cell surrounded by a wire-pen enclosure. She'd spotted a dozen or so of them when they'd carted her out into the night in a rusty wheelbarrow.

I was too heavy to carry.

Not like the little girls.

Girls. More than one. On the short wheelbarrow ride, Carolyn had counted six little girls of various ages dressed in similar pajamas as the first girl in the house, each in their separate cell.

What kind of sick monster did this?

No, she thought. *Monsters.* More than one. Henrietta Hogarth, evil author, and her bedeviled daughter, Cynthia Fox.

C wasn't for Carolyn. C was for Cindy.

Once again, Carolyn wondered how many strokes her brain had suffered, and when exactly had the first one occurred. *TIA. Transient ischemic attack.* One of her mother's friends had suffered such a stroke years ago. Carolyn recalled how when she'd visited the hospital with her mother, half of the woman's face drooped. If Carolyn remembered correctly, the woman had gone home a few days later, no worse for the wear than a slight limp and a blood thinner prescription.

If only Carolyn could be so lucky.

The Sneaking Woman.

Yes, that was how Bunny thought of her foil. Her counterpoint. Her opposite.

Sneaking into bedrooms. Doing these terrible horrible things.

Bunny was going to be sick. She turned to run away, managed one short hop before she halted.

Was forced to halt.

Using witchery-magic, the Sneaking Woman had stopped Bunny in her not-so-very lucky-bunny footed tracks.

Bunny turned to face her foe.

Why?

Why would the Sneaking Woman do this? This wasn't like her at all. This darkness wasn't in her, this evil.

Bunny had no time to ponder how she knew this as the Sneaking Woman took the moment to turn her tear-stained face directly at Bunny.

Bunny shivered all over. Here, she'd thought herself invisible to the woman, but the woman had known of her presence all along. Another bit of sneakiness on the woman's part.

How foolish she'd been.

The woman grinned before she opened her mouth wide. The hungry maw grew larger, but then Bunny felt her body lift from the ground and realized the Sneaking Woman drew Bunny toward her and her even more horrible emptiness.

Bunny had enough time to think, Curse my bad luck, *when the Sneaking Woman's warm moist lips swallowed her whole.*

Death almost sounded attractive.

Carolyn spat at the padlock on the wire gate then turned and hobbled back toward the cell. Her left foot scrapped against the pen's hard-packed soil leaving the barest mark.

Hopeless.

She reached the opening, and bending at the waist, went inside.

Dead, she wouldn't have to endure this mounting fear.

She went to the small window at the structure's rear and peered across the darkened lawn at the still darker house. She rubbed her left arm with the right, forcing blood into the deadened limb.

A light went on inside the house. Inside her chest, her heart fluttered.

"Don't have a heart-attack now, Bunny." She laughed - a hollow sound that echoed off the cinderblocks.

A second window in the Hogarth home came alive.

"Early risers, mother and daughter both. Bitches."

Bitches, rhymes with witches.

She didn't have much time left. They would come for her. She could only imagine the end. More poisoned soup? Or would the odd pair go full-psycho, one of them dragging Carolyn screaming to the cutting block, while the other clutched a hatchet like Farmer Fritz in *Bunny*?

In the story, Bunny had escaped, surprising Fritz with a rabbit kick to the farmer's stomach, allowing Bunny to scamper away to the safety of the farm's refuse heap where she found the title's lucky slipper. Unfortunately for Carolyn, with Bunny's author in the Farmer Fritz role, any surprise ending would have to spring from Carolyn's imagination.

Yet hadn't her imagination gotten her into this mess? If she'd faced reality from the start, accepted her fate, taken responsibility for her wrongdoings, none of this would be happening. Her future may have included a prison term, but surely, no death penalty verdict, as was her quickly impending destiny.

Childish.

That's what she'd been. Running away from home like a spoiled little girl who didn't get her way. She couldn't blame anyone for her current troubles but herself.

A silhouette crossed one of the lit windows in the Hogarth home.

"Tough luck, Bunny. Deal with it."

Bunny worked her way deeper into the abyss. Lost, she couldn't tell up from down. Or right from wrong. She was lost, utterly and completely. Alone in the dark, she felt herself dwindle with each hop until she became a speck of nothingness in a vast desert of nothingness.

For a timeless time, she despaired of ever finding her way back home, but then, from out of the abyss, a voice spoke her name.

"Bunny?"

Carolyn flinched from the window, startled by the voice and the sudden appearance of a girl's face right outside the glass.

The girl - the same one she'd seen inside the house? - tapped the glass. "You wanna play wiff us? We gonna play hidey-seek."

When the girl grinned, Carolyn realized this was a different girl, younger than the one from the house. The girl's missing front tooth gave her away.

Carolyn went to the window. Behind the girl, a group of four other similarly dressed figures hopped about, pointy rabbit ears attached to pajama hoods, puffy white tails pinned onto saggy backsides.

Carolyn felt revolted and overjoyed at the same time. Disgusted at the thought of what Henrietta had done to these children - was still doing - and thrilled at the prospect that there may be a way to escape.

Meanwhile the girl squashed her nose and cheek up against the glass. "Huh, Bunny? You wanna? It's lotsa fun."

"Sure honey ... uh, that sounds super. But I can't get out."

The girl went cross-eyed and twisted her face sideways. "I'm Bunny, not Honey. Honey's for bees. I like carrots."

The other girls began a game of leapfrog, bounding over each other in obvious joy.

"Listen ... Bunny. How did you girls get out?"

For a second, Carolyn was sure the girl would tell her they just hopped out - silly-billy.

The girl blew onto the glass, her lips puffing wide on the surface like a fish out of water gasping for air. Steam clouded the glass, but a second later, a dirty fuzzy elbow wiped it clear. "It's easy-sneezy," she said. "We opens the windows."

Bunny walked a strange path. She couldn't remember when she'd first spied it, but that was okay. She knew the path would lead her home.

The voice had told her so.

The voice had told her much more, things she knew she'd forgotten the moment she'd heard them.

But that was okay too.

Ahead, upon the next rise, she spotted something red.

Dashing up the hill lickety-split, she came upon Maurice Mole's overturned wagon.

Given time, Carolyn would have noticed the hidden latch. Unfortunately, time was a commodity in short supply. The eastern horizon already glowed bright when the window swung upward and outward to the children's combined cheers.

Carolyn glanced to the still quiet house. All it would take was one look outside from Cindy or her mother -

"Listen ladies," she called to the girls, "we're going to play a new game, but you have to be quiet."

A girl tisked. "Aw, quiet's no fun."

"This will be, I swear."

Another girl looked at the house. "Besides, we gotta get back soon. Gamma doesn't like it if she catches us out."

Carolyn said, "Gamma won't catch anyone."

The girl didn't look convinced. "She always catches us. An thens we gets in big t'wuble."

Another girl, this one in pink pajamas said, "The Big Black Kettle."

All the girls turned toward the same building - a dilapidated farm building, smaller than a real barn. Wide gaps between the planking didn't reveal anything horrible within, but many of the girls visibly shook.

Carolyn didn't wait for an explanation. The fit through the small window would be a near thing. Thank God, she hadn't inherited her mother's hips. Lifting her left arm with the right, she shoved the still-unresponsive limb out the window first.

The lucky slipper sat inside the wagon. Climbing onto the wagon first, Bunny slipped her foot into the slipper. Far down the hillside, she glimpsed the old oak tree that shaded her hidey-hole-in-the-ground home. Grabbing the handle, she urged the wagon to move, scooting her body forward. The wagon leapt ahead in a small hop. Bunny kept at it until the hill grabbed hold. The wagon's wheels picked up speed. In no time at all, the little red wagon flew down the hill lickety-split. Bunny, the wind whipping her ears backward, cried out in fear.

And delight.

Carolyn couldn't believe her luck.

Cindy Fox or her mother had moved the station wagon, but the girls - *the Bunnies*, she told herself, recalling how each girl had replied when Carolyn asked them their names - had taken her by the hand, leading her to its current whereabouts: parked behind the infamous *Big Black Kettle* barn.

Carolyn smiled at the key in the ignition before she craned her head sideways. Four Bunnies sat in the back seat grinning at her, the fifth, the Bunny with the missing tooth, sat beside Carolyn in the front passenger seat. It probably wasn't legal to have the girls sharing seatbelts, but under the circumstances...

"Everyone ready?"

The excited voices behind her confirmed her passengers' eagerness.

Carolyn felt light-headed, not stroke-dizzy-light-headed, but *soulfully light*, as if a great weight had lifted from her shoulders.

"Time for roll call." She adjusted the rear mirror. "Bunny, are you here?"

All the girls giggled and called out, "Here!"

All except the girl beside Carolyn, who pouted and said, "When Auntie Fox wizzits, she needs Bunny ta help her get her ta sleep."

Bunny didn't see the stone until it was too late. She tried to steer round it, but the handle had a mind of its own and twisted viciously out of her grip. The wagon tipped and Bunny went flying.

The tire iron felt wrong. Its heaviness unsettled Carolyn, like a fading nightmare she'd gladly forgotten upon waking. She didn't want to use it for violence, but she would, if she had to.

She hobbled around the corner of the house.

Somewhere inside was the last missing girl. Bunny Number Six. Seven lucky bunnies, if Carolyn included herself. *Mama Bunny*. She would do anything to protect her foster litter.

She paused beside a rose-covered trellis. The fragrant, vibrant blooms stretched to the rust-speckled rain gutter. An open window within reach of the trellis invited her up.

Anything?

The tire-iron weighed down her right arm. She relaxed the muscles there letting the bar's pointed tip rest against the dew-covered ground.

Yes, she'd stolen from the temple, but petty thievery did not a tire-iron wielding murderer make. Carolyn could easily *imagine* herself doing awful terrible things, but in the past whenever *reality* demanded she choose between a difficult route or an easy path, she'd always chosen the later: hiding in her sub-level apartment, letting the real world pass her by while she dreamed imaginary scenarios one more preposterous than the last behind her triple-locked door. No, she couldn't fight Cindy Fox. Wouldn't dare. Women like Cindy and her mother were monsters - real monsters - and Carolyn, in all her life, had only faced those of the make-believe kind.

Carolyn contemplated turning around. The easier path led back to her mother's station wagon and the waiting five girls. Five was better than zero. Once she reached Skaneateles, she could notify the police about the last girl.

She gritted her teeth and looked again at the trellis and the open window.

No, she had to do this. Who knew what would happen to the last girl once the two women found the others missing? Luck was with her after all. Fate wouldn't let her down now.

Would it?

The tire-iron dropped the rest of the way to the ground.

Facing the trellis, Carolyn reached up with her one good arm and began to climb.

Cindy Fox said, "Oh, you bad *bad* bunny."

Carolyn groaned inwardly while she gripped the little girl's hand more tightly. Cindy Fox stood on the top stair, dressed in a flannel nightshirt, her flaming red hair in disarray.

Carolyn tried, and failed, to raise her free hand in a warning gesture. "Stay back."

"Really, Bunny? Or what exactly?" Cindy Fox's blue eyes fixated on the girl. "Come here, sweetie." She raised her arms, hands wide. "Come to Auntie Fox."

The little girl tugged at Carolyn's hand until Carolyn let her go. The girl rushed into Cindy Fox's arms, who quickly wrapped her in an embrace.

"What a good little bunny you are."

Around the girl's floppy ears, Cindy Fox leered at Carolyn.

Carolyn's heart sank. It had been too easy. Not the climb, but once she'd gotten inside. The window had let onto the stairway landing. She'd found the girl in the nearby bathroom, her pajama bottoms lowered, relieving herself of her morning water. They'd made it back to the open window when Cindy Fox had discovered them.

"You won't get away with this," Carolyn said.

Cindy Fox's smug look intensified. "But we have, Bunny dear. For years now. And no one the wiser."

Carolyn's palms were wet with sweat and blood from the climb. She wiped her hand on her pants and noticed the slight bump from the pocket. "I ... I left a note."

Both of Cindy Fox's eyebrows rose. "A note? I don't think so."

From downstairs, Henrietta Hogarth called, *"What's going on, Cindy?"*

Cindy Fox turned her head. "Nothing to be worried about, Mother. We've got a loose bunny."

"The girl?"

"No, the big one."

"What in the hell is she doing up there?"

"I think she was trying to steal our little bunny here." She looked back at Carolyn. "Isn't that right, Bunny?"

Carolyn backed up against the windowsill. Maybe she could still save the other girls.

"You take the cake, Bunny dear. I can't believe how misguided and delusional you are. You know that, right?"

"Stay back." Carolyn glanced over her shoulder. Even if she made it out to the trellis, Cindy Fox or her mother would be waiting below before she'd made it halfway down the damned roses.

The little girl started to squirm. "You squeez'n too hard, Auntie Fox. Bunny can't bweathe."

Cindy Fox twisted her face sideways before she asked, "Once again, Bunny dear. *Or what?*"

Carolyn flinched when the screen door slammed behind her. "You don't have to do this."

"Keep moving."

"Please, I promise, I won't tell anyone."

Cindy Fox snorted. "And I should take the word of a lunatic to mean anything?"

They reached the porch step. Carolyn grabbed the handrail with her good hand. "I ... I'm already on the run from the law. I was heading for the border -"

"You!" Cindy paused. "What did a pathetic creature like you do? Steal lunch money from schoolchildren?"

Carolyn stumbled but Cindy Fox steadied her. The woman had been so close to the truth. *Pathetic.* Yes, Carolyn was pathetic, dreadfully so.

Already out on the lawn, Henrietta Hogarth waved them forward. The large knife blade in her hand glimmered in the morning sunlight.

The little girl, Bunny Number Six, hopped a wide circle around the elderly woman.

Carolyn shivered. The truth would only make Cindy Fox laugh.

Henrietta wore the same housecoat as the day before, although she'd put on a cardigan sweater to go outside. She hadn't bothered to put on any shoes. Carolyn noted the woman's quilted granny slippers as they sloshed through the dew-dampened lawn. She'd just about reached the first *bunny pen.*

Carolyn wondered how the woman would react to the missing child, but didn't have to wait. To Carolyn it looked as if the woman's body shrunk - if only for a moment. Then Henrietta turned about, the terrible butcher knife shinning in her grip, and shouted, "Where is she?"

Beside her, Cindy Fox asked, "What did you do, Bunny?"

Carolyn blurted, "I... I think I killed my mother. I took her pillow, put it over her sleeping face and..."

This time it was Cindy Fox's turn to flinch. Her features showed sudden revulsion, but then the fox returned. She grinned. "You *think* you killed your mother? I think you're a liar. No, I know you're a liar, Bunny. A loony-bin fib-teller, with delusions of grandeur. But that's not what I meant, and you - as off your rocker as you may be - know that. *Where's the girl?*"

"Don't you mean *bunny?*" Carolyn smiled, but the gesture felt false on her face. Yet she thrilled at the reaction she received from Cindy Fox who snarled and stepped off the porch, dragging Carolyn along with her.

Bunny had forgotten the Sneaking Woman.

Which was strange because, after all, the Sneaking Woman had gobbled Bunny up once upon a time. Stranger still was the bellyache Bunny now suffered while she flew through the air. Yet it was this pain, which brought the Sneaking Woman back to mind.

F is for flying.

Flying was not fun.

Bunny opened her mouth to scream, and the strangest thing yet happened: the Sneaking Woman leapt from her mouth.

Inside of Bunny, the Sneaking Woman had used her magic to grow magnificent black wings. While the ground approached Bunny lickety-split, the Sneaking Woman used those wings to fly away.

Carolyn knew her small victory was short-lived. Still, her heart leapt into her throat when the station wagon's horn honked like a riled goose.

Henrietta, who'd been checking the other empty pens, glared over at Carolyn before she stormed off toward the barn and the hidden wagon.

Bunny Number Six chased after her, laughing.

Beside Carolyn, Cindy Fox leered before she let go of Carolyn's arm and started after her mother. With her red hair, flopping like a foxtail behind her, she called back, "Nice try, Bunny. But you're out of luck."

What luck? Good luck or bad, Carolyn knew deep down in her soul, there wasn't any such thing.

She followed at her own slower pace. She supposed she could try to run for it, escape, but seriously, how far would she get in her condition? Besides, if there was any way to help the little girls...

The unmistakable revving of the wagon's engine sounded and reality hit home.

Oh, dear God.

She'd left the key in the ignition. One of the children had started the car.

It happened when Henrietta, with Bunny Number Six right on her heels, rounded on the barn.

The red wagon, with five sets of bunny ears peeking up from behind various windows, sped out from behind the barn's shadows and made a beeline for Henrietta Hogarth.

Carolyn had a second to register the unreality of the moment, when the car smashed into the old woman. Her body bounced off the wagon's hood, careened into the windshield before it flipped onto the long roof and tangled itself in the empty luggage carrier.

Cindy Fox screamed and rushed toward the still moving car.

The wagon had just missed the little girl dressed in the bunny pjs. She stood frozen in place near to the barn, holding something in her hands, her mouth a large O in the middle of her face.

Carolyn ran to her, scooping her up into a hug. "It's okay, honey. You're not hurt. Everything's going to be fine."

Carolyn wasn't sure about that. She looked around the girl to see Cindy Fox, screaming at the bunnies in the wagon. Carolyn didn't think the girl at the steering wheel could even see outside. The scene would have been humorous, if it wasn't so horrible. The car swerved toward one of the bunny pens. It wasn't moving as fast now. Still, the car coasted through the wire fence with ease before it collided with the concrete block structure. Blocks went flying, and the car lurched to a stop.

Slowly, one at a time, bunny ears reappeared.

The little girl in her arms squirmed. "Gamma drop this."
Carolyn let her go, her eyes fixated upon the wagon.
Five pairs of ears. Thank you, God.
The collision had disentangled Henrietta Hogarth's body from the car.
It lay slumped on the ground. Cindy Fox ran to the crumpled form and
dropped to her knees, taking up her mother's dead body in her arms.
Carolyn would have to do something about Cindy Fox. The woman's
anguish would turn to anger.
What she needed was a weapon.
Remembering the older woman's knife, Carolyn scanned the ground
for any telltale glimmer.
Beside her a voice asked, "You want, Bunny? Gamma drop this?"
Carolyn started: What if the girl had found the knife?
"Gamma drop," the girl repeated.
Panic stricken, Carolyn turned, but the girl didn't hold a knife as Caro-
lyn feared. She held a quilted and blood-splattered slipper.

*Bruised, battered and bleeding, Bunny stood and brushed herself off. Up the hill a
ways, the wagon lay on its side. One of its wheels spun lazily.*
She turned her back on the hill and the mischievous red wagon.
She'd had enough fun for one day.
*Hobbling more than hopping, she continued her journey homeward, never noticing
she'd lost the lucky slipper during her horrible fall.*

Carolyn hung up the phone. The 911 operator had asked her to remain
on the line until the sheriff's car arrived, but Carolyn had another call to
make.
One she dreaded.
She had coaxed all six of the missing girls into the house playing Fol-
low-the-leader soon after an equally enjoyable game of *Tie up Auntie Fox.*
None of the girls had yet taken off her bunny pajamas. Carolyn knew
each of their futures would entail years of counseling. Yet, they were still
young. They probably didn't fully grasp the extent of the horrors they'd
endured.
To them maybe it was all a game.
One of the little girls approached Carolyn, tugged on her shirt.
"What is it, honey?"
"Not honey." The girl scowled. "*Bunny.* Honey's for bees." A tongue
appeared through the gap where a tooth would soon grow.
"Sorry, Bunny dear. I need to make a phone call."
The girl scratched her nose. "You gonna caw your mommy?"
The girl's prescience startled Carolyn. Yet whom else did a little girl
have to call when she was in trouble? She caressed the girl's cheek and

chin. "Why... yes, that's exactly who I was going to call."

"Oh, okay." The girl hopped out the kitchen into the adjacent living room where the other girls watched cartoons on the television.

Carolyn heard childish laughter.

Her body shook, while she swallowed back tears.

She could do this. She lifted the phone back to her ear and dialed the number, biting her inner cheek as she did.

A faraway ring.

One lucky slipper, two lucky slippers, three -

"Hello?"

A dam work of hot tears burst free. On the Hogarth kitchen table, *Bunny's Lucky Slipper* blurred into nothingness.

"Carolyn, that you?"

"Yes, Mama."

"Good gracious! I been worried sick. That silly note you left -"

"I'm so sorry, Mama."

There was a pause on the other end before Carolyn Rosenbaum's mother replied, *"Of course you are. Now, is my little bunny going to tell me what this foolishness is all about?"*

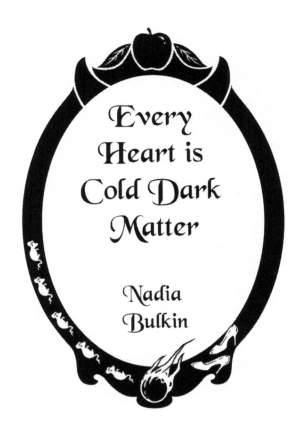

Every Heart is Cold Dark Matter

Nadia Bulkin

JONAH KAHMER, "THE GILDED AGE." IN *MASTERS OF BAT-TERSEA: A COMPLETE HISTORY*, ED. JONAH KAHMER AND THOMAS WHYET (ELON: UNIVERSITY OF ELON PRESS, 1998), P. 219:

Prince Gilford was the first in his line to marry a commoner: Melanie of Krepshire, whose father had been a wealthy landowner but not a noble. Melanie is described as a "righteous beauty, with flaxen hair and sky-blue eyes." She was just eighteen when she married Gilford. The ceremony was pompous and ended in misfortune. As a wedding present, Gilford had presented Melanie with a pair of genuine glass slippers (it was said that what he admired most about her were her slender arched feet); however, the Princess fell during the newlyweds' waltz and shattered the shoes. A particularly large shard that broke off her heel blinded the earl of Damant in his right eye. The Princess's injuries were limited to her reputation, and for the rest of her time at court she was considered clumsy, unlucky, and cursed. Some saw the accident as evidence that the prince should not have brought a commoner into the royal blood line. Anonymous letters calling for a divorce began to circulate. Gilford, outraged, declared that an *Apodemus Batterii* - the local species of field mouse - had tripped his bride, and ordered that the castle be scourged of all rodents and for ten thousand field mice to be drowned in a river. This act of ruthless pest control might have saved Battersea from the plague, but it did not entirely assuage the concerns of the superstitious public.

MELANIE OF KREPSHIRE DIARY, 4 OCTOBER, MELANIE OF KREPSHIRE PAPERS, ELON UNIVERSITY LIBRARY (ELON):

I am living with strangers. I do not know where Gilford is. He is so seldom here that I do not think he has enough to do at court, and neither do I, especially when he does not let me tend to him - but he is at least allowed to wander. I write this on a stool, in my bath, with my feet in a tub of vinegar because he wants them to be "soft as baby flesh." He calls them "dancer feet" but he hasn't let me dance in months. Soon he will probably not let me walk so I do not stress them. Yes, *them*, because he seems to think they are not part of me. Meanwhile his father the King is very concerned about the conception of real human babies. He called me "sweet daughter" at first, but now he only squints at me, as if looking for a little foetus inside. A little star. I know he isn't going to find one.

My own handmaids won't befriend me, even though I am a much kinder mistress than most. They're whispering just outside the door. I hear them saying "Black Moon," "Ashen Princess." Their white hoods and their hunched shoulders - I had another nightmare about them hiding in the wardrobe last night. I think they have heard a lot of talk about the comet, and it is making them skittish, the way horses get before a storm. And I cannot deny that the rain is coming down hard outside, and the thunder is more frightening than I have ever heard in my life, and the sky is more green than blue. I do not know what all that means. I do not really want to know. I am no astronomer, I just say my prayers.

Regardless of the comet - at times I think I have had enough, I would like to leave, I would like to leave before the misery drowns me. I told Gilford last year that the heart is a living organ, raw and excitable and warm-blooded. I told him I would use mine to love him fully, if he only let it *breathe*. He claimed to understand, but there is fuzz between his ears, and these old brick halls are a mausoleum. I see this now. These walls are not so different from the walls at home. It does not matter that the sconces are always lit. The shadows are still long (maybe longer?).

When I was young, I thought if I ran away from my father's house and Krepshire and *Yolande*, everything would set itself straight and the stars would align, but I was wrong. There is darkness everywhere. Even in Kings and Princes and their poor dead Queen Mothers. It saddens me more than words can say. If the light doesn't touch us here, where in the world can it reach?

I must go to pray. I trust in God, and I trust in goodness. There is a reason they tell children *everything will be all right*, because it will, the world keeps turning, the sun keeps rising...

Looking back at this entry I feel ungrateful, because I know I am very lucky and have absolutely no right or reason to complain. God has blessed me. I must have faith in His protection. Nonetheless I have called for Adamine, even though I'm sure she will be ill-received here at court. I pray she leaves Mistress Yolande at home. I do not miss being called "Bitch!" and "Murderer!" at every turn...

SIBYL BENNETT, *HERMETIC SECTS OF BATTERSEA.* STAMMELTON: FOUR ARCS PUBLISHING, LTD., 1971, P. 130:

The most fascinating and momentous development of the hermetic movement in Battersea was precipitated by the appearance of the Great Comet Mayday (alt. spelling: *M'aider* or *M'aidez*). Lesser sects had made erroneous projections about such unconfirmed cosmological entities as the Ghost Star and the parallel planet Doppelganger approaching or even colliding with our planet. But the Celestial Order of the Hermetic Truth was the first to correctly identify Mayday and its trajectory. Their leader at the time was a Prophet Abellio - he sometimes called himself a "shepherd's son," though the earliest record that can be traced to him is of an Abellio Good (a sure pseudonym) enrolling in King's College. A family in the village of Eastfork claimed he was their cousin Matthias Johnson, but this claim remains unsubstantiated.

Prophet Abellio was a singularly gifted astronomer and astrologer, though his views were non-orthodox. He published his own text to accompany the teachings of Hermes Trismegistus: *The First Book of Psychocosmosis*. He differed from other hermeticists of his time in his obsession with retribution, with the 'fire and brimstone' associated with more austere faiths, and unlike his contemporaries in Battersea was not content to simply read astral alignments and cosmological events as indicators of political phenomena. Abellio claimed to be taking the Hermetic doctrine 'as above, so below' to its logical conclusion: as injustice is done below (our planet), so will justice be administered from above (the cosmos, or Universe). This radical approach to theurgy stressed the idea of a direct, active connection between microcosm and macrocosm. Under Abellio, 'Sic Itur Ad Astra' (Thus One Goes to the Stars) became the Order's motto. It will be noted that a modern descendant of the order, the Celestial Temple of the Great Pine Lake, is a great supporter of space travel.

Abellio staked the Order's entire reputation on the great comet May-

The
Watchmaker
of Filigree
Street

Natasha Pulley

Rob Thurman

day. While other hermetic sects explained that the comet heralded the onset of some great change (whether this was a change for the better or worse usually depended on their relationship with the monarchy) the Celestial Order of the Hermetic Truth declared that Mayday was a manifestation of Universal displeasure with Princess Melanie's rise to royal court, and would strike Battersea if Princess Melanie was not removed. The association was likely made because Mayday was first charted in the twilight sky a few hours after the Palace announced that Prince Gilford had married Princess Melanie. As far as Prophet Abellio was concerned, one was a clear reaction to the other. This was, of course, an extremely dangerous declaration to make in Battersea. Just sixty years earlier, King Fionn I had burned fifty-four 'heretics' who claimed his pale Queen Jenae was a *zombi* of the Vodou tradition who had been brought back from the dead (despite some convincing evidence on the heretics' part; see Villeneuve 1967 for a comprehensive study). But Prophet Abellio was buttressed by a flurry of independent reports of strange behavior among people and animals of all sizes and breeds, a spate of particularly terrible weather, and incidents of mass hysteria at schools and markets. He was also a political ingénue who had no affiliation with anyone of high standing and no ambitions for the crown. "I do not know why the Ashen Princess is not favored by the cosmos," he stated in a town square speech. "I only know that the cosmos cannot be fought and cannot be argued with."

MELANIE OF KREPSHIRE DIARY, 17 OCTOBER, MELANIE OF KREPSHIRE PAPERS, ELON UNIVERSITY LIBRARY (ELON):

A horrible thing happened today. Gilford and I went to the poorhouse to give alms and our carriage was egged. Of course the guards suppressed them, and I worry this violence gave them even more cause to hate me. Because they do hate me, I know it. I feel it. I would give them all my possessions if that would make them happy. I would happily give up the crown! If the people do not want me, if I displease them, then I *should* leave court! I only fear it would not be enough.

I tried to tell Gilford this - my proud husband, he did not even want to go to the poorhouse. He ignored me. He asked me why the lunatics call me the Ashen Princess. I told him about Daddy and the lightning storm and the old house in Krepshire. He said he did not know my father was dead. I almost cried! Maybe he does not even know my name? Maybe he truly thinks I am named 'Prettyfeet'? Is it possible that is all he sees and knows?

Speaking with Gilford did make me wonder why they call me 'the Black Moon.' I have asked after this. I hope it is not something terrible. I suddenly find myself regretting that I didn't read all those nasty books

Yolande brought to our house, the ones Adamine read by candlelight. I never thought I would need them. I really did think piety would be enough.

CARIDEE WILLIAMS, *THE ENCYCLOPEDIA ASTROLOGICA.* SANTA LUCIA: DESERT ISLAND PRESS, 2003:

BLACK MOON. The Black Moon (also known as *the Black Moon Lilith*) has historically been considered a highly negative influence, as well as a distinctly female one. Some astrologers regard the Black Moon to be a long-lost or long-destroyed 'phantom planet' that in the hermetic tradition 'haunts' the periphery of our subconscious. That this ominous force is feminine is no doubt a reflection of the patriarchal nature of our society.

MELANIE OF KREPSHIRE, LETTER TO ADAMINE LUCCA, 8 NOVEMBER, FOLDER 3, BOX 1, ADAMINE LUCCA CORRE-SPONDENCE, ELON UNIVERSITY LIBRARY (ELON):

Dearest darling sister,

I trust by now you have safely arrived home at Krepshire. First, I must apologize on Gilford's behalf for calling you "Hoof." Your feet are just fine. He can be clumsy with his words - I am sure he only meant it as an endearment. Second, I cannot get out of my mind the image of you licking the blood of that poor unfortunate fawn off your fingers. Please, please wash your hands very well. Not only because it is generally odd to swallow the blood of an uncooked animal, but because that animal had two heads! The groundskeeper was kind to put it to sleep. He says it's Mayday's fault the fawn was born that way. I do not understand how so large a force as Mayday could be troubled to hurt something so small.

I know you are very disappointed in me for not being, as you say, "more upset" with my predicament. But as I explained, I am a firm believer in patience and quiet virtue. You are right to say that I try very much to be 'good.' Indeed, everyone should. This does not mean I go blindly forward. I understand the trial I am undergoing, and I sincerely believe that God will protect me and keep me in His benevolence, no matter where or how I go. If my death would truly save Battersea, then I would gladly forfeit my life to save this kingdom. And if my death would not save Battersea, then I suppose all our lives are forfeit anyway. It's just as well for me to accept my destiny calmly and patiently, and try to give the people some solace.

Please do not carry hatred in your heart for the Order and their followers. You have very little restraint in expressing your emotions, and I understand your mother Yolande is a distinguished member of the Order now. She will not appreciate your comments, even if you are only protesting on my behalf. Please try to show them empathy. As I told you, Addy, I think it is more than anger they feel toward me. I think they are afraid, so terribly afraid of Mayday, that they are willing to grasp hold of any faith and follow any instruction to protect themselves from Mayday's wrath. You know what panic feels like, we were both raised by Yolande. Yes, you've always covered it up with rage and insolence and shouting, but dear sister, you knew fear. It needs to be consoled.

I have been thinking often of our father. I suppose it is thanks to Mayday, and Yolande's telling everyone that the lightning storm and the fire were meant to kill me instead of father. Sometimes I wonder if she is right. I know you think all of that is garbage, but you were very young. You were spared the sight of his charred body. And the lightning bolt that started the fire did strike the roof of my room. If your mother is right about that night, then you must know that I am very sorry I deprived you of a father.

Last night I dreamed I was skating on the pond behind the house (the one you fell through when you were twelve, even though I told you the ice was too thin!), and father was watching me from the pines. He was wearing his furs. Everything was drowned in snow. I told him I knew the ice was getting thin. I said - and this is very unlike me, I know! - that I was very angry with him for dying. I still regret saying this, even if it was only in a dream. He said, "Things change, my dear." Then the ice cracked. I saw myself falling, in my golden wedding dress. He did not help me, but watched me sadly and solemnly. I believe he said something else: "You must learn to stand up." What do you suppose this means?

Of one thing we can be sure, that Mayday is bringing great change upon us all. How funny that I have been talking about Mayday as if she is a person instead of a comet. Maybe she is the third sister? The long-forgotten one? The most misunderstood of all?

I pray for your love and support and understanding, Addy, you who knows me best of all. I hope nothing but the very best for you, and I have <u>no doubt</u> that with a bit of cosmic fortune you will live a joyous, vibrant life and marry a very suitable (and handsome!) suitor if you improve your manners and your countenance just a little. You have a very pretty smile. You have no reason to scowl. Life, and God, are good and wonderful.

You are most kind for visiting. I have faith that I will see you in time.

Love,
Your Devoted Sister Melanie

SIBYL BENNETT, HERMETIC SECTS OF BATTERSEA. STAM-
MELTON: FOUR ARCS PUBLISHING, LTD., 1971, P. 131:

Despite the growing hysteria surrounding the comet - by November of
that year, as many as a dozen peasants had committed suicide in preparation for Battersea's collision - the Celestial Order of the Hermetic Truth
likely would not have gained an audience at royal court if not for Yolande
Rampel, stepmother to Princess Melanie. Yolande was a frequent guest at
the capital's most lavish esoteric gatherings, but did not seriously commit
her money to any until she encountered the Order. Some claimed that
Yolande was jealous of her stepdaughter and so engineered her down-
fall, though most consider her to have been a 'true believer' in Prophet
Abellio's predictions. In her testimonies to the order, Yolande confessed
that her stepdaughter had been "marked for death by the cosmos" since
childhood. She cited as evidence crosses on Melanie's palms, a family estate that grew only pumpkins, an infestation of rodents, and a lightning
bolt that finally destroyed the property.

Yolande had charmed the widowed King Fionn III during the prince
and princess's wedding, and so she brought Prophet Abellio to court
to meet the King. Fionn III began summoning Prophet Abellio to private meetings from which the King always emerged 'wild-eyed and determined,' according to servants. This was Abellio's well-documented
effect on others. The Order's highest minister preached a careful balance between fear and deliverance. In this way he was actually quite for-
ward-thinking for his time: Abellio encouraged proactive empowerment
among his followers, not passive acceptance of a terrible fate. Whatever
the bloody consequences, he should at least be recognized for this.

MELANIE OF KREPSHIRE DIARY, 10 NOVEMBER, MELANIE
OF KREPSHIRE PAPERS, ELON UNIVERSITY LIBRARY (ELON):

My dinner-banquet with fate draws near. I imagine gongs being beaten
outside my door (I have actually opened the door to check, twice). I have
been reading *Little Martyrs I Have Known*, which my mother gave to me. I
have found it to be most wise. In the book they call moments like mine
"dinner-banquets with fate". And they say the best thing you can do - the
thing all martyrs do, anyway - is accept it quietly, without fussing, and sit
down and eat the meal that has been presented to you.

Yolande came to court and she brought those men in green robes and
odd hats, the ones who found Mayday and say she has come to have my
head. It seems many people across the countryside are very angry with
me, though I have hurt them not at all. I do not even know them. Their
prophet called me 'ashen princess' and said I have offended the cosmos,

and no one - not the King, certainly not dumb Gilford - said a word to defend me. It makes me wonder if they ever loved me. I told the King afterwards that I looked to him as a father, and I loved him very much. He only patted my arm and turned away. Me, his "sweet daughter"!

Maybe he is wrestling with his ministers. I know the King's heart is heavy with worry. He has many concerns to look after. I should not be so selfish. I must focus on bigger things now: Mayday, death, the end of all things good and wicked.

Every morning I open my curtains and look to the sky and pray that I will not see Mayday, my dark sister (of course she does not look dark, she is actually whiter and brighter than the sun, a gleaming little fireball). But she is there. I think she does seem bigger every time I see her. Her radiant hair trails behind her. She is beautiful and terrible. Everyone goes silent and watches as she passes over our heads. Children cower behind wagons and hedges. It saddens me to see people so upset. But maybe she does *not* bring death and destruction. Maybe she brings transcendence! Maybe God's final plans remain hidden still!

JONAH KAHMER, "THE GILDED AGE." IN *MASTERS OF BAT-TERSEA: A COMPLETE HISTORY*, ED. JONAH KAHMER AND THOMAS WHYET (ELON: UNIVERSITY OF ELON PRESS, 1998), P. 223:

In the midst of the tumult of the Mayday comet, King Fionn III gave a speech asking his subjects for calm. "Come and let us behave ourselves like civilized men," he stated. "Remember that strong and mighty people will always be faced with the hardest trials, because God knows we can take it." He apparently had less faith in the hardiness of his kingdom than his words might indicate, as he had already built three brick underground bunkers (ironically named Mars, Venus, and Jupiter) and stocked them with supplies to last the winter. Fionn also consulted with military leaders on the possibility of an aerial assault on the comet (they advised him against the idea).

Given these inclinations of the King, it should be no surprise that he believed soothsayers who claimed the sacrifice of Princess Melanie would save the kingdom from the comet's wrath. Historians such as LeVan (1995) and Zelma (1997) have argued that the sacrifice of the Princess indicates the widespread practice of human sacrifice in Battersea. However, there is no evidence to support this conclusion. This sad case simply illustrates the extraordinary lengths a state will go to under extreme duress. The desperation at all levels of society in Battersea was such that householders were conducting murder-suicides of their families in preparation for what they believed to be an apocalypse so total that "fields would be barren for one hundred years" and "the land will be drowned in ash." Individuals have been known to resort to such behavior when faced with enemy invasion, and there is after all no hope of fighting a comet. Under these circumstances any state is susceptible to sacrificing even a Princess.

ADAMINE LUCCA, LETTER TO MELANIE OF KREPSHIRE, 13 NOVEMBER, MELANIE OF KREPSHIRE PAPERS, ELON UNIVERSITY LIBRARY (ELON):

Sister - there are ways out of this. You can make an escape. You can pretend to be pregnant (I sincerely believe this would forestall any killing). You can blame someone else! Point the finger at Gilford, for the heavens' sake. Point it at that Abellio fool, point it at my mother, point it at *me* if you must. By the time you receive this letter I will be across the sea in Hannegard, so yes, point the finger at me. I swear I do not care. And yes, I am trying to run from the comet. I do what I must. You should do the same. There are people who can help you. There is a Miss Kaltrin in town, she will make arrangements for you. Or there is also the court barber. I spoke to him when I was there. He seemed to give you sympathy. Please talk to these people, Melanie. Please *try*!

PRINCESS MELANIE'S FOOT. PLACARD. *LATTER-ERA ARTIFACTS OF THE BATTERSEA ROYALTY.* NATIONAL MUSEUM OF PRE-COLONIAL ART, ELON:_

Plaster cast of Princess Melanie's right foot, commissioned by her husband Prince Gilford prior to her scheduled sacrifice to the comet Mayday by the Celestial Order of the Hermetic Truth. Gilford, who was known to call his wife "Prettyfeet," called the plaster cast "Melanie" and kept it in his room until his own death. Its original plaque read 'In Honor of Melanie the Good-Hearted.'

MELANIE OF KREPSHIRE, "MY WORLD IS EVER GOLDEN IN THE SNOW," 20 NOVEMBER, MELANIE OF KREPSHIRE PAPERS, ELON UNIVERSITY LIBRARY (ELON):

My world is ever golden in the snow
When farmers rest the plow and shut the barn
And all the stoutest men are laid down low
My eyes still find the daisies on the cairn
I find rejuvenation in the ice
When others find it difficult to strive

And see no virtue in enduring twice
I still thank mighty God that I'm alive
How sad I'll be when death does usher me,
Because I cherish even minor bliss
Though I am loyal child of Battersea
I do not welcome death's concluding kiss
The thought that haunts my soul as I lie curled:
How much I do not want to leave this world.

DUNCAN LOOM, *MY LIFE & TIMES IN BATTERSEA*. OFFICE OF THE NATIONAL HISTORICAL SOCIETY, 1950, P. 347:

On 21 November we gathered in the House of Stars. There were many people in attendance in the hall and I was lucky because I arrived early and found myself a place to stand on the base of a pillar in the middle of the room. Babies sat aloft their elders' shoulders. While Prophet Abellio prepared himself, his assistants recited his speeches. The crowd played simple music. A man beside me shared that his wife, while pregnant, was so concerned about the comet that she had taken ill and died. The longer we waited the more we feared the Princess would not come and the sacrifice would not happen. A butcher stood and shouted that we had no more time, that we had to act quickly now. Some foolish soul even suggested we storm the palace. I confess I too began to grow anxious in fear of the end. In all my time spent watching M'aidez I never truly believed it would strike us until this moment. But in the midst of the weeping and yelling in the Hall of Stars, I did feel fear of God.

At sundown there was a cry from the crowd outside the hall - the black hearse carrying the Princess had arrived! We let out a resounding cheer for our heroine but when soldiers brought her into our hall I was shocked to see her in tears. The King had told us she would come in peace but her feet dragged and she begged the soldiers to let her go. She said such strange things: that she had never had the chance to go to town, that she wanted to walk in the pine woods of Krepshire. We yelled to her: "God Bless You, Princess Melanie!" but she only flailed her head and howled for His Most Honorable King Fionn III and His Honorable Prince Gilford. She howled for her father to save her, even though as we all understood the old man was dead, burned by the stars when they hunted for Melanie the Ashen Princess. It was most unseemly, and very disturbing. For we all loved the Princess, and thought she too loved us enough to make this sacrifice willingly.

I still wonder why the Princess was struck by this sudden madness. Did she forget that all of Battersea was at risk if she did not give herself up? Did she forget the blood and sweat we all have spilt for Battersea, in battle and hardship? Did she not believe the Hermetic truth that M'aidez wanted her?

Prophet Abellio stepped out from his chambers and stood behind the altar, the Knife of Reckoning in his hand. We were so glad to see him, come to put an end to our kingdom's misery that we cried out in jubilation, but the Princess threw herself into such a fit we thought she'd become a wild animal. Her tears became screams of anger. I thank God the Prophet commanded us not to listen to the Black Moon's protests. And I confess she did look less like a Princess of our glorious kingdom and more like a woman possessed, perhaps even a witch. This was not the sweet and light-hearted princess, the 'jewel of the countryside,' who sat in a golden carriage on her wedding day and waved her slender hand. By my eyes this was a condemned witch, a mad-woman. Where did this gorgon come from? Her poisoned heart was revealed to us all by her malicious words: "I Curse You All Until The End Of Time!"

I was shaken by this declaration. Prophet Abellio raised his arms for silence and warned us again not to pay her any mind, because the Black Moon lies, he said. So onward the soldiers brought her, to the altar beneath the emerging stars, where she would meet her destiny in full view of the Cosmos. She stumbled several times. It was a disgrace. The man beside me reminded me of the story of her wedding dance, at which she fell and broke her glass slippers. I had heard this story many times, usually told in humor, but now I felt all was foretold. None other than our good Prophet in Green divined this truth!

I clung to this faith while the Princess bled to death. A few in the crowd cheered but others cried "Thank You" and called her 'Saint Melanie.' I was still quaking from her curse and when I walked home I did not dare look behind me, but my faith was confirmed when M'aidez did not strike us, but instead burst into a thousand golden sparks. The sight was so beautiful I could not speak. The rejoicing lasted three weeks. I have never been so glad to be alive.

LYDIA VARGAS, *ADAMINE LUCCA: WOMAN AT DAWN*. ZANNABERG: PINNEROSE BOOKS, 1985, P. 107:

It is highly unlikely that Adamine Lucca would have reached her heights as a bandit if not for her independence and extreme moral relativity. These personality traits, however, were highly unusual for young women in her time. Adamine's resistance to authority and traditional symbols of power was evident from a young age, and it is likely that the death of her older sister Melanie consolidated Adamine's approach to life. In addition to developing a lifelong hatred of obscure religious cults such as the Celestial Order of the Hermetic Truth, Adamine came to believe that the world was deeply unjust and one's fate pre-determined. This revelation, in turn, made all actions taken between birth and the deliverance of this fate irrelevant and in moral terms, inconsequential.

"If one so good as Melanie could meet that gruesome end then clearly there is no purpose in being good," she wrote to her cousin Johann Walsh after her first documented crime. "So I have stolen the purse of the old woman sitting in my train car. The loon was so buried in her furs and feathers and so drugged on opium I do not think she even noticed. I immediately used two pieces to buy an almond cake and nothing struck me dead for using stolen coins. Poor dead Melanie and papa and mother, always admonishing and tongue-clucking about good and proper behavior, they have all taught me wrong. There is no reason not to simply do what you want in the time that you have. If I die damned, I was born damned."

JONAH KAHMER, "THE GILDED AGE." IN *MASTERS OF BAT-TERSEA: A COMPLETE HISTORY*, ED. JONAH KAHMER AND THOMAS WHYET (ELON: UNIVERSITY OF ELON PRESS, 1998), P. 233:

The sudden and total collapse of Battersea remains a contentious subject among historians. Initial theories that Battersea was invaded by highland tribes have been widely discredited. Le Van (1995) argues that famine coupled with a revolt among an over-burdened peasantry was to blame, citing the death of the leader of the Celestial Order of the Hermetic Truth, Prophet Abellio, who was broken on the wheel by a mob after he incorrectly predicted a year of plenty. His assistant Yolande of Krepshire is also sometimes considered to have been murdered by arson, although it is unclear why a mob would have burned her in her home - thus eliminating the opportunity for any looting - instead of burning her at the stake, as was typical at the time.

It is unlikely that a peasant revolution would have succeeded were it not for the startling deterioration of the royalty. King Fionn III's reign came to an end when an iron chandelier in the palace's winter sitting room suddenly fell on him while he was signing property transfers. The King had taken to doing his paperwork in the winter room even in the summer, when he kept it artificially cold and dark. He was still mourning the death of his sole heir Gilford, who had lost both feet to gangrene after an ill-fated trading expedition left him stranded and frost-bitten in the Waycass Mountains; the Prince had been so distressed that he had taken his own life. Gilford, of course, had agreed to surrender his own Princess to a sacrifice less than a year earlier and had neither remarried nor sired any heir, legitimate or not. When General Michael Alexander of the early Cormorant Empire launched a campaign to colonize Battersea, the weak and conflicted kingdom buckled. The elaborate rituals of the Gilded Age were supplanted, the schooling system overhauled, society restructured, and eventually, the kingdom's collective memory lost. It may seem intellectually lazy to blame a kingdom's rapid demise on a set of bizarre accidents, but happenstance is often the stuff of fate. As the famous Battersea poet Chrystal wrote on the occasion of the Cormorants' taking up residence at the royal palace, "We have become a people bereft, wandering in the wilderness."

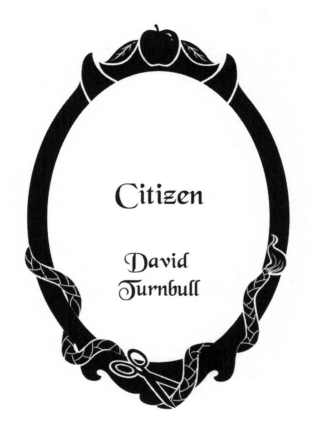

Citizen

David Turnbull

The long hot summer that had superseded the Marchen spring was in turn about to give way to a dour autumn. A fact that seemed patently obvious from the murky clouds that swelled and billowed in the gray skies above starkly austere architecture of the headquarters of the People's Commissariat.

On this downcast morning the door of the cramped cell deep in the festering bowels of the building was thrown open and a young woman with a ragged scalp of horribly shorn hair was forcefully led by armed guards along a dank, cockroach-infested corridor and up a narrow stairwell. Her bare feet smacked against the cold stone floor as the ragged hem of her prisoner's smock flapped around her skinny ankles.

She was directed to a large, well-heated room and ordered to sit upon a crooked wooden stool that seemed completely out of place amongst the lush pile of the rug on which it stood. Once the guards had taken their leave, the woman stared silently at a mahogany desk, behind which a tall chair, upholstered in startling blue velvet, was turned toward the window. A thin blue plume of cigarette smoke, dancing in the air above this chair, provided the only clue that anyone might actually be sitting there.

Almost afraid to breathe, the woman remained perfectly still, hands resting on her lap in an effort to halt their trembling. Of all the items sitting on the desk two stood out and completely enraptured her. A large cupcake, covered in pink fondant icing, and a steaming mug of what smelled deliciously like hot drinking chocolate. Her undernourished belly let out an envious groan. She felt her mouth fill with covetous saliva. It had been weeks since she'd eaten a proper meal.

Still she waited, intermittently dragging her eyes away from the gastronomic delights to watch the curling blue spirals of cigarette smoke snaking upwards to the ornate ceiling. Every now and then she would hear a rustling noise from behind the chair, suggesting papers being shuffled and pages being turned.

This prolonging of her agony was no doubt deliberate. She had already waited for a month in that cold, dismal cell for her interrogation to finally commence. To keep her waiting now was cold and malicious. After a while, when she could no longer tolerate the torturous silence, she cleared her throat and spoke out loud.

"Is anyone actually there?"

The chair swung around instantaneously. Almost lost inside it was a small, seedy looking individual. His long black hair was greased flat against his scalp and pushed back behind his ever so slightly pointed ears. Tracing the top of his repulsively moist upper lip was a pathetic and dismal attempt at a pencil thin moustache.

He needed no introduction. She knew him by the description other prisoners had whispered through walls. He was a man of unrivalled infamy - none other than Hopkin, the People's Inquisitor. This was as bad as it could get. It was claimed that if the Inquisitor took a personal interest in you then pain of the worst possible kind would undoubtedly follow.

Digging her bare heels firmly into the rug she tensed herself so that he might not see the shudder of revulsion that went juddering through her body. He fixed her with a cold stare of his beady eyes and laid down his portfolio onto the desk. *My file, no doubt*, she thought.

Slowly he stubbed out his cigarette into a wide crystal ashtray and proceeded to break off a chunk of the cupcake with his dirty, long-nailed fingers. His eyes never left her as he delivered the chunk to his mouth and began to chew noisily. When he was finished he took a slow sip from the mug of drinking chocolate before wiping his mouth with a white handkerchief.

Then, apparently done with his taunting, he pressed his fingers together and leaned forward across the desk, much as a spider might edge towards a helpless fly caught in its web. "Citizen," he said, in a voice that rasped like cold water poured on a hot pan. "How good of you to join me."

"As if I had a choice," she replied, head and shoulders defiantly straight, deciding in that instant that if these were to be her last moments they would pass in as dignified manner as possible.

Absently Hopkin tapped the pads of his little fingers against one and other.

"But I had a choice," he told her. "I could easily have had you shot. I have the order right here on my desk."

"So why didn't you?" she demanded. "You executed my husband. Why delay? Just get it over with!"

"My dear," he said, in a patronizing tone. "One thing the revolution has taught us all is that nothing is ever predestined. Just as Kings and Queens, who believed that they had a divine right to rule, can be toppled and deposed, so too can pardons be granted to enemies of the people - under the right conditions."

"Where are my children?" she interrupted, hoping to deflect him from his cruel teasing. "What have you done with them?"

"Your children are perfectly safe," he replied. "Unlike the previous regimes that held sway across the Marchen, the People's Assembly has provided sufficient orphanages for pitiable unfortunates such as your son and daughter."

Her heart fluttered wildly at the mention of her family.

"They are not orphans," she said. "I am still alive."

"At present."

"Then do it!" she challenged. "Call back the guards. Have them march me out to the execution yard."

As he stared her down through those nasty little pin prick eyes his pink pointed tongue popped quickly out of his mouth and traced the narrow contour of his unfortunate moustache. "I have a proposition for you," he said, goading her once more by popping another fat chunk of cake into his mouth.

"You can't bribe me with cake," she spat. But the sudden spasm in her stomach suggested that the day might not be so far away when he might be able to do just that.

Hopkin took a noisy slurp of drinking chocolate and again dabbed his face with his handkerchief. "I may be able to offer you more than cake."

The sham seductive timbre of voice sounded sly and snake-like. She felt herself bristle with anger. This was surely some sort of trick. Nevertheless she pressed him to continue.

"I'm listening," she said.

The Inquisitor seemed to consider this some sort of victory over her. He smiled as he outlined the terms of his proposal.

"What is on offer is your freedom. All charges dropped. We can set you up in a small garret room in one of the state owned tenements. You can live out the rest of your life without fear of persecution or prosecution. Which, in my humble opinion, is far more than you deserve."

"And my children?" she asked.

"Custody would be out of the question, of course," he answered. "But a visit on the odd occasion may not be beyond the realms of what is possible."

"And what exactly would I have to do in exchange?" she asked.

Pushing himself away from the desk Hopkin climbed down from the chair. At a quick guess she would have put his full height at no more than four foot. Despite the seriousness of the situation she had to bite her lip to stop herself from smiling at the thought that while he had been seated there with such menacing authority, his feet had clearly not been touching the ground.

Placing his little hands behind his back he paced up and down in front of the drapes. The internal ledge came up to his shoulder. He would have had to stand on tiptoe to see anything out of the window. The proposal he put to her as he strode arrogantly around the room was precise, clearly articulated and full of the type of dogmatic rhetoric that had become depressingly commonplace amongst those of the Inquisitor's particular political persuasion.

"The Assembly is determined to stamp out pernicious pantheon of myth and superstition that was previously encouraged and engendered by aristocracy," he declared. "This was quite patently a crude and callous attempt to deflect the attention of the exploited mass of the workers and peasants away from the misery of their enforced and unjust condition of servitude and oppression."

"And that's why you have people like my husband shot," she snapped at him, brazen now that it seemed she might have something he wanted.

The Inquisitor stepped up in front of the stool and pressed his ugly face so close to hers they were almost nose-to-nose. Had she stood up she would have towered over him. "This is the deal I am authorized to offer you, Citizen." He whispered the words as if they were an intimate secret that should only pass between the two of them. "In exchange for your liberty you are to sign a public confession, stating that your story, the preposterous *tale* that people once told about you, is a complete fabrication. A corrupt pack of lies. Nothing more than foul Royalist propaganda."

She had to forcefully prevent herself from jumping up from the stool. Digging her heels into the rug again she pressed her fingernails angrily into her emaciated thighs. "I won't do it!" she snapped back. "I won't deny who I am. Or what happened to me!"

"Take some time to think about it," said Hopkin, stepping away from her. A crafty grin spread across his wet lips. "I have discretion to choose the exact timing of your execution. Alternatively, if I deem it to be in the interests of the revolution, I can keep you locked up in here for a long, long time."

"I have suffered incarceration before," she reminded him.

"Then suffer some more," he said and called for the guards.

Back in her cell she quickly came to appreciate how rash her last statement had been. As a young girl her incarceration in the stone tower, with its narrow window looking out across the lush green canopy of the forest, had been a positive luxury compared to this clammy cell where the sunlight never penetrated. In the tower the sorceress had come once a day to feed her and brush her long, long hair. And later her Prince had come - with gifts that were increasingly scandalous and physical in nature.

Despondent, she lay down on the hard mattress, pinching her nostrils against the reek of stale urine and old vomit. After a moment she allowed herself to cry. The tears came thick and fast. Tears that mourned the unjust murder of her husband. Tears that bewailed the appalling conditions of her confinement. Tears that expressed the hollowness she felt from the enforced separation from her children. With the tears came a strangled yowling screech that seemed to rise from the very pit of her soul.

"Don't let the bastards hear you crying, Rapunzel!" yelled someone in a nearby cell.

She sat up, dabbing her wet cheeks with the heels of her hands.

"You know my name?" she called back.

"I recognized you when they took you away this morning," came the reply. "It seems to me that it would do you good if you yourself could remember just who you are."

"And who are you?" she asked. "Who is it who offers such advice?"

"Just someone who was also once the subject of a *tale.*"

She tried to place the voice that echoed through the gloomy catacombs.

"But who?" she called out again.

"Shut up down there," came the angry voice of the duty guard. "Any more noise out of you lot and no one gets any rations tonight."

From the other cells there came shouts of indignation and wails of desperate pleading.

"Shut up!" asserted the guard more forcefully.

The hush that followed was like a breath being forcibly held.

Biting her lip to maintain her own silence she pushed her face into the foul smelling mattress. *Rapunzel*, she thought. *I am Rapunzel. I am who I am and no one should expect me to deny that.* Gradually she drifted into an exhausted sleep. Her dreams were of her children. Her handsome boy and her beautiful girl.

An entire fortnight may have dragged slowly by before she was once more escorted to the Inquisitor's office. It was difficult to be entirely sure. In the melancholy gloom of the cell her perception of passing time was severely hindered and distorted. In fact when she once more took her place on the little stool that stood on the plush rug she found that she couldn't quite settle in her mind whether it was morning, afternoon or evening.

Inquisitor Hopkin did not have his chair turned away from her on this occasion. He watched in silence as she arranged her tattered smock around her knees. In the time between their meetings the unkempt fringes where her hair had been hacked away had grown a bit more. It was not yet as long as it had been when she was dragged, kicking and screaming to this place. And was certainly nowhere near as long as it had been in the *tale* that the Inquisitor found so offensive.

Once more he forced her to wait for a long time in total silence, his beady, rodent eyes fixed unflinchingly upon her. *This is all part of his strategy,* she assured herself. *It's how he seeks to unsettle you and emphasize the power that he holds over you.* She dug her heels into the rug and prepared obstinately to sit him out.

As she did so her eyes fell upon the items that on this occasion were laid out before him on the mahogany desktop. A crusty pork pie, glazed lusciously brown and emitting a strong and seductively meaty aroma. Next to it a tall beaker of milk, so icy cold that rivulets of condensation were winding slowly down the side of the glass. Her stomach, tortured by her infrequent diet of gruel and tepid water, complained noisily

Hopkin crumbled a piece of crust from the pie and tossed it nonchalantly into his mouth. *This too is deliberate,* thought Rapunzel, forcing down the ravenous saliva that filled her mouth. *All part of his cruel tactics.* A wicked smirk formed on the Inquisitor's face as he picked up the beaker of milk and took a long, premeditated drink.

"Tell me, Citizen?" he asked, placing the milk carefully before him. "Have you taken the time to consider my proposal?"

"I have," she replied, careful not to reveal any emotion, buoyed by the encouragement of the frequent whispered discussions she and her mysterious neighbor had engaged in over the past fortnight.

"And?"

He dabbed his lips with his handkerchief.

"Give me back my son and daughter and I will sign your lies," she replied.

Hopkin's pasty white face flushed red.

Anger flashed in his eyes.

"You are in no position to negotiate!" he hissed at her.

"Nevertheless," she insisted. "That is my condition."

"Let's be clear," he said, seeming to regain his cold composure. "Custody of your children is not an option and never will be. The revolution will not be put at risk in such a reckless manner. If we were to allow someone such as you to raise them, who knows what Royalist nonsense you would fill their heads with? Reactionary forces tend flock to so-called 'heirs to the throne' like horseflies to dung."

Rapunzel felt her breath choke in her throat. *I won't let him see me cry,* she cautioned herself. *I must be assertive with him.* But when she went to protest her case further he held up a grubby finger.

"I am going to read something to you," he said, shuffling the papers before him on his desk. "And I want you to listen very carefully."

He unfolded a ragged scrap of paper.

"This is a statement from a former scullery maid who once worked at the Palace."

Clearing his throat he read from the paper, clumsily attempting to affect the coarse accent of a scullery maid. *"It was a terrible scandal, so it was. The young Prince went and got a peasant girl from the village in the family way. His mind was well and truly fixed on marrying her. A Prince and a commoner? It was unheard of.*

But nothing the King and Queen could say would make the stubborn boy see sense. So the King sent him and the little trollop away for a long time. And when they came back and she had twins, a boy and a girl, the King made up this story about how she had been locked up in this tower by a witch and how the Prince had saved her and all..."

Hopkin looked up from the paper and fixed her with his trademark stare.

"Do you want me to continue, Citizen?"

She shrugged her scrawny shoulders. "It doesn't worry me," she said. "It's all lies. You probably bribed her or tortured her to say those things."

"Lies?" He shook his head wearily. His long greasy locks slipped from behind his pointed ears and flapped heavily around his chin. "You and I know precisely where the lies stem from."

Now he held up another sheet of paper.

"This is your story - as I understand it."

He cleared his throat once more.

"When you were a small child your parents were caught stealing radishes from a neighbor's garden?"

"True," agreed Rapunzel.

"The neighbor turned out to be some sort of sorceress?"

"Precisely."

"As a punishment you were taken from you parents by this 'sorceress' and locked away in a high tower in the woods?"

"In the same way that I am locked away now," she said.

"And she had you grow your hair to a somewhat impossible length, so that when she wanted to come to you in the tower she would call to you to lower your hair out of the window - then she could climb up it?"

"Exactly."

The Inquisitor heaved a long, exaggerated sigh, as if his patience was being stretched to its limit. "And after you had been locked in that tower for a few years the Prince came riding by?"

"The poor, dead love of my life," nodded Rapunzel.

"And he too climbed up your hair?"

"He had watched the sorceress from behind the bushes," Rapunzel explained. "So he knew to call out to me and what to do when my hair came tumbling down the side of the tower."

"And you fell in love?" sneered the Inquisitor.

"We did," agreed Rapunzel. A single tear went rolling down her cheek.

"But when the 'sorceress' found out all about you secret liaisons she cut off your hair and cast you out to live in some bleak and barren far away place?"

"She did," said Rapunzel. "And I gave birth to my children there. All alone. With no one to help me."

"Do you know how preposterous this all sounds?" asked Hopkin. His face looked furious.

"It is true nevertheless," insisted Rapunzel.

"And this ending," he continued. "The most ridiculous part of all. The 'sorceress' tricked the Prince into climbing up the hair she had shorn from your head. Then she tossed him out of the tower into some thorn bushes that tore out his eyes?"

"And he wandered blindly through the forest for years," Rapunzel finished.

"Till he found you again?"

She nodded in agreement.

"And when you kissed his eyes he miraculously regained his sight?"

"Never underestimate the power of true love," said Rapunzel.

"And you lived happily ever after?"

Rapunzel bowed her head. "Till now," she said, quietly.

"You were a lowly peasant girl who, through a series of somewhat dubious events and convenient coincidences, became a Princess?"

"I was," she nodded.

"This is precisely the problem with these *tales*," he said, glowering at her now. "Dangerous, subversive nonsense. Peasant girls become Princesses. Idiot boys turn out to be Princes and suchlike. Everyone has the chance to live happily ever after."

"As I did, till quite recently," Rapunzel pointed out.

"But that is precisely the lie," said Hopkin. "These tales gave false hope. Not everyone could rise from the base condition of his or her crushing poverty. The very nature of the nobility required the subjugation and alienation of the peasantry and the mass of working people."

Rapunzel rolled her eyes. When backed into a corner zealots like Hopkin inevitably began spouting rhetoric. "Personally I neither subjugated nor oppressed anyone," she told him. "In fact my husband, on my urging, was the author of a number of progressive reforms."

Hopkin shook his head. "You showed no class loyalty what so ever, Citizen. You ate cake while your subjects starved for bread!"

"And am I not starving now?" she challenged. "While you eat cake and pork pie?"

"And have I not given you a chance to resolve that particular problem?" he challenged her back.

"You cannot manipulate history by forcing people like myself to change their account of what happened to them," she insisted.

"Pah!" spat the Inquisitor. He scrunched up the paper and threw it violently across the room. "This is exactly the type of irrational nonsense we are trying to stamp out!"

"Suppress you mean," said Rapunzel raising her head to face him.

"Call it what you will," said Hopkin. "But we won't have any of it. You hear?"

"And I will only agree to denounce the truth of my past if you allow me to have my son and daughter back," she said, just as forcefully. "If you won't grant that then you may as well kill me. I would not want to go on living without them by my side."

The Inquisitor rose to stand upright on his chair. He leaned over and placed his little hands on the desk. "In a moment I'm going to have the guards take you back to your cell," he said. "But before you leave I am going to give you something else to ponder on before we meet again."

"I've told you my conditions," insisted Rapunzel. "I won't change my mind."

"The orphanage where your son and daughter have been placed is a large institution," he said. "The matron who runs it has so many children she simply doesn't know what to do. Jacks and Jills she calls them. It saves her from having to remember their names. Despite her best endeavors accidents happen with depressing regularity. Jacks have been known to fall down the stairs and Jills to go tumbling after…"

"You wouldn't dare!" cried Rapunzel.

"Oh but we would," insisted Hopkin. "*Dare* is precisely what we do. Revolution is daring by its very nature. They said that we wouldn't dare to overthrow the morally corrupt monarchist system. But that is exactly what we dared to do."

Uncertainty gnawed constantly at her as she lay in her cell.

She began to doubt everything that she had ever held to be true. Echoed snatches from the scullery maid's statement reverberated maliciously around her head. She had to concede that the words had a nagging ring of authenticity about them. Couldn't the *tale* of Rapunzel who had let down her hair quite easily be a fabrication to cover a distasteful liaison between a Prince and peasant girl? Would it be so hard then just to concede that her story was so sordid that she had somehow convinced herself beyond the shadow of a doubt that a fanciful fabrication was the truth?

Why not simply do as Hopkin asked? Sign a public statement, denouncing her *tale* and confirming the alternative version of events? In doing so to be released from this terrible place and at least see her children once more? Perhaps find a chance for the three of them to escape?

But where would she turn to?

Who would help her if she became a fugitive?

Had not the ordinary people, the subjects of the realm, responded willingly to the call of the insurrectionist Till Eulenspiegel and risen up against their masters? It came to her that she had forgotten so easily the poverty she and her parents had once endured in the days before she was imprisoned in the tower - poverty that large sections of the population had clearly continued to endure whilst she'd been cosseted in the lap of luxury in the Palace. Why would any of them risk the wrath of the Commissariat by offering assistance to someone they perceived, perhaps with good reason, to be partly to blame for their former oppression?

She called out to her neighbor, the nameless man who had somehow become her rock.

"Are you awake?"

Silence.

"Hello? Are you there?"

"He's gone," snapped a voice from farther along the corridor. "The damned fool had a big mouth. He's either gotten himself executed or transported to one of the work camps."

The news shocked her. That was how easy it was for the Commissariat. They could simply cause a person to vanish - no magic required as part of the equation.

"I am Rapunzel!" she called. "Do you know *me*? Do I know *you*? Who else is locked away down here?"

"*Nobody* is down here," came the response. "Our *tales* are denied and written out of history. We are nothing now. We are *nobody*…"

"Shut up, both of you!" pleaded someone else. "Shut up, or we'll be starved and beaten."

Seeing the futility of arguing with people who had clearly become devoid of hope, Rapunzel held her tongue and wrestled her dilemma in silence. *If we are all nothing now, why shouldn't I put my children first? Sign what Hopkin wants and hold them once more in my arms? But then, once he has what he desires what will be left to keep him to his word?*

She slept and dreamt of the stone tower where she had spent her formative years. The tower where the sorceress had called to her every morning to let her hair down. The tower where her sweet prince had finally come to seduce her and save her. The dream was so vivid that it could not possibly be a false memory.

And in the dream she recalled the angry words the sorceress had spat at her as she sheered away the long yards of her hair after finding out about her secret suitor. "You fool! Don't you realize the power that your own will could have exerted over these enchanted tresses? The wicked things you might have had them do, if only you had tapped in to your own potential and not allowed some sordid sexual liaison to dominate your thoughts and actions?"

On those words she awoke - the seeds of a plan rapidly forming in her head. Hopkin could not be trusted. For her own safety, and that of her beloved children, she needed some leverage - the fact that the Commissariat denounced magic did not mean it could not still serve a purpose.

Hopkin had tweaked his tactics slightly.

On the mahogany desktop this time sat a dinner plate bearing the remnants of a recently finished meal. A creamy curl of gristle cut from a sirloin steak. A lone marrowfat pea, floating in a tiny puddle of glossy, dark gravy. A pale yellow streak of congealed hollandaise sauce. Beside the plate an almost empty glass with a dreg of ruby red wine settled down in the bevel.

The message was clearly intended to taunt her.

My belly is full, while yours is empty.

She was so hungry now that she would have gladly licked the plate clean had she thought that he might allow it. From his velvet chair the Inquisitor coldly watched her as she settled on the stool. If he intended her to endure another dose of torturous silence she was in no mood for it. "Are my children safe?" she demanded.

Hopkin blinked at her as if slightly taken off guard. His tongue traced the line of his narrow moustache, slowly left to right. "They are in rude health so far as I am aware," he replied. "Although I would be loathe to guarantee it. Boys and girls of that age can be impossibly reckless and incautious when it comes to risking life and limb."

Rapunzel shivered with relief. She could tell from the malicious expression on the Inquisitors unsightly face that he was telling the truth and still intent on using the safety of her son and daughter as his trump card.

I have a card of my own now, she thought and smothered the grin that threatened to curl on her lip. "I have considered your proposal some more," she told him.

"Have you now?"

He smiled liquidly.

"I am of a mind to agree," she said.

"You are of a mind are you?"

Rapunzel felt her hackles rise at the scornful sarcasm in his voice.

"I have a request," she told him.

Hopkin was unable to hide the disappointment on his face.

"As I explained previously," he said. "You are in no position to bargain."

She pushed ahead with her request.

"I wish to see my hair!"

The Inquisitor cocked his head to one side. His sharp little eyes danced up and down.

"I hardly think they would have kept it," he said.

"Not the hair that was shorn from me when I was brought into custody," she explained. "My original hair. The enchanted hair that I grew when I was locked away in that tower. The hair that the wicked old sorceress cut off."

"You were never locked in a tower," insisted Hopkin.

She fancied that he seemed on the verge of some sort of temper tantrum, but she kept her response composed and measured. "My hair exists," she said. "And you know it. My husband sent some of his men to the tower to fetch it shortly after we were wed. I kept it all coiled up in a tall old hat box as a reminder of all that we had been through. And it is here now. Somewhere in this building."

The Inquisitor was clearly growing more and more infuriated by what she was saying. His brow was creased and his cheeks were flushed rhubarb red. But he was holding back, somehow bottling in his ire.

"I know about the *fetish* laboratory," she told him.

His little eyebrows went up.

"I am aware that magical fetishism is outlawed by unanimous decree of the People's Assembly," she continued. "But that does not mean that the Commissariat is not interested in isolating and defining the inherent power of the *fetish*. And so you have amassed a collection to experiment upon. Lamps and looms and mirrors. Golden eggs, glass slippers and such like..."

She watched the pulse throbbing wildly on his temple as his nostrils flared and hushed out a gush of air. "Amongst these items is the hatbox containing my hair and it is my simple wish to see it."

"Enough!" roared Hopkin. He slammed his little hand down on the desktop. The sound it made was more of a smack than a thump but it was enough to topple the wine glass and make the dinner plate rattle.

"Enough of this!" he shouted at her. "This... this... nonsense. This waste of my time!"

She simply could not afford to back down now. Not when she was so very close.

"You think that it's all so secret don't you?" she asked him. "The things that go on behind these walls."

"Whatever we do in here is for the benefit of the people," he spat at her. "To protect the achievements of the revolution from those who would unravel and undermine them."

"Then you *do* have my hair, don't you?" she pressed.

Hopkin became suddenly calmer and more in control of himself.

"So you know of the laboratory." He shrugged his little shoulders as if this had become completely unimportant to him. "You believe we have this... this hair of yours?"

Rapunzel nodded.

"And I wish to see it."

"What could you possibly - ?"

"I simply wish to touch it," she interrupted. "To remember my tale one last time before I am forced to deny it ever happened."

Hopkin stroked his chin. "And in exchange for this concession you would sign a statement of denial for public consumption?"

She was careful not to risk giving the game away.

"Reluctantly," she said. "But yes. Should you see fit to agreeing to my request I would indeed sign such a statement."

"Then," said the Inquisitor, "on this occasion, I am the one who will require sufficient time to reflect."

Rapunzel awoke to the retort of a single gunshot. Her first thought was that it must be dawn. They always carried out executions at dawn. She blinked, trying to adjust her eyes to the gloom of the cell, looking for any small trace of sunlight that might have crept down the stairwell and snaked its way under the cell door.

It had been dawn on the dreadful day that she and her husband were brought here. The Republican Guard, assisted by two of those accursed Clockwork Soldiers, had raided the safe house where they had been hiding. Her children had been dragged screaming and kicking from her side. When her husband tried to intervene his frantic protests were swiftly silenced by a blow from the powerful arm of one of the mechanical men.

They were brought immediately to the execution yard and she recalled thinking how swiftly and unceremoniously it was all going to end. Through eyes that were swollen and half-closed from the flood of tears she had shed for her son and daughter she saw that her husband was bleeding profusely from the wound to the side of his head.

In the yard two teenagers had been lashed to wooden posts and blindfolded. A girl and a boy. The girl frail and skinny. The boy grossly bloated and overweight. Had there not once been a *tale* about a lost brother and sister and a strange cottage in the woods? In her distressed state she had been unable to recall.

The magnified retort of the firing squad's volley had caused her to jump and cry out. When she looked across the boy was clearly dead, slumped into the folds of his own obesity. But the skinny girl was still twitching and groaning. The Sergeant at Arms marched briskly across the yard and fired a single shot from his pistol into her head. She twitched no more. Clockwork Soldiers came clanking forward to remove the corpses.

The Sergeant turned to his men.

"This one is for the cells," he said, pointing to Rapunzel with the smoking barrel of his pistol. "This one is for the chop." Indicating towards her husband. "Orders of the Assembly."

"No!" she had screamed as her husband was dragged across the yards towards the bloodied wooden posts. "No!"

But there was nothing she could have done. She herself was dragged through the back doors of the Commissariat building. As she was bundled down the filthy stairwell that led to the cells she heard again another heart stopping volley of gunfire.

Now a key turned in the door of her cell. *The Inquisitor has considered my proposal and rejected it,* she thought. *I'm on today's list. I will be lashed to a wooden post. A single pull on the trigger and then I'll be gone. The last thing I'll see outside of these barren walls is the execution yard. And what will become of my poor children then?*

She slumped down onto the little stool, the relief of being wrong almost too much for her. No food on the desktop this time. No games or convoluted strategies. No long, deliberate silences.

Just the hatbox.

She could barely see the diminutive Inquisitor over the top of it as he sat in the velvet chair.

"You found it then?" she asked, savoring the warmth of the rug on her cold, cold feet.

"I hope you don't think for one moment that I'm going to bring it to you," he replied.

"Pardon?"

He sighed irritably.

"If you want to look inside the box. If, as you say, you want to touch what is there one last time then you will have to come here to the desk."

Rapunzel rose somewhat unsteadily onto her feet. They were stained and filthy. Bits of dirty straw from the damp floor of her cell poked up through her toes. Her legs had become so thin and birdlike now that they could hardly manage to hold what was left of her weight. She stumbled across the rug, swaying like a drunkard, and reached out to steady herself against the desktop.

Hopkin narrowed his eyes and looked up at her. As she reached for the lid of the hatbox his small hand shot forward and grabbed hers. His flesh felt cold and leathery.

"You will honor your side of the bargain, won't you?" he asked.

A panicky trickle of sweat ran down her back. This was no time to arouse his suspicion. She answered with a question of her own. "And you will honor yours?"

The studied nod of his head only served only to confirm her conviction that he could never be trusted. But he removed his hand from hers and opened his little arms in a gesture that said, *go ahead then, do as you please.*

Trembling ever so slightly she lifted the lid and looked down into the hatbox. The dazzling yellow locks of her youthful hair lay there, as lustrous and radiant as the day they had been angrily hacked from her head. You could tell from one look at the texture and girth of each luscious strand that they still retained amazing tensile strength and fortitude.

Squeezing her eyes tightly shut she reached into the box and touched the soft and silky hair. *This is enchanted hair,* she reminded herself. *Oh, the things that I might have it do.* Still with her eyes squeezed shut she tried to force the hair to respond to her will. Nothing. It simply hung limply and heavily in the palm of her hand. She heard the Inquisitor drumming his tiny fingers impatiently against the desktop.

Despondency clawed at her. *I've played my card and my gamble has failed.* With those words an image of the angelic faces of her children formed in her head and the despondency gave way to a burning anger. Anger at the notion that she may well have robbed herself of a last chance to embrace them and tell them how much they were loved.

And now, as if the energy in this anger was the key to her latent power, something stirred inside the hatbox. Her hair began to fidget and squirm as she willed it towards a supernatural animation. Within seconds it began to creep and crawl up the length of her arm, spiraling around and around as it went.

"What on earth?" cried the Inquisitor. "Stop that! Stop that at once! You hear?"

Rapunzel opened her eyes.

Hopkin was balancing upright on his velvet chair. His face had turned the color of beetroot. His rodent features were contorted in rage. His little fists were clenched in fury.

"I know you don't believe in the power of magic," Rapunzel told him. "But this hair of mine may have the capacity to do impossible things."

Now the hair began to separate and stream away from her, spreading over the carpet and around the legs of the stool, climbing up the drapes and weaving across the Inquisitor's desk. Some of it wrapped itself around her neck. Around and around it went, like a long winter scarf, pulling tighter and tighter - until she was gasping for breath.

"My hair could help me to choose the manner of my own death," she croaked. "And the extraordinary manner of my choosing would be something that you would be hard pushed to explain to your skeptical comrades in the People's Assembly."

Hopkin climbed onto the desktop and scuttled across to her, his little feet desperately trying to avoid becoming tangled in the strands of hair that writhed there like a seething pit of serpents. His hands pawed and grabbed impotently at the constricting hair around Rapunzel's wan and filthy neck.

"Stop this!" he screamed at her. "Stop this treason!"

"No use," wheezed Rapunzel. "My hair is strong. Strong enough to carry the weight of a wicked old crone. Strong enough to carry the weight of my beloved Prince. Strong enough to resist the feeble efforts of a pathetic little specimen like you!"

She collapsed to the floor and Hopkin was dragged down with her. The hair squeezed tighter around her neck as the Inquisitor's efforts to tear it from her became ever more frenzied. She could feel her eyes bulging out in their sockets and big purple veins straining on her forehead.

"What is it you want?" he cried. "I can't have you dying in this manner."

"Wouldn't - this - be - a - *tale* - to - tell?"

She laughed, choking at the same time and willed the hair on her neck to loosen a little so that she could force out the words she needed to say. "My dying wish will be for you suffer the very same fate as me. Be in no doubt that my enchanted hair will most certainly carry out this wish. You will not have the strength or the wherewithal to fight it off. Wherever you run it will surely follow."

It was important for him to understand this - but there was a delicate balance to be achieved here. She knew that if she carried out her threat to kill herself the safety of her children would be placed in immediate jeopardy. If, on the other hand, she deployed her hair in an act of murder against the Inquisitor she would never escape the building with her own life. For her plan to work they both had to remain alive and he had to appreciate how much the balance of power between them was now weighted in her favor.

The Inquisitor stopped clawing at her. He rolled onto the rug and sat there with his tiny legs splayed wide. He picked a wriggling strand of hair from his trouser leg and then another from his shoulder. He watched wide-eyed as the twisted tresses on the carpet and the drapes spun in wild circles and spirals. He coughed and spat out a mouthful of hair. He coughed again and plucked up a single golden strand from his tongue, alarm and panic etched on his repulsive face.

"Do not underestimate the aptitude of these enchanted locks of mine," she warned him. "If you run for the door they will be upon you as swiftly as a striking snake. If you call for the guards they will fill your mouth till they suffocate you into silence."

"What do you want from me?" he pleaded, fighting against the multitude of golden hairs that crawled all over him.

"A promise," she replied

"Promise?" His eyes never moved from the writhing knot of summer blond locks that tightened and slacken around her neck

"I will sign your confession," she told him. "And in return my children will be released back into my custody. You will see to it that we are allowed to live quietly and unmolested as citizens in this Republic of yours."

"But the Assembly would never..." he protested, spitting out as hair as dozens more wove themselves around his wrists in a set of malicious bracelets.

"You can find a way," she insisted. "Are you not the People's Inquisitor?"

Hopkin sneezed as a strand of hair attempted to creep into his nostril.

"Fine!" he blurted. "I will agree to your terms. Just end this abomination."

Rapunzel willed her hair to stop. The strands around her neck unraveled themselves and the seething multitude of wisps snaked away from the Inquisitor. Then slowly she had it dissipate from the curtains and the carpet to escape the room. Beneath the door it went, under the little gap where the window had been left slightly ajar, through the tiny cracks in the ceiling and the walls and along the skirting board.

Hopkin jumped to his feet, obsessively brushing at his arms and his shoulders.

"What is this?" he demanded. "Have it coil itself back into the hatbox so that it can be sealed up and stored safely away."

Rapunzel also rose to her feet. She rubbed her neck as she looked down at the pathetic little creature who had tormented her so. "This is my insurance," she told him. "Hair can be so bothersome, don't you think? Strands of it can turn up just about anywhere. If you dare to go against your word I swear I will summon it once more to hunt you down."

Hopkin rifled amongst the paperwork on his desk and handed her a quill and inkpot, his hand still trembling in fear. "Just sign, damn it!" he spat. "Sign the confession and I'll have your little blue-blooded brats brought to you."

Placing her signature on the dotted line she allowed herself an inward smile.

This would take time. The People's Assembly, by its very nature, was a slow moving beast. A resolution concerning the future custody of her children would need to be moved, seconded, debated and voted upon before the inevitable paperwork could be prepared in triplicate. Sooner or later though she would at last be reunited with her son and daughter. Meanwhile she would take the opportunity to consider what other mischief she might have her exceptional hair engage in.

Everyone Else has Two Eyes

Nicki Vardon

Mama Louhi carved the meat on the dinner table, but the knife could have scraped against my bones and it would have felt the same. My sisters laughed while I sat in ash and stared into the hearth, hoping to burn my last tears into my skin as they dried up. My only friend was dead, and they laughed while feasting on his flesh.

"It tastes delicious, Mama." Yksi licked her fingers, and I could not be sure who she was winking towards. Her one eye sat in the middle of her forehead and her gestures could have been aimed at anyone around the table.

"It's your own fault, Sister," huffed Kolme. "You with your secrets." All three of her eyes looked down at me with disdain. She had two where most people have them and one in the middle of her forehead, like Yksi.

Not like me. I am Kaksi: born with two eyes. I look like everyone else. Or so Mama Louhi told me.

I've never known how many eyes Mama Louhi had. People would say she had two, but she called them liars, cut out their tongues, and fed them to her snake. Then no one said it anymore.

Mama had one blue eye, like me. A second eye so white, like milk, it almost slipped in with her skin. She had a third, in the middle of her fore-head, carved into her skin in crimson lines. She could have one or three. Not two. Never two. Never like those girls behind castle walls, at village markets, in towers, harbors and gardens, all looking the same. Those were the girls men left her for after they'd sired another daughter on her.

That was why Mama Louhi hated me. I knew my sisters did, too. And it was fine. I had a friend who kept me company in the meadows: our little goat. When I was hungry, he brought me food. When I was sleepy, his pelt was my pillow. And when he told stories, I listened and laughed.

Then Kolme spotted us together.

"Why don't you sing again, Sister? Sing that wonderful lullaby of yours." Kolme dropped back into her chair, drooped her mouth as if asleep, closed two eyes and kept her third peeled open with her fingers. Yksi laughed again, sauce from her lips spurting over her napkin like blood.

Mama Louhi kissed her snake, let it curl around her shoulders and mur-mured. When she slammed the table, Yksi stopped giggling and Kolme sat up straight. Like perfect little girls, though scared, they had nothing to fear from her. Mama stumbled over to me, but I'd stopped feeling fear. She had taken my friend and slaughtered him. His bleating screams still echoed in my ears. There was nothing worse she could do to me.

Mama Louhi pulled me to my feet. "Lazy child. Should we wait until you feel good enough to clean the table?"

Mama never used the word 'child'. I replaced the word in my mind every time she said it, because what she did say was the ugliest of words.

She pushed me and the table plunged into my stomach. The plate of roasted goat flesh nearly touched my skin. I shivered and pushed away from my friend's carcass, rubbing my face with my sleeve. Mama smacked my cheek.

"Ungrateful child," she screeched. "Go then! Go clean the kitchen if clearing the table is beneath you."

Yksi and Kolme said nothing. It wasn't until I left the room that Kolme hummed the lullaby again and Yksi sputtered out her ale with laughter. I clenched my fists and lifted my head.

The kitchen dripped with blood. Criss-cross patterns streaked over the windows. Mama's knife stood upright in the meat-block, buried two thumbs deep. I could not pull it out, so I cleaned it in its place and wiped away the spills of meat. Such thin shreds of flesh. She killed him slow.

As I scrubbed the threshold of the kitchen door, a whisper floated outside. If such sounds weren't a trick by my sisters, usually whispers were good and far away. Mama Louhi never whispered, so it was not her.

I tiptoed around the house and the whisper became a moan. A cry for help floated from the rubbish tip. Without hesitation I dug my hands into the pile of rotten meat. The moan became louder, bleating with a shiver. "Help me."

My hands found pelt that I had slept in and a snout I had talked to. "My friend, Mama did not even give you a grave." I pulled his skin and head out of the rubbish heap and held him close against me.

"I'm so cold, Kaksi." He spoke on the verge of tears.

"Don't cry, my friend." I carried him like I used to when he had a sore hoof, although he felt much lighter, draped limply over my arms. "We're together. They cannot part us again."

I covered his eyes as we passed through the kitchen and I hid him under my bed. Downstairs my sisters sang of brave princes coming to ask for their hand. Mama Louhi screamed that she needed more wood for the fire.

"They do not treat you fairly, Kaksi," said my friend, and his eyes shone like dark glass.

"It has always been this way." I sighed and wrapped a shawl around my shoulders. The woodshed was far outside and winter had begun to touch the night. "I am the plain one, with two eyes, so it is me who must get dirty."

"But your sisters have only four eyes among them, like any two other sisters would."

My friend's words clung to my mind like the blood on Mama's knife. When I returned from the woodshed, arms full of kindling, I passed Mama's chamber. I tipped the heavy curtain and slipped inside. Black and red candles burned at each wall, most of them quenched as I passed. Even the candles knew I was there, so I should be fast.

The branch, for Mama's snake pointed like a gnarly finger at the vessels I needed. For once, I was glad for the times Mama Louhi sent me out at night into the forest to pick herbs. I could find them in the dark just fine. I knew which ones I needed, how they smelled and crumbled between my fingers. I quickly tainted a fresh jug of ale for my sisters. All would be fair once dawn peeled back the night.

I slipped out of bed when the moon said it was time. My sisters' beds lay empty. Instead, Yksi and Kolme had slumped in drunken sleep over the table, their blonde and dark hair twined through spilled gravy. Mama Louhi seemed to have crawled to her own bed.

My sisters were heavy like logs and limp like sheets as I set them in chairs next to one another and let their necks rest on the back of their seats. I sharpened a small knife and fetched my needle and thread from the box.

Kolme slept with her three eyelids firmly closed. I prodded to check. She gave no shrug. Mama Louhi's herbs worked wondrously. No song would wake Kolme tonight.

When I turned to Yksi, I touched the skin below her one eye. My finger squished on flesh, not bone. She had eye sockets, even if they were not filled like Kolme's. I touched my own forehead of solid bone. I had no third eye. I was never meant to.

For a moment I held the knife still in my hand and the light from the hearth glinted off its edge. I looked at both my sisters, asleep, almost sweet. Then the light, as if to guide me, glinted off something else. In Kolme's black strands hung a gnawed bone. I snatched it out, catching some of her hair. She barely stirred. Even while chomping down their meal of goat flesh, they hadn't flinched once in sympathy for my friend's life. I smacked the bone among the others and sharpened the knife with a few more swishes of the whetstone.

I cut through Yksi's skin to open her closed sockets, then spooned out the flesh kept within. I'd been their seamstress for years; I could make some decent looking eyelids for her and embroider eyebrows where they should be.

Carefully, I cut around Yksi's eye and placed it into the right empty socket. Kolme's top eye became her left. I sewed their top eyelids closed with perfect little stitches and light-coloured thread, then dabbed away the blood on their faces. Their foreheads would need powder for a while, but otherwise they looked like ordinary girls. Like me.

I pulled my friend from under my bed and let him sleep on my pillow. "It's done," I said. His eyes seemed oddly sad.

On the morrow, screams filled the house and it wasn't long until Mama Louhi dragged me out of bed by my ear. "Come look at what you've done, you little wretch!" Her nails pierced my flesh and she did not use the word 'wretch'. As I swatted flies away from my friend, I looked at both my sisters, crying in front of Mama's mirror.

"You've made us ugly," Yksi howled as her fingers traced the bruised and swelling flesh. "You've made us like *you!*"

"How dare you think you're better than us!" Kolme had already bound a headscarf around her scarred empty eye. "You were jealous, so we had to look like you, but worse."

Mama Louhi said things as well, but they were so ugly they blurred into each other until they weren't even words any more. Nothing had changed. Mama made me break every mirror and pick up the pieces with my bare hands. I clenched the shards as I brought them to the rubbish tip until they cut my skin and blood ran between my fingers. Then Mama had me cover up all the windows of the house with dark cloth. My sisters could neither see themselves nor be seen. After that, my punishment still wasn't over.

Mama Louhi didn't notice I took my friend with me into the cage she put me in. We dangled outside the house, where she used to keep her crows, and she covered my cage with the dark cloth. I huddled up with my friend and hoped winter wouldn't come before Mama Louhi forgave me or tired of cleaning the house by herself.

Several days must have passed. When I was thirsty, I suckled on bits of the pinned down cloth, hoping enough rain or dew would cling to it. Once I began to crave food, a foreign hand rattled my cage. A man's hand, with fingers thick as the bars of my cage and with hair on the back. At first, I shoved the hand back with my foot.

"Who are you?" asked the man. Much like his hand, his words were firm as iron, but soft as if they carried some fur as well. "What is this house with covered windows?"

"The windows are covered because my sisters are hideous," I said.

"Then why are you in a cage?" he asked.

"Because I made them hideous." I lowered my voice and huddled closer to my friend. "And because I'm the most hideous of all."

"You don't sound hideous to me," the man said and his footsteps came closer. He lifted the cloth around the cage and I glimpsed a mantle of thick woollen thread and sturdy make, dyed in the deepest, richest red I'd ever seen. A golden clasp in the shape of a wolf held it in place on a broad shoulder. But before I could see his face and he mine, I heard the creak of the kitchen door. I knew it was Mama Louhi. Her snake hissed, her staff ticked against the threshold and her teeth ground as if crushing sand.

"You're devil-touched," she screamed at the man, her voice hoarse yet sharp. "Away! Only a struck fool would chase after the ugliest daughter I've borne."

I grasped for the golden wolf as the man stumbled backwards and he tried to calm Mama Louhi with words that would not mean a thing to her. The clasp came off and I hid it between my friend's teeth.

The man screamed and I pulled at the cloth where he had loosened it. I could not see anything except for Mama Louhi swinging her staff at the man, who had tumbled forward into the hedge of thorny rose bushes around our house.

"Be cursed if you so wish to be," Mama Louhi cried out in her dark voice. I did not wish to see what she would do, but I heard the man groaning until she'd chased him away.

Once Mama Louhi had left, I reached for the lock and pried it with the pin of the golden wolf. It took me until dark to unlock it, but my friend broke my fall as we tumbled through the trapdoor. "We're free, little friend," I whispered.

"You're not safe, Kaksi," he said. "Take the cloth to keep warm and wear me over your head as your disguise. Then go find a town far away from here."

I did as my friend said. Before I left the house, my friend asked me to return to the rubbish tip once more. "Find my heart," he said, "and bury it along the road. It will help you when you need it."

When I walked past the rose hedges and saw them shimmer in moonlight, I touched the branches and smoothed the blood on my fingers. I hoped the man was not fatally wounded. I wore his golden wolf on my cloak to remind myself to look out for the cursed stranger.

The morning came soon on our way through the marshes. Gnats bit my bare legs and flew up inside my nose. Mud suckled on my toes. My cloak was damp and drew the cold against my skin. My friend's heart lay against mine in my kirtle and kept it warm, but my friend cried over my face and through my hair. His ruddy tears streaked my cheeks.

"Don't be afraid, my friend," I said, but as I spoke, I shared his fears.

The trees held secrets and did not want to comfort me. I looked behind every time I thought to hear a sound, but nothing could be seen, even though I felt there were eyes out there following me.

When I kneeled down to drink from the swamp, a rustle sounded from the reed and I held still. Claws gripped into the muddy grass close to me. A black shadow lunged, growling and pointing its sharp teeth at my throat. With my mother's strength I clasped at the grey fur in the wild animal's neck as his saliva splattered into my face. He was wounded; his ears torn, his nose dripping with blood and his eyes closed by deep wounds and scars.

"Ulf!" I cried out, for that was the name I knew for wolf. The claws slipped and its muscles loosened underneath my fingers. The beast cowered and slunk away into the forest. Breathless, I sat in the muddy shore amidst the reed and touched the clasp at my shoulder. The golden wolf. I'd found and lost him again.

The sun rose in mist and set in silence. I lived on blueberries and swamp water. Reindeer clacked their hoofs on the mountains and snorted like unkempt men. The first time I heard the snorting of unkempt men was when I passed the hunters' tavern of a small village after days on foot. Only then did I find out such hoofing did not need be reindeer. Rumours were spat over canisters of mead and ale. Stories of princes lost during a wolf hunt, of witches deep in the woods, of devilish creatures on the prowl for cattle. Drunkenmen's talk.

I wandered through the village and ended up near a churchyard. An empty space became the burial spot for my friend's heart, as he'd asked. I dug the cold soil with my own hands, laying his heart to rest. I wrung out my kirtle and slept next to its tiny grave with the last sun on my back. "Goodnight, sweet friend."

What awoke me the next morning was not the sun or the gnats, but a host of people from the village standing over me. They weren't looking at me, of course; I was the most hideous child Mama Louhi had ever borne. Instead, they gaped at the tree that had grown where I had buried my friend's heart. It was in full bloom despite the closeness of the winter gales and golden apples wore down its silver-leafed branches. Yet, no matter how many villagers tried to climb on each other's shoulders, no one was able to reach the golden fruit.

Their lust for treasure made me look, but I still held the golden clasp. It had not been stolen, yet I stood - to leave, for the crowd unnerved me - and as soon as I got on my feet, the tree's branches bent towards me and one of the apples fell into my hand as if it had perfectly ripened once I laid eyes on it.

Around me, the village gasped. "She's blessed!"

"I'll give you the best dress from my tailor for that apple," said one. I looked down. My kirtle was dirty and my cloak drenched. "I'll build you a house," offered another. I chewed my bottom lip. I had slept so many nights under the naked sky.

"What should I do?" I asked my friend, but he remained still and silent.

"She's cursed," they now whispered. Whispers always win. The villagers came closer and their demands, while ever growing, stoked the fire in their eyes. I crumpled against the church walls when offers of houses and dresses were replaced with drawn knives and swords. I threw the apple on the ground and ran as they fought. Although I still had nowhere to go.

A hand closed over my wrist and pulled me behind the churchyard wall. A man, dressed in rags and walking with the aid of a large cane, yet he stood straight and strong. His hair was wild and scruffy like his beard, his face pale underneath grime, but his eyes seemed hollow, scarred with thick lines, healing in ugly crusts of bloody clumps.

"Careful of those madmen, child." And he did say the word 'child', so I followed him, towards a small, forsaken shack just outside the village, covered in filth, but warm. The blind man stumbled only a little as he boiled water on the stove and filled a small tub. I bathed until my skin showed wrinkles.

"You are too trusting of a stranger," he said as he stirred a strongly smelling stew over the fire.

"You are no stranger," I answered and placed the golden clasp in his hand.

He sat back in a large chair, covered in ratty furs, and let his fingers slip over the gold, tracing the outline. He must have recognized the shape, because his face twitched and tears fell from his hollow eyes. He wept, the lost prince. With shame, I feared, as he was touched by a witch's curse and had become the beast that was hunted - the wolf that jumped for me. His curse was cured, but his eyes were not. My cry of his name while he still wore the skin of the wolf had not returned his sight.

I stayed. To earn my keep, I cleaned the shack from top to bottom, beat out the rugs and replaced wood that needed replacing. My friend had kept silent ever since the tree had grown, but I washed him too, and he still was my pillow when I slept in front of the hearth. Ulf was skilled in laying traps and breaking kindling, anything as long as he could do things slow, but he shuffled through the shack and never quite learned where the door or his bed was. Yet, whenever I asked, the castle was too far away and a blind prince too useless.

"Would the king not take you back even if you are without eyes?" I asked one evening.

"You should not ask such things, Kaksi." His wounds had healed by then. The crusts had fallen off and revealed new skin, but the pink lines still drew shadows of the rose branches across his face. "You must understand if you are as hideous as you claimed. We are better off in this shack. Without even a single eye, I could do nothing that a prince should do. I would mean nothing."

I uttered not a word that night until he was asleep and tossed and turned in his bed. "But we have two eyes among us both," I said, "like any other child."

The next day I traded a golden apple for a standing mirror and a new set of thread and needles, while I ignored all looks and gossip. I sharpened the smallest of Ulf's knives and picked the herbs Mama Louhi would have me pluck at night. Tainting the ale was troublesome as I needed to drink it myself. I took only small sips. Ulf drank much more and passed out in his chair while I sang to him. My high notes were difficult to reach and my hands would not keep steady when I reached for the knife, but I knew what threads to cut and I could do so again.

Carefully, I cut open Ulf's right socket and removed the torn eye, a sad and limp husk, much like a crushed, overripe plum. The hardest was cutting around my own and keeping the eye whole. The threads were difficult to reach and the knife slit deep into my cheek. Mama Louhi's herbs worked well; I did not feel much, but I bit down on Ulf's leather belt to keep myself from screaming. I managed at last and my eye toppled into my hand to be placed neatly into Ulf's socket. Sewing it into place was much harder with only one eye. My hand was not where I thought it was and the needle often poked where I hadn't meant it. The sun was nearly rising once I finished and I still had not sewn my empty socket closed. I could not go to sleep yet even though my body wanted to slump into a puddle.

I was a lousy seamstress on myself. Scraggly lines limned my eyelid and cheek and in the wrong colour, too. But I finished, let the needle slip and dropped into Ulf's chair.

When I woke, Ulf tenderly washed my face with a wet rag and traced the stitches along my cheekbone while I regarded my handiwork. I liked to imagine Ulf had blue eyes before I met him.

"Why did you do this?" Ulf asked, as a question, not merely head-shaking. "You gave up half your face for a man who had never seen it before."

"Maybe my face was never complete," I answered. "Maybe that is why I was the most hideous daughter Mama Louhi had ever borne."

The rest of the day I sat back in Ulf's chair with a raging fever and drank the rest of the tainted ale until my bleeding had stopped. Meanwhile, Ulf had noticed the standing mirror and though he flinched at his image at first, by the end of the day he had shaved his beard, combed his hair and pinned the golden wolf to the rags draped over his shoulder. And I did not do much else but smile through the pain and the rush of alcohol.

Ulf brought me to his father's castle and we were each other's left eye. At the court, he shunned every suggestion of masks and hoods from the king. Indeed, I did not even wear a veil when we married.

Though our firstborn had two eyes - one grey, one blue - I did not name her Kaksi. I did not see in her what Mama Louhi saw in me. She was born and taught my eye to look in a new way: there was not a spot on her that I wanted to cut away, or hide from the world.

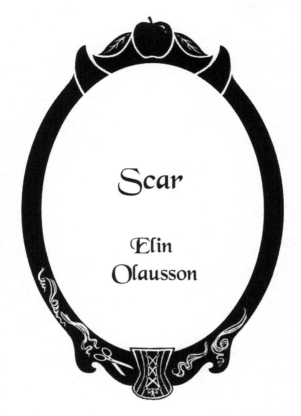

Scar

Elin Olausson

Ravens circle the tower. Hundreds of black eyes. Their voices pitch higher for every strand of hair that falls to the floor, every golden lock.

Hair that will grow no more.

Nine years earlier she sits quietly in the throne room with her hands clasped. The back of her chair raises high towards the ceiling. She has to stand on the seat to admire the snow crystals carved into the wood. Now, with other people present, Princess Stella would obviously never do such a thing.

She can hear faint noises through the music, and doesn't have to look to know that Lune and Leal are kicking each other under the table. That is how boys are, says Ganda. They can never stay quiet for any length of time. Beneath the hem of her heavy dress, Stella's tiny feet are completely still, as she has been taught. She knows better than to cause a ruckus, and even though Lune is sitting close, he has never once kicked her. Stella is different. Her brothers protect her. Not even Luc, whose temper is so bad in the mornings, is ever mean to her. She is the princess of Debre, the only one. Beloved by all.

The girl who plays the flute has long, red braids and leather shoes in the same beautiful color on her feet. Even Stella knows somehow, what the look means, the one Leo gives the girl. He has just turned fourteen, and in the kitchen the maids are giggling about his curious fingers, while Stella sits hidden under the table with the cat. When she looks out through her window before bedtime, she can see Leo in the courtyard with his swords and his pistols. His stabs are swift and he never misses a shot. Stella does not have to be afraid of anything, as long as Leo is around.

The boy who beats the drum is pretty, with rings on every finger, but Lantos only looks at Sabir. That is how it has always been. Mother speaks of a wedding and Stella is looking forward to feasts and new clothes - and the joy on her oldest brother's face. It is a day that will come, and after that four more, until it is her turn. In the evenings, Ganda tells stories about Maris and the white city. About the palace made of glass and the sovereigns there. When Stella is all grown up she will be Maris's queen, her mother has promised her so. She is five years old. She already knows her future.

When she remembers the songs in the throne room nine years later, she does not know if she heard them before or after the scar.

Maybe she was still right.

For Ganda, there never was a scar.

"Bend your neck, Your Highness, we need to rinse out the soap properly." Stella's neck is slender and beautifully rounded. All the young girls at court are envious. Sometimes, when she thinks they have deserved it, she lets them touch it.

Ganda rubs the hair clean with her hard, red hands. Even if the water is hot, Stella is freezing in the tub, for the window has a slight crack and it is windy in the mountains of Debre. Not even in summer, when the apple trees down in the valley bloom, is it ever warm in her chamber.

"Her Majesty has chosen a dress." Stella has of course seen it: purple velvet and shoes in the same material, golden roses stitched to the waist. Royal colors that suits her hair, which her mother has said shines brighter than the sun.

"It is wonderful, Ganda."

"It truly is, Your Highness." Ganda places the thin linen towel around Stella's narrow shoulders and she rises, climbs out of the cold bath water and down on the floor. Her hair is a large, heavy mass twisted in linen on top of her head. Stella's whole body is white.

"Very good, Your Highness, now put on your chemise." The old chambermaid's movements are slow, and her fingers clumsy, when handling Stella's silk stockings.

No, Ganda never sees any scar.

The Queen of Debre has five sons, they are all tall and light of hair. They will defend the kingdom. The councilors at court speak highly of Lantos' presence of mind, his seriousness. Every soldier in the country looks forward to following Leo, or Luc, in the future. At the university in Riza, the professors are waiting to receive Leal and Lune with open arms.

But Queen Adrisa has only one daughter. What luck, one can hear the women at court whisper. At her age - it was her last chance. The Queen of Debre sprinkles gold and precious stones over her princess, lets her take classes with the best singers and artists, gives her kittens and puppies who are gone without a trace when Stella wakes up a few weeks later. She personally powders Stella's cheeks so they shimmer and plucks her eyebrows until Stella has learned to stand the pain. In the throne room, Stella is at her mother's feet, while the ladies in waiting entertain with their chatter, flattering the queen and complimenting Stella's new emerald bracelet. Her father is tired and ill from his duties, she seldom sees him. For him, Lantos is important, Lantos and the rest of her brothers. But in the Queen's eyes, Stella is the most important, most beautiful of them all.

Through her mother, Stella gets to know the far away Maris, their neighboring country by the great sea where the sovereigns travels in carriages on paved roads behind white horses. Where lanterns lights up gardens and parks, and no one is ever cold. In Maris, her mother says, even the maids wear corsets and powder their curls. The mistress of such a place does not have to sit bored in dim lit halls, just because her husband values tradition, not comfort, and because the country she lives in is placed outside the map of the world. The heir in the glass palace is a boy Stella's age, pale, just as dark-eyed as Sabir. Queen Adrisa has met him.

"You will be a beautiful queen one day. Everyone will praise you." Stella receives the caress on her cheek and knows that she will be a queen, just like her mother.

Stella dreams of the glass palace in Alba. The lights and the masquerades and the constant warmth.

She is ten and does not know yet what sovereigns want. What men want.

The forests are deep around the castle in Debre. That's where the five princes ride their horses, string their bows and lift their spears, hunt like their forefathers. They come home at dusk with servants almost kneeling under the weight of the game. The ravens follow them.

Princess Stella only visits the forest during summer. This is the only time she is granted permission to go there with her own young ladies-in-waiting, to gracefully walk the narrow paths and pick the flowers of the earth. The grown up women are watching them from their seats in the carriage. Stella can hear strange birds in the trees. She receives the other girls's messy bouquets of flowers with a distant smile, one she reserves especially for them. They are daughters of chancellors and councilors, chamberlains and duchesses. They all hope to become her confidant, her closest friend.

Stella cannot stand them.

Still, Aurelia's flowers seem the least appalling, and Aurelia's laughter hurts her ears the least. Aurelia is the daughter of one of her mother's most favored companions, she has curly brown hair and dimples in her cheeks. When Aurelia speaks, Stella almost thinks it is nice.

"My mother was at the masquerade when she was young," says Aurelia when they are twelve and the moss beneath their feet makes their shoes wet. The tree branches above their heads are braiding a roof that conceals the mountains, the clouds and the castle from view. "She says that there is no place more beautiful than Alba." It is somewhat annoying to Stella to hear someone else talk about the city that belongs to her. That will belong to her.

"My mother, the queen, has been there many times." She does not have to say more than that, to let Aurelia know her place.

"Her Majesty must have been the most beautiful woman in the ballroom," Aurelia flatters, and Stella does not point out that the masquerade in Alba is a large event, which hardly plays out in one ballroom alone.

"But Your Highness will, if I may say so, become even more beautiful." Aurelia's eyes are large. The violets are already dying in her hand.

"No one can be more beautiful than my mother, Aurelia."

The other girl reddens. When she speaks again her voice is more quiet, thinner. "I am sorry, Your Highness. Your Highness must not misunderstand."

Stella waves her hand. *It is fine. You are forgiven.*

"I am just hoping that Your Highness will take me with you to the glass palace in Maris. When Your Highness becomes queen there."

Sometimes Stella wonders if she has a friend in Aurelia.

She had thought friendship would feel different.

Stella watches her brothers grow. Even Lune becomes long-legged and strong, gains a dark voice and determination in his gaze. While the king's sword hand is withering, while his eyes cloud, Lantos speaks to the lords of the council and makes treaties with the dukes in the north. The queen's eyes are wet and Stella knows her father is dying.

Stella watches her brothers grow, but she herself does not change. She is a piece of jewelry, a doll to dress. Even the young men in Lantos's guard must smile when she walks by. Queen Adrisa buys pearl necklaces and velvet gloves for her daughter, and Ganda does up her blonde hair with combs, clamps, needles and artificial flowers. Stella sees her face in the mirror and knows that she is beautiful.

A beautiful doll with dreams of Alba.

When the king of Debre dies, Princess Stella is thirteen years old. They will not let her watch when the funeral pyre is lit.

Her brother's wedding finally arrives. In the cramped chapel at the castle grounds Lantos takes Sabir's hand in his, and Stella is cheering like everyone else. Ten underskirts billow around her ankles and her belly is heavy with pastries. Beside her, Aurelia is clapping her hands hard.

Later, they are leaning over the banister of the great hall, watching the feast below. Their gowns are in the same colors, as Stella's mother decided, and everyone - not just Aurelia, has complimented her tonight. The other girl's dress is of course not quite as beautiful as Stella's, and yet it is as though Stella wishes she was the one carrying it. The one who had the body it conceals. Aurelia's hips are already round beneath the dress, as are the budding breasts in her neckline. Stella has not shown any signs of such things yet. Every morning Ganda laces her tight, tight, and when passing a mirror she can almost believe that she sees something; buds that have started to grow. But without the lacings and the mirrors, there is nothing there.

"Luc is so handsome. Mother says he is cruel to the poor maids, what do you think that means?" Aurelia is giggling. They are older now, she has begun addressing her princess as 'you'. Stella had thought that it would annoy her, but she does not care very much.

"I do not know." A lie, of course. But Aurelia knows better than to discuss Prince Luc in such a way.

"I for one think he is awfully handsome..." Aurelia says. "Leal too, but everyone knows he already has a girl." Stella has nothing to add to the court gossip about her brothers. Her eyes follow faces, smiles, voices. People moving, alone or together. She can see her mother laughing. There are representatives from Maris, slim, black-eyed women in sheer fabrics. No heir, no sovereign's son from Alba.

"Who do you... Stella, if one of the men down there were to ask you to dance, who would you want it to be?"

People moving, alone or together. Faces. Stella tries to imagine that one of the men in the hall down there should touch her, and all she can think is that she does not know. That she cannot know.

"You have no right to ask me such private questions," she snaps at Aurelia, who is instantly remorseful. They go quiet, their gazes drop.

The question remains in Stella's head.

That night, when Ganda is combing her hair, Stella is dizzy with wine and does not want to sleep.

"They are a handsome couple," she says. Ganda merely chuckles; she has listened for quite some time to Stella's chatter about the dance, the food, the music... "It is a shame they cannot have children."

"It is not that serious a matter, Your Highness." Ganda's voice is calm, but Stella knows her well enough to know that she is tired and wants to go to her own bed. "The King will produce an heir that his husband will be foster father to. After that, they can have as many foster children as they like, as long as the line of succession is secured."

Stella lifts her arms to let the nightgown slide, chilly and smooth, over her torso. "I shall have many children," she says. "At least five." Ganda nods, tucks her in.

"Surely you will, Your Highness." She does not look at Stella as she speaks.

She breathes in the knowledge, slowly, like toxic fumes and ashes.

The night before Christmas, the men of the castle bathe in the great hall. Lantos and Sabir, the rest of the brothers. The pageboys run with scalding hot water up and down the stairs, filling the tubs. On a night like this, no women are allowed.

Is that why Stella lingers in the door? Why she sees Lune standing there, hair falling wet around his shoulders, until Sabir slams the door shut and laughter rises inside.

He is like her. Back in her tower room while the gusts of wind comes crawling through the windows, all she can think of is their likeness. Under cloaks and billowing shirts, under dresses and corsets they are alike. Only in one place is he different, beautiful Lune with his lute and his poems.

The one place where Stella has only a scar.

Stella sits with a straight back on her throne, she is tall now, and can see the snow crystals just by turning her head. Other than her length, she is not growing.

They say that the girl from the village has a huge belly already. That Lantos will soon hold his child in his arms. He is in the High Seat and Sabir has taken their mother's place. At night, Queen Adrisa strokes her only daughter's hair. They talk about the white city, Alba, about the glass palace. About the life Stella will lead there.

"I remember it so well," Ganda often says. "Her Majesty so dearly longed for a girl. And in the end she finally got one."

Princess Stella sleeps alone. Lantos and Sabir lie with the newborn twins close to their bodies. Leo never lacks companions. Luc is distributing his interest evenly among the young maids, and Leal has his black haired courtesan. Everyone knows that Lune's pageboy is sharing his master's bed.

But Stella sleeps alone.

The castle in Debre was built to resist attacks. Cliffs surround the towers, hide them, and from the north castle wall one stares into an abyss. No hostile armies can arrive from that side.

The wind is lashing. The five princes are dressed in black leather boots and fur trimmed cloaks, carrying heavy swords in their belts when they ride out in the forest, or practice the arts of war in the courtyard. But the princess is cold in thin silk slippers, and her cloak is not trimmed with anything but velvet.

The brothers go to bed with kitchen maids and servant boys. Stella is shivering between icy sheets.

They are men, brave, strong. She is nothing but a scar, red and rosy between hairless legs.

Her young ladies-in-waiting play the harp and recite poetry, curled up on pillows in her chamber. Some are small of build, others soft around the cheeks, or skinny. But they have all developed breasts, all of them complaining about stomach pains and the blood once a month.

Everyone but Stella.

She prefers when it is only Aurelia, though she would never admit to such a thing. Aurelia does not talk as much of boys anymore, and she freely lends out ribbons and jewelry, if Stella asks.

Stella thinks that she might take Aurelia with her to Maris after all.

With her mother the Queen, she talks about the future.
    "I want a hundred white horses." Her mother laughs, patting her hand. "I will have new clothes every day and ten chamber maids to wait on me." Stella was raised to weave large dreams.
    "Of course you will, my darling. And no one in Alba shall be able to resist you." She enjoys hearing her mother's flattery. Needs it. True, she is beautiful, with flowing hair and dark eyes, but Stella never looks in the mirror in the morning. Not before Ganda has laced and dressed and brushed and painted. The deepest layer, she will not see.
    "Lantos goes to Maris to meet with the sovereign within a few weeks. He will deliver your portrait." Stella looks up at her mother. She does not dare to ask why it is that Queen Adrisa is crying.

The knowledge grows when nothing else does.

Stella has been fourteen for some time when Leo comes home drunk one night. There is talk of bad company, but it is Lantos who must decide what to do, and Lantos will do nothing. Brothers take care of each other. She does not know why his gaze lands on her.
    "Little Stella." Serious eyes follows him, they are all there. They shall all be witness to her humiliation. Leo, so strong that when he grabs her shoulders, she flinches.
    "Tell me, little sister, why are women so…" He has some difficulty finding the words. "So goddamn false."

"Let her go, Leo." Lantos's face is stern. In the crook of her eye, Stella can see her mother whisper something she cannot hear.

"You should eat better," Leo says and gives her pathetically padded chest a hard pat. "You cannot look like this if you want to get married." He laughs before leaving her. A joke, Stella tries to think. A joke, and he is drunk, and it does not mean a thing. But on the other side of the table her mother's face is white.

Stella begins to wish that Ganda would let her dress herself. She is ugly, she knows that now. The old chambermaid moves with heavy feet, hanging up dresses, picking out new ones. Stopping the draft from the windows with the same cotton they use to fill out Stella's neckline.

"Ganda," Stella says. Spring has arrived and Lantos's twin boys are laughing down in the courtyard. "Why do I have a scar?" Ganda is standing with her back bent, looking away. Maybe that is why Stella dared to ask.

"Scar, what do you mean? Your Highness looks just like everyone else."

"Lune does not have a scar. None of them do."

"It is not proper to speak of such things, Your Highness. Girls are different from boys." Ganda still has not turned around. She has picked the stockings from the drawer as she said she would, but she has not turned around.

"I am not like the girls, either." The words fills the air, accusing. Stella is freezing. Winter has left, but she is freezing.

"That," Ganda says, a little bit unfriendly, before approaching with the stockings in her hand. "Your Highness will have to talk to Her Majesty about that."

Stella knows that she should. But she is not sure if she dares to. She is thinking about the portrait, her own portrait, which Lantos left in Alba. She remembers her mother's tears.

One night she walks up to the north wall and feels the abyss before her feet, hears the birds screeching. She is half - she knows it is so.

She is not right.

Aurelia makes it a habit to stay when the other young maidens disappear for the night. Sometimes she is the one to comb Stella's hair. She does not hear any news from Maris. She has hidden that dream inside. Sovereigns want curvy girls, or boys with broad shoulders. Sovereigns do not want scars.

Queen Adrisa no longer leaves her bedchamber. Stella asks to see her and they say that she is tired, has no strength to talk.

They whisper that she will not live through this.

Stella overhears Lantos talking to Sabir about the queen. That she has been taken by regret. That she wants his forgiveness for something, but that she cannot bring herself to tell him what it is.

"She is not making sense," Lantos says and does not know that someone else can hear him. "But it is all about Stella."

She can see him disappear into the Queens's chamber, one evening a week later, and she knows that her mother will die. That Lantos is to know the truth.

It might be because Aurelia sees her tears, that Stella allows her to follow her into the bedchamber that night.

"I want you to cut my hair," Stella says. There are silver scissors in the small chest on her nightstand. Ganda uses them sometimes.

Aurelia's eyes go wide.

"Can I? Just a little, surely?" Stella merely nods. She sits, curled up on her bed, can hear Aurelia moving behind her. Braids and pearls and combs must be removed before anything can be cut.

"You can cry as much as you want," Aurelia says while the hairbrush scratches against her scalp. "I mean, if you want to."

"Thank you." Stella wonders if the Queen has taken her last breath yet. If she has put her lips to Lantos's ear and told him that which everyone is soon to know.

What the sovereign in Alba will know.

"This dress is so pretty." Aurelia is pinching the fabric, tittering. "Violet really suits you." Stella could say that Aurelia too looks good in violet, because she does - and Aurelia has been kind to her. She has always been kind to her.

I have something to tell you.

"I can cut it now." Stella moves to stand by the window, and Aurelia brings the scissors.

I am not a girl.

"How much do you want me to cut?" Stella is measuring with her hand, a caressing motion across one of her shoulders. "Like Lune. Just the same length as Lune." Aurelia stares at her, horrified, and then she starts laughing.

"You almost fooled me there! Oh my, what a sight that would have been."

Stella just smiles, while Aurelia cuts the tips off her hair. As if that would make a difference. She is cutting, talking. When she is finished, Stella feels her round arms around her waist, just for a moment. Aurelia who likes her, even if she is not right. Who is warm and who likes her.

"You look nice," Aurelia says before pulling away. "Really nice." Stella picks up the scissors to put them back in the small chest. Thin strands of hair are scattered on the floor, outside the window are faint sounds of bird cries. She crosses the stone floor on bare feet.

"If you want to —" Aurelia is suddenly close to her, her cheeks are glowing red. "I could sleep here tonight. If you want to."

"It is getting so cold," she continues in a rush. "And maybe you do not want to be alone right now."

Stella is thinking that Lantos might already know. But Aurelia does not know and she likes Stella and wants to sleep beside her. No one else has ever wanted that.

"You can sleep here," she says and Aurelia must help her with the lacings, because Ganda is not there. Ganda who has always known. The dress falls to the floor, heavy, lifeless. The skirts, stockings, and Stella's heart is racing. Aurelia likes her. Aurelia will still like her.

"You are laced so hard," Aurelia says amused and the corset comes off, she is only wearing her chemise now. When she turn around it takes a while for Aurelia to regain her bearings. "It starts late for some I have heard." A pat on the arm. "Don't worry." Yes. Aurelia will still like her.

Stella's narrow hips slide easily out of the thin chemise. Ganda has stitched it in many times.

A scar. That is her truth, the only one she has. And Aurelia screams.

"What is that?" She takes several steps back, fumbling for the bed behind her for support. "What is that?" Stella wants to ask her to be quiet, but no voice emerges from her throat. She is a body, just a scarred body. And Aurelia does not like her at all anymore. Stella is standing over her, trying to calm her down. Wants her to be quiet. They will hear, they will come running up the stairs and they will see her. Aurelia must not scream.

Then the scissors glitters in her hand, over and over again, until Aurelia does not scream anymore.

Stella climbs down on the cold floor. The scissors drips darkly over the stones. She is naked, but she is not cold anymore. Outside the ravens have already begun to gather.

I have something to tell you.

The scissors are sticky but she does not leave them be. The birds are screaming. The birds see.

I am not a girl.

The locks of hair fall to the floor. The hair on her head is soon shorter than Lune's. Shorter than Leo's. The scissors flutters around her neck and ears, tendons and skin. Follows the the shape of her head. Stella cuts, she does not stop. The hair is gone, but she does not stop.

I am nothing.

Raven wings are flapping by the windows. On the stairs, down at the bottom, she can hear steps. She cuts, will not stop. Like the hard hands that time, when Queen Adrisa decided to have a daughter.

The scissors are still moving. Princess Stella's eyes are closed.

I am nothing.

I am a scar.

Harsh Beauty

Martine Helene Svanevik

Blood soaked through Belle's white silk slingbacks. It felt like standing with her feet in the sand when the tide came in, only this wave was slow, thick and lukewarm, just like Reginald used to be, before he rediscovered his passion.

Reginald wasn't much, now. The skin around his lifeless eyes was contorted and stretched, frozen in a wax cast of pain and anger. One hand reaching for her, the other closed in a fist.

On the night they met he'd been formidable - a great beast. She hadn't liked him much, then. But he'd burrowed his way into her heart.

The theme of the party was New Beginnings, and everyone wore vintage clothes. Belle was sporting a floor length yellow dress, layered like a stack of Twinkies. She'd even put her hair up, to fit in with the posh crowd. Her father had scored her a ticket after fixing the starry-night overhead lighting in the giant ballroom. The host, a Mrs. Dewitt-Howard, had been so grateful she presented him with two passes and he gave one to each of his daughters. Belle had been delighted, Cora had sold hers on eBay.

She danced all night with a young entrepreneur named Benjamin Gaston. His hair had been black, she recalled, in contrast to Reginald's golden mane. Reginald the fair, they used to call him. The first time she heard it, she'd thought they meant fair as in evenhanded. They didn't.

Reginald's hair was long that night, blowing in the evening breeze as he leaned against the balcony with one arm slung over the edge. He spoke to a scrawny man wearing an ill-fitting suit and a nervous disposition. Her eyes slid off the other man, but when they fell on Reginald, she was lost. She forgot about Benjamin's breath against her neck, about the heat of the dance floor, about the nervous flutter of her heart. Without a word, she dropped her hand from Benjamin's shoulder.

Dancers scattered as she stalked across the marble floor. The overhead lighting shimmered like the stars over the meadow outside her childhood home in Beaumont, a stark contrast to the black sky outside. But she didn't notice the darkness when she looked at Reginald, only the smile on his face and the call of his frame.

The kiss of chill October on her naked arms shook her out of the trance. She stepped through the open doors and onto the terrace. He was only a few feet away, and she still hadn't cut eye contact. He smirked at her, winked, and then grabbed his partner by the neck and pants and hoisted him over the edge. A scream. A crash. Belle rushed to the edge, looked down, and saw blood and guts sprayed across a 1977 Lamborghini.

She'd never gotten the name of the man who fell to his death on the New Beginnings party. She had an inquiring mind, but there are only so many answers a heart can bear. Still, she felt a twinge of sadness now that it was too late to ask.

She hadn't expected to see Reginald again, but she couldn't help asking about him. Who was this man? What did he do? Why had he been at the party? Her new acquaintances were vague. No one seemed to like Reginald, but none of them knew how to articulate the unease they felt around him. Finally she talked to the daughter of some diplomat, a young girl who dared speak the word. To call him monster.

The carpet slurped like summer bog moss under her feet as she walked the ten paces to the body. She leaned forth and searched for some emotion etched on his face, some hint of past crimes, past affections, but there was nothing there. Only jagged teeth and frozen pain.

He'd smiled that same wolf grin the second time they met. Belle had been tending her father's shop, like she did every Thursday. It was a quiet evening. Her father worked on one of his inventions in the back while she dusted the shelves. *The Timeless Tinkerer* made most of its profits off watch repairs, but her father's passion was inventions. He had a mind for it too, but the market for solar powered screwdrivers and indoor clouds was limited, so they repaired broken tools and sold refurbished electrical equipment and scraped by.

The bell above the door chimed. She looked up. Her breath caught in her throat. Time stopped. The sun itself - brilliant and blindingly terrible - had come down from the sky to see her. His teeth were sharp, his cane broken and his golden hair flowed across his shoulders. A long, jagged scar split his left eyebrow in two, but his gaze pierced right through her.

"How may I help you?" she said, breathlessly.

He marched towards her and didn't stop until he was painfully close. "You've been asking about me. Why?"

"I didn't expect to see you again," she said with a shopkeeper's smile; bright and empty.

He took another step, forcing her into a corner. "Answer the question."

The glass monitor she'd been polishing was cold against her arm, the empty shelf on her right a sad reminder of her lack of defensive weapons. There were more than thirty feet between her and the exit.

The image of him throwing the man off the balcony played a *Punch n' Judy* show behind her eyes. But she'd been the smallest kid on the playground for as long as she could remember, and she wasn't going to back down now.

"I don't know," she said, her smile balancing on the edge between bright and vicious. "I guess I just wanted to find out what kind of man drops someone off a balcony with a grin, and then assumes no one will tell the cops."

"I don't know what you're talking about," he said, coolly indifferent. He tightened his grip around the cane and she noticed spots of red in the splintered wood.

"Fuck you," she said, conversationally. "Of course you know what I'm talking about. Why else would you be here?"

He blinked, then laughed and stepped back.

She tried to read this new expression.

"Have dinner with me," he said.

"Excuse me?"

"Candlelit, romantic, the whole nine yards."

"You want me to have dinner with a murderer?"

"I want you to have dinner with me."

I'm sure they'll say I knew what I was getting myself into. She dropped the Beretta next to his cooling hand and let one finger slide along his cheek, feeling soft, wrinkled skin give beneath the stubble. She bit back the tears. *Or at the very least that I should have.*

Reginald had designed his apartment to fit his complexion - all gold and white - and it was still his apartment even though they had shared it for years. The white sofa with silk brocade cushions made Belle feel like sitting at attention and the chairs lining the giant, white dining table were old enough that each fidget or adjustment made a creak like the ancient wood was about to collapse beneath her. But Reginald didn't fidget.

He later claimed that their first dinner had been the scariest and most tantalizing experience of his life, but she hadn't been able to see it. He had seemed to her the perfect gentleman: cold, calculating, with impeccable poise and a killer eye for detail.

He took her to some fancy place with a forgettable name where the patrons all spoke in hushed tones and the waiters wore masks and wigs. She was sure he meant her harm, even though she couldn't suss out why he bothered buying her dinner first.

"Why the interest?" he asked, picking up their conversation from the store.

"You mean most people don't find you interesting?"

"Most people know better."

"Well, I'm not most people."

"You've got that right."

You've got to love your man for who he is, Cora always said, meaning that she had to polish and sparkle the parts of him she did like until those shone through. But Belle had known by the end of the first night that the parts of Reginald she liked were intimately connected to the parts she didn't.

Their first affair was quick and violent. It was as if he was consumed by sweltering heat, holding on to sanity by a thread. Incredible strength strummed under his skin. He took her like no man had ever taken her before. Like she was light as a feather and solid as a rock. After he was done, she felt spent, run through, and unbroken.

On the last night of that first affair, he fucked her like he wanted to crush her beneath him. Once he was satisfied, she lay limp beside him, unable to move. He put his arms around her and turned her towards him. He held her with incredible strength and sudden tenderness, as if she was trapped in the embrace of a beast. She had been ready for pain, for hurt, for mindless sex, but she hadn't expected the raw emotion in his eyes. She did what she should have done that first day in the store: she ran.

He didn't chase her. They would meet at parties and social functions of her new crowd, who tolerated her despite the fact that she was far below their annual income level. The Emilys and Catherines and Margarets of the Upper East Side didn't even raise their noses at her secondhand dresses, instead they called them chic and found her style fascinating. And through every conversation, she would smile and chuckle and desperately ignore the man at the corner of her eye, the golden crest of her Reginald.

When Benjamin reappeared, back from a six-month stint in Zimbabwe, she fled into his arms. They'd dance, their bodies moving with passionless ease across the floor. They'd have coffee, their conversations flowing without pause or compromise. And they'd watch movies, their taste utterly compatible. He was perfect for her, her sister said, and Belle nodded and tried to kindle an answering spark inside her chest.

On the cold November evening when he tried to kiss her, she was unprepared. The leaves had fallen, leaving bare branches pointing accusingly at the sky. They promenaded home from a romantic comedy where the heroine had to choose between two men and ended up picking neither. Benjamin took her hand and she let him. It felt nice, safe.

"I'm leaving for Malawi," he said.

"Oh?" She stopped and looked up, waiting for him to continue.

"I'll be gone for a year and a half."

"A year and a half," she repeated, her voice hushed.

"And I was hoping you'd come with me?"

"Come with you?" She sounded like a confused parrot.

"Yes," he smiled. "These last few weeks have been the most wonderful of my life. I'll be gone for so long; I don't think I could stand being there without you."

"But we're just friends," she said.

"Friends." He dropped her hand. "You think we're friends?"

"Well, yeah," she said, quietly, and put one hand on his chest, strong and warm under his woolen coat. "Really good friends."

"Do friends do this?" he asked and grabbed her shoulders. His eyes were dark and sincere in the glow of the street lamps. She sighed and then his lips met hers. The kiss was soft but insistent. She tried to pull away, but he held her fast. As she opened her mouth to speak against his lips, his tongue entered her, exploring her mouth.

Suddenly, he was ripped away. She stumbled back and blinked and there he was, her Reginald, pounding Benjamin into the ground. He had his hands wrapped around the fabric of Benjamin's coat, and he used it to smash his head into the ground over and over. Belle screamed, but he didn't listen. Benjamin's face went slack.

"Stop! Reginald, please," she cried.

In the streetlight, the blood looked candyfloss red. Each impact made a crunch. Benjamin's eyelids fluttered closed. She couldn't tell if he was breathing.

She grabbed Reginald's arm. As he let go of Benjamin to shake her off, his fist hit her straight across the sternum. She was airborne. Her head cracked against the ground. Then everything faded out.

She woke up to his worried eyes and gentle embrace. She couldn't have been out for long because the moon was still in the sky and she was still outside. She shivered.

"It's you," she whispered. "It's always been you."

He kissed her.

Nothing ties two people closer together than disposing of a body.

Everyone knew Benjamin was planning one of his long trips to Africa, so it was relatively easy to fake a few farewell emails. He'd never been one for long goodbyes. They ladened the body with rocks and dumped it in the East River. Reginald did the heavy lifting, but Belle still felt faint at the end of the night.

"I don't want to be alone tonight," she whispered.

How young they had been, that night. How filled with hope. If they had known the ending of their story, if they had known what festered just past the happily-ever-after, would they have kept going?

She placed one kiss on his too-still cheek, and let her hand run through his thick mane. The metallic scent of blood mixed with his warm, spicy smell made him seem other, her Reginald no longer.

"It's always been you," she whispered.

They were married the following spring. Her father walked her down the aisle, hiding his worry behind teary, fatherly hugs. Cora perched uncomfortably beside Belle's assortment of new and old friends, while Reginald's associates made up his side of the church. His parents were long dead, and he had no other family, so he'd filled the church with people who didn't really matter.

Tailored weeds fit best, Cora always said, meaning you should groom a man to your ideals rather than wait for one that fit them. But Belle had never seen Reginald as some lost puppy to be trained.

Still, during their first year together, he grew softer, kinder. He mellowed, others said. Cora would nod to Belle approvingly, as if it was her doing. Their lovemaking turned gentle, caring, and his business deals publicly acceptable. It was as if a curse had been lifted, revealing the prince beneath the violent beast.

But Belle had loved him for who he was, not what he might become. Soon every conversation turned strained, every silence too long. Their dinner parties became awkward affairs where they circled the room in opposite directions, trying to keep everyone else from knowing that something was lacking.

On the night he confronted her, they were tucked in bed. He'd usually spoon her, but this time, he stayed on his side.

"Belle," he said. "You awake?"

"Mhmm," she said.

"Can I ask you something?"

Her Reginald wouldn't have asked for permission. "Sure."

"Why are you acting this way?"

She turned and watched him hug himself tight.

"What way?"

"As if... as if you no longer want me."

Resentment bubbled to the surface. Her Reginald wouldn't have said that. Would never have needed that type of confirmation. "You're not the man I married."

He blinked. "I'm better. You made me better."

"Not better," she said. "Just different."

After that night, he grew his hair out and began spending more and more time away. Business trips, long nights at the office. She didn't ask questions. She was ashamed to admit that she was relieved.

She wasn't sure when he started drinking, but she couldn't forget the first time he came home drunk. She'd been working on the seating chart for one of Margaret Rennan-Dobrowsky's benefits, when he stumbled inside. She didn't look up to say hi, so she was surprised when she felt his hand close around her neck.

His breath was hot and smelled of wine. She swallowed, heart suddenly in her throat. As he threw her down on the sofa, she felt passion rip through her for the first time in months. She threw her arms around him and kissed him. That was the second time he hit her.

After that night, he left for three weeks and she bought her first gun. When he returned, he wasn't the same. He'd be cold and distant, then mean and all too close. The beatings got worse. She finally had to put her short-sleeved dresses in storage.

When she spent Thanksgiving morning in the hospital, Cora finally spoke up: "You've never been one of those women."

"What women?"

"The ones who stay with losers. The ones who let people hurt them."

"Reginald isn't a loser," she argued, propping herself up in the hospital bed.

"Then why is he hurting you?"

She couldn't explain it, but the three broken ribs, seventeen stitches and a fourteen-day concussion spoke for themselves. She filed for divorce.

Rigor mortis hadn't set in yet, but his fist was clenched tight. The golden band around his finger glimmered in the light. He still wore the ring. That was what made tears leak from her eyes. He was her Reginald. Her Reginald.

When she told him she wanted out, it had been too easy. She sat him down on the white loveseat, took his hand in hers and told him she no longer felt the same way about him. He didn't argue. Just nodded and said he understood.

"Do you want to do something together? Share a last meal or something?" she asked.

"What did you have in mind?"

"I don't know. I could make your favorite?"

His shoulders hunched forward. "I don't think I could stand that."

She packed a bag. Her life neatly folded in one suitcase. Tears pushed at the back of her throat, but she swallowed them away. At the front door, she hesitated, turned and asked again: "Is there anything I can do?"

"Just go," he whispered, and she saw the smile break on his face. "I just need you gone."

She went to a hotel, but couldn't sleep. She wanted to talk to her sister, but she didn't know how to share this hurt, so instead she stared at the walls. Four days later, she managed to keep a meal down. Six days later, she was back at work.

By the time he called, she had almost put her life back together. She walked through her old routines, suspended in time, but at least she was walking. The sound of his voice, raw and haggard, jolted her back to reality.

"We need to talk."

The clock on the mantelpiece read five past midnight. Long past the expiration date of enchantments. She stepped inside the white-on-white apartment, meticulously clean, and came face to face with him.

"What do you want from me?" she asked, not knowing what she wanted him to answer.

"I want you to come back," he said, without a glimmer of hope in his eyes.

"I can't do this again," she said and turned towards the door.

He grabbed her arm and held on too tight. She stared at his hand until he let go.

"I never meant to hurt you. Not you."

"Who did you mean to hurt?" She asked, and hated how bitter her words tasted.

He closed his left fist. "I just wanted to make you happy."

And therein lay their problem: she had not wanted him to change for her, and what was broken between them couldn't be fixed.

"I can't," she said.

"You can't? That's it? You can't?!"

She nodded, and walked across the room to perch on the straight-backed chair by the window.

"I killed for you," he said.

"I know."

"I came back for you," he said.

"I know."

"I... you don't know what I've done for you."

"No, I do know," she said. "And I'm sorry."

"I don't want you to be sorry. I want you to love me."

"Reginald, I... "

"No," he spat. "You don't get to play the better person. This is your fault. This. All your fault!"

He grabbed one of the dining room chairs and flung it at the wall, it smashed into kindling and he closed his fist and sprang towards her. She drew the gun she'd carried with her and his eyes widened and he reached out to her and she couldn't read the look on his face, and before she could decide if it was pride, longing or hatred, she pulled the trigger.

He'd just wanted to make her happy.

She looked at the scene again: the ripped curtains, the broken mantel-piece, the blood. Was this all on her?

Sirens sounded in the distance. She let her white dress fall to the floor, revealing bruises and old aches, the epilogue to a battered fairytale writ-ten on skin. As she felt the phantom cold of steel around her wrists, she prayed for someone to claim that true love was worth it.

Cloaks
and
Hoods

Angela
Rega

Soleil flipped the sign on the door to *Fermé* and extinguished the oil burner. No matter how much fragrance she used, it was hard to compete with the smell of camphor that kept the clothes she sold moth free.

Tonight there was another odour, of fresh soil and leaf litter. She stared through the glass to the world outside. The streets of Paris were wet; the rain rivered down the shop windows washing away the day's dust.

She snapped the deadwood twig that appeared under the front door. She couldn't put it off any longer. She had been so busy these last few months with alterations, stitching loose hems and buttons, giving new life to old frocks, she didn't have time to remember the memories that crept like tendrils around the borders of her mind. Busy meant no time to remember who she was before Soleil, Wardrobe Mistress of one of the best vintage clothes shops in the 4th arrondissement, Paris.

Often she imagined folding away the unraveling memories like the metres of fabrics she sold, stacking them neatly into the back walls of her mind. Today's customers hadn't noticed the woods that grew within

CLOAKS AND HOODS | 135

the shop, the vines crawling up the wall, the moss gumshoeing the carpet. Perhaps they were too consumed with searching for the right dress to notice? Perhaps they thought it quite usual for the wilds to grow within a shop in the middle of Paris? Or perhaps, she thought, more disturbingly, they didn't see them at all.

Soleil drew the crimson velvet curtains across the shop windows and ripped out the vines that crept up the walls and twined around the dress racks. Already they sprouted roots and stung her palms.

There was much work to do when the woods Soleil had left behind began to grow around her.

She went into her workroom, hidden behind the racks of sales dresses and bargain boxes, opened the door to the sewing machine cupboard and took the fur out. It smelt of game and dried blood. The memories came flooding.

"Ouch!" She plucked a few of the long coarse blonde hairs from her head and threaded the sewing machine with the longest one. She pressed her foot on the treadle and fed the pelt through. St st st st st st st st st st stitch. She released her foot from the pedal. The machine's stitches were fast but inaccurate; wolf skin was hard to work with. Underneath the fur, the hide was fibrous and in some places still viscid. Between times, when no woods grew and her memories were like sleeping dogs, Soleil seemed to forget how difficult it was to work with wolf skin. With each stitch, she remembered.

St st st st st st st st st st st stitch...

His name didn't matter. Soleil was made to call him grandfather. Grandmother had re-discovered love. She wore garish red lipstick and sang love songs with her shard-sharp voice.

"Need a man about the house to keep things safe. Don't want to be like those young women that go missing in the woods, now, do you?"

Soleil shook her head. Her grandmother was right. She had seen the signs up of little girls gone missing in the wild woods that lay between their village and the next. The posters were nailed like little crucifixions to the thick trunked trees.

Soleil was happy for her grandmother but sad for herself. Her new grandfather was stricter than her grandmother had ever been; he forbade her to go out and took away her bone needles and whittling knife.

"Those are boy's toys. You're at an age when you should be learning how to care for the home, cook and clean, be ready for your husband, which is not far around the corner, hey?" And he would tweak her chest or pat her behind and laugh.

Soleil didn't laugh. She found his coarse fingers, hairy at the knuckles and joints, and the stench from his gums repugnant. Instead, she grew angry. Why was he allowed to roam the woods, sometimes for days on end, and she was not allowed out for a small snip of time to smell the grass and feel the wind on her face?

He returned with the rain and let the dampness in on his homecoming. Soleil heard the decanter pour, and their laughter and kisses as she fell into a restless slumber, dreaming of running against howling winds, of branches scratching her legs, of pursuit.

His scrabbly fur had scratched her skin as he lifted the covers and crawled next to her in the bed. "Soleil," he whispered; his nose wet in her ear. She struggled. His hands were heavy, the weight of his body crushing.

"I won't hurt you," he whispered. His breath was pungent with whiskey. No doubt Grandma was sound asleep from the same draught. "You're just a little too young, yet. But when you become a woman, you'll be mine."

Soleil held her breath. Become a woman? She knew that time was nigh. Already her friends had boasted of womanhood. To Soleil, it seemed like a curse. The air in the room became thick and in her panic she felt she might never breathe again. She felt hemmed in, the desire to run making her legs spasm. The room spun.

Soleil became a woman quicker than she expected; there was mild cramping, a spattering of blood that made her thighs stick together and a feeling of defeat. Her grandmother clucked her tongue and said she should stay indoors. She did not listen. Ever since that night he had come to Soleil, marking her like a wild dog that brands a child before his bite, she ran wild in the woods as she pleased.

She climbed oaks, finding hiding places in the nooks between two branches or the hollowed out remains of what once were majestic trees. She learned to jump high, run fast and crouch low. Her hair and skin grew tawny like a moth and she learned how to merge unobtrusively in her surroundings.

Grandmother slapped her when she got home, saying she was an unruly girl. "If the wolves eat you up, don't say I didn't warn you!"

Soleil never answered; she knew her grandmother would never understand, never believe that grandfather would betray her. Instead of replying, she went to peel the potatoes and skin the rabbit her grandmother had left for her to prepare for the evening meal.

She'd cried the day she skinned her first rabbit, because it had been very easy to do. A simple swift nick and its fur had come off in one peeling. She made slippers out of the hide, trying to keep her feet warm at night; the house was bitterly cold in the evenings, as if no door or window could keep out the oncoming winter. Grandmother was too preoccupied with her lover to notice that roots stabbed through the cracks in the floorboards and moss carpeted the walls.

She told her she was a lazy girl and should fetch daub to repair the floor and walls. "Or else we'll all freeze to death! And take your grandfather with you to help get a good price."

"He's not my grandfather!" she wanted to say, but her words were no longer forthcoming. She let him walk behind, her ears pricked. Somehow the air was not as bitter as in the house, the sun shone through the spaces between the branches bringing light and warmth to her cold cheeks and nose. She wore rabbit hide slippers and could keep ahead of him with her hare-like hop.

She was thankful for the fur slippers that made her quick on her feet, but even they were not enough to keep him at bay. Her bleeding had come again, and Grandfather somehow sensed it. He had been poking at her with his index finger in places that not even she had dared to explore; the unfamiliar terrain of her own developing body, the blood, sticky on her inner thigh.

She made to run, but his hold was strong. Instead of skin, there was bristling fur. His nose had elongated, his canines lengthened.

It was like the rabbit, really. A swift nick at his throat with her penknife and his wolf hide peeled off, though not as easily as the rabbits'. She had to tug to peel his hide away, and a harder yank down the back of his neck pulled at the sinew that stretched taut. She cut into it, separating the pelt from his being. He was left whimpering with bloodied skin.

"I'll tell your grandmother what you did to me!" he screamed. "You'll never be allowed back home again!"

She laughed and cloaked herself in his sticky pelt that stank of metallic blood and lust. It draped the saddlebag thighs that she carried for her new journey as woman. On her feet, she wore her rabbit slippers.

"See if you survive the woods!" he shouted.

Soleil thought of the vines and moss, of the root and branches that had grown within their walls since his arrival.

"I know my way out of the woods!" she screamed back. "I have lived in them ever since I met you!"

She took her foot off the treadle. She shivered. It was time to wear it. *His skin*. Worn to remember that once she had been brave enough to fight, bold enough to escape, and young enough to reinvent herself and live again.

But the wolf skin didn't make the memories less haunting. It didn't take much: bad weather, a customer with bad breath, an old lady and her granddaughter. And even though it was a long time ago, she still remembered. It's never easy to slay your demons, the ones left lingering inside your mind, the ones you unleash when your memories unravel.

The last stitch she did by hand and lifted the wolf skin up to the dim light. Complete, the pelt resembled a cloak. She draped it over her shoulders. Tonight, she would walk the Bois de Boulogne in his skin and remember that once she'd conquered them, she'd killed one, she'd become one.

She took her keys and little else. She would not need an umbrella, or her purse.

The Queen of the Woods only needs her cape.

She walked the Bois de Boulogne. The rain had left the night crisp. She inhaled, taking the air into her lungs.

Memory must come like a virus infecting many: she saw other girls wearing cloaks and hoods, scales and skins. There were those who wore feathers instead of pelts, and swan masks. There were those girls that wore pelts like hers and women of donkey skins. There were men who wore gowns prettier than the ones she sold in her shop. There were many stories about the Bois de Boulogne, about how unsafe it was in the evenings. But tonight, she was not alone in her remembering. Even the park itself remembered that it, too, was once part of a forest that stretched from Paris to Normandy. The oaks remembered their wildness. They would protect Soleil, the feathered and furred girls and the men in frocks.

Tonight, they were safe, all walking alone, smiling silently at each other.

She would return with dawn's moisture beading in her fur, and her nose cold when first light peeked through the gaps between the clouds. With sunrise would come the undoing. She would pull at the hair threads, unravelling the stitches, until there were just pieces of skin and fur. Then she would fold it neatly away into its hiding place inside her sewing machine, draw open the curtains and turn the sign to *Ouvert*, the roots and vines gone.

She would always find her way out of the woods.

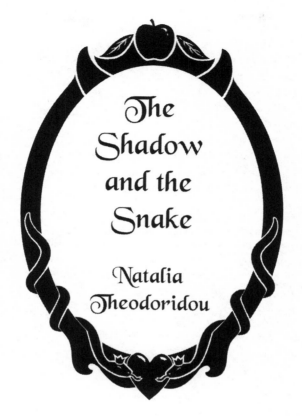

The Shadow and the Snake

Natalia Theodoridou

There was a palace, once upon a time, a palace stranger than most. For there were voices in that palace, whispering in the dark, echoing through the empty chambers. And the voices in the palace said:

There was a King, once upon a time,
and there was a Queen, once upon a time,
who had a daughter with raven hair.
She liked to play with the water snakes by the pond, once upon a time,
and she knew them all by their proper names:
Enhydris and Liophis, Xenochrophis and Nerodia,
and Hydrodynastes, which was her favourite, because his name meant 'Master of the water.'
She put her hand in the pond, unafraid, and the Master danced around her fingers, and she felt powerful and strong.
The Queen did not like her dangerous game and scolded the Girl, with kindness and love.
But the Queen died, once upon a time,
and the King wept, and fell sick for a whole winter.

And then spring came, and the King rose from his bed,
and he took a new wife, once upon a time.
The new Queen was jealous of the raven daughter,
scared of her snakes, and of the master in the water.
And so, she asked for a witch, to curse the Girl,
to live unhappily ever after.
And the witch came, once upon a time.
"I can do what you ask," the witch said,
"but you have to pay the price."
And the voices in the palace said:
The Queen is with child.
May her child be prosperous and wise.

Look at her, skipping down the slope. Going to that pond again. She looks happy.
She has grown since her mother died. Her figure is rounder now, her breasts fuller.
She will be a woman soon. She is lovely, really. Perhaps I could have loved her, had it
not been for those nasty things she likes to play with. Play, only? Maybe she's a witch.
Don't be foolish, she's no witch. No need to fear her. She's just a girl. Why don't I
love her? She could be my little girl. She could be a big sister to my baby son. Isn't that
right, son? Perhaps I could have loved her like a mother. How I wish I could love her.
Perhaps that would make the fear go away. Perhaps not.

She is watching from her high window.
The Girl could feel the Queen's eyes burning holes in her back. Without wanting to, she reached for the spot, trying to protect herself. She knew it wouldn't work. What could ever protect her from the hatred of a pregnant woman?
She skipped down the slope as lightly as she could, faking carelessness and joy.
Father says she's just scared of the snakes. He says I should give them up, stay away.
She knelt by the pond's edge and disturbed the water lightly. It was their signal. They always came when she did that.
How could I ever give you up?
The Master gave a subtle nudge to the underside of her palm, then his head emerged, familiar and kind. The kindest.
"Good morning, Master," she said.
The snake dived again and looped its body around her wrist.
"Do you love me, snake?"
The Master wrapped himself on her arm and allowed her to drag him halfway out of the water. She caressed his head.
"I know," she said. "I know."

Look at her, playing with her snakes again, thought the King. *She is so unlike her mother in her fearlessness, yet so similar in form. Her back is the same, the curve of her shoulder, the dark shine of her hair. If she stayed with her face turned away like this, I might think it was her, brought back from the dead for me. How can two people so unlike be so similar? I have to let go of the mother, and in letting go I must forsake the daughter's form too. But how could I ever let go of you, dear daughter? My dear, dear girl.*

"What are you looking at, my King, so thoughtful and sad?"

The King turned away from the window and drew the curtain shut.

"My Queen."

He approached the woman and knelt in front of her swollen belly. He put his arms around her waist and pressed his ear against her navel.

"Can you hear your son's heartbeat, my King? He is becoming strong; a worthy heir for you."

He looked up at her.

How can she talk like that? I don't care for strength. Unbroken lines, they say. What line can remain unbroken, with all that death besieging our lives? Death is like a snake, wrapped tightly around us, squeezing out our life.

"I just want him to be happy. That's all," he said.

She withdrew from his embrace, looking hurt.

What things women care about.

He suddenly felt foolish, kneeling like that in the middle of his own chambers. The King's chambers. "Get some rest, woman," he said. "Give me a strong heir, as you promised."

That seemed to satisfy her somehow. He watched her leave the room, her royal posture maintained flawlessly, despite the ripening fruit that disfigured her body.

Let my son be happy. Let her be as good a mother as she *was. My love.*

The palace was woken by the Queen's unearthly screams that night. The King was banned from the labour room by a nurse with a hollow look in her eyes. The Girl stood in a corner and watched the Queen writhe and struggle against an enemy seen only by her. The blood seemed endless; the mattress was soaked through. *How can a woman hold so much blood?* the Girl wondered. *Where does all that blood come from? So much. So much. Can she live through this?*

She did. And when the blood ran out, there was the Prince, dark and wet, reaching for his mother's breast when the nurse snatched him from her body and threw him on the floor.

And the voices in the palace said:
Alas!

142 | NATALIA THEODORIDOU

The Prince is a snake.
Alas!
Who will nurture the Snake?
And the Queen rose from her bed and looked at the Snake. She
dried her brow and said:
"The Girl has such love for her snakes. Who better to
breastfeed my child?"
Alas! the voices said.
Alas! The Girl is lost.

"Drink this. It will bring milk to your breasts." The witch held out a cup
filled with a steaming white liquid. The smell reminded the Girl of the
pond after a good downpour of rain.

"How will I do this? Why is father allowing it? The Snake will bite my
breast and I will die. It's what the Queen wants. Isn't it?" The Girl sat on
the bed and held her head in her hands. She wouldn't cry. She refused to
cry.

"You will find a way," the witch said. "Mothers always do."

The Girl looked up at the witch. *Mothers?* she thought. *Mothers?* "You
say this will bring me milk to feed the Snake?" she asked.

"Yes."

"Give it to me."

She held her breath and downed the liquid as fast as she could. It tasted foul, but she barely noticed. Her mind was working fast. They would
both survive this.

She ordered the metal smith to her chamber. She was soon lying on
her bed half-naked, her bare breasts groped by the craftsman's ragged
hands. Her tender skin turned red under his touch, but it had to be done.
The metal smith breathed heavily. He tried to work quickly, obviously
embarrassed.

"You have good tits, Princess," he said, and turned a bright pink.

"Don't forget your place," she thought of telling him, but didn't. What
did that mean, anyway? What was his place? What was hers? She laughed
it off.

He had the bust ready in a few hours. A bronze vessel in the shape and
size of her breasts for the Snake to suck on without wounding her. But it
wasn't enough. She had to make sure.

She ordered the butcher to her chamber.

"Do you know how to handle snakes?" she asked him.

"I know how to kill them good," he said. "But that's the Prince. I want
no trouble."

"That is not what I want from you."

"What, then?"

"Get me a vial of the Snake's venom. Can you do that without hurting him?"

"That's easy," the butcher said. "But whom do you want poisoned, Princess?"

"It is not death that I desire," she said. "Get me the vial, and never speak of this again."

Two strong men carried the royal crib and put it in her chamber. The Snake lay there wrapped in fine silk. He flicked his forked tongue and looked at her.

She took a drop from the vial and diluted it in a large cup of blood-red wine. She gulped it down and stripped naked from the waist up. She put on her breastplate.

"This is our armor, brother," she said. "May it guard us both well."

She approached the crib. "Easy now. You won't bite me, will you?"

She took the Snake out of his crib and placed him gently on her chest. Within moments, the smell of her milk had drawn him to the bronze nipple. She shivered. And as the Snake lay on her chest, she could feel his heart beating against her own, until she could no longer tell them apart.

The poison she took made her sick. She ran a fever for days, but she refused the doctor's orders to stay away from the wine. The Queen watched her closely. She watched the Girl breastfeed the Snake, watched her bathe and care for him, but she never once laid a loving hand on her child. *She hopes I'll die*, the Girl thought. *She hopes we both die. And where is my father? How did he let this happen?*

After seven days, the fever subsided and the Girl felt strong again. She looked for the King but he was nowhere to be found. She asked about him but the people avoided her questions with mumbled excuses and tight lips. She even went down to the pond and looked for answers amid the water snakes. She found none. The pond was empty.

She disturbed the surface of the water like she used to, but the Master never came.

"Where are you, Master?" she asked. "Where are you, my love?"

And the voices in the palace said:
The King went mad, once upon a time,
and killed the water snakes,
for he could not bear to kill his own son.
And he climbed on a horse, once upon a time,
and rode, and rode, until he was a distant spot in the horizon,
and then he was no more.

The Girl kept taking the drop of poison every day, but she never got sick again. Feeding the Snake was getting easier every time. She even caught herself enjoying it, looking forward to it. She missed him when they were apart. With her water snakes gone, he was her only company. And he was sweet, and affectionate.

"Do you love me, Snake?" she asked him each morning, and he wrapped himself around her arm.

They now slept together every night; the Girl on her back, the Snake coiled three and a half times by her left breast. And years passed. And he grew strong and kind, always tender, always mindful of her human frailty; taking care so that his embrace was never too tight, his fangs never in contact with her skin. And she grew too. She grew beautiful and fearless of his beastly form. For she knew his heartbeat as if it were her own.

> But then the voices in the palace said:
> The Prince wants a woman.
> Alas!
> Who would ever marry the Snake?
> And the Queen looked at the Girl and the Snake
> and she envied them, for she was alone and bitter.
> "She has such love for my snake," she said. "Who better to lie
> with him in his bed?"

"First she made me a mother to my brother, now she wants me to marry my child. What will she ask next?" The Girl grabbed the cup from which she used to drink the poisoned wine, earning her immunity against his venom, and smashed it on the floor. She immediately regretted it, threw herself down and started collecting the broken glass, cutting herself as she did so.

"How will I do this, witch?" she cried. "Tell me. How will I do this?"

The witch sat carefully next to her on the floor, took her trembling hands in her own and said:

"Listen to me. There is a way for all things that are meant to be in our life. This is the way of yours. You will light the fireplace. Build a good fire, let it blaze high. You will then wear seven shirts and invite your husband to lie next to you. Then you will say, 'how hot it is, my snake,' and you will take off one of your shirts. Then the Snake will take off one of his. You will do this six more times. When the Snake takes off his last shirt, there will be a man underneath. Only his teeth will be the teeth of the snake. Love him and walk the path of your life in peace."

"How hot it is, my Snake," she said, taking off her last shirt, her breasts naked for him, bare for the first time.

He slithered close to her, and took off his own last shirt, and then there he was, her man, her love. He rested his human head against her chin, and took her nipple in his mouth. Such a familiar move, and yet so different now.

"No armour this time, my snake," she said, her voice quivering. His fangs pressed against her skin, then broke it, and his poison flowed inside her for the first time, and it felt warm and sweet.

And the voices in the palace said:
Thus the Snake became a man, once upon a time.
And the Girl loved him, and he loved her.
And only his sharp teeth and his forked tongue remained,
to remind humans of his old form.
But rumors travelled to the nearby kingdoms,
about the new King who was a snake, deep down.
And the Snake was called away to war, once upon a time.
"Do you love me, snake?" the Girl asked, once upon a time.
"With all my heart," the Snake replied. "My sister, my mother,
my wife."
"Come back to me," she said. "My brother, my child, my love."
And then the Snake went off to war, and was away for a long
time.

Is she unhappy? Has she ever been truly unhappy? Like I've been?

"She has everything," the Queen screamed. "A brother, a child, a husband, all of which she took from me. Tell me why I should not punish you, witch."

The witch took a step backwards.

"Life works in mysterious ways, my Queen. I told you you had to pay."

"And what do I have to show for it?"

"My Queen..."

"You are useless! You gave me a snake for a child and robbed me of my King. I should kill you with my bare hands."

The witch knelt before the Queen and hid her face in her palms. "You need to cast her off, my Queen," she said and her whisper was the saddest sound the Queen had ever heard. "Write to the Snake, tell him she died. And cast her off into the wilderness."

The Queen's anger subsided a little. "What will that accomplish?" she asked.

"It is what needs to be done. She has to walk her life's path, and so do you."

And the voices in the palace said:
Thus the Girl was cast off, once upon a time.
And no one in the palace knew what happened to her next,
for it was years before she was seen again.

The Girl walked for many hours. She took the path that led from the pond into the dark woods, and from the woods into the great marsh that surrounded the kingdom. She slipped and fell, and she got mud in her raven hair. She reached the sea and wet her aching feet in the cold water. And just before nightfall, she found a cave to sleep in. The rocks fit her weary head nicely, and the wind spoke of a home far away, and of a snake lost.

She woke when the wind had given way to the midday heat, and the sun was already high up in the sky. She got up and stood at the cave's entrance, where the light could reach her and warm her tired bones. She was hungry and thirsty. She glanced at her clothes and found them torn and dirty. *Not even my Snake would recognize me, if he saw me now*, she thought.

She looked out at the water. She had heard stories about it, even visited it once with her father when she was small. Mother was alive then. The ocean was still as wild and magnificent as she remembered it. She walked out of the cave to face it. She stood at the edge and let the waves spray her with salt. *Why don't you take me now?* she thought. *Just take me now.*

There was a flicker in her vision, like a wave of heat passing in front of her. Then the fleeting impression of a shade on the ground. Then a voice.

"Girl."

"Who is there?" she asked.

"Who is there?" the voice repeated.

"Are you mocking me? Where are you? I can't see you."

There was a movement, and then she thought that a man's shadow stood in front of her.

"You are the Snake's wife," the Shadow said.

"Yes. I was."

"Yes, you were. I've heard about you."

"From whom?"

"What happened to you? Are you lost?"

"I was cast off."

"Cast off. And where is your snake now?"

"Away."

"Away," the Shadow repeated. Then he paused. "You remind me of someone I knew, long ago," he said after a while. "Come. You need water and food. I will take care of you."

She was too exhausted to refuse. And why would she? The Shadow took the Girl along the shore and led her to a much larger cave than the one she had spent the night in. His palace, the Shadow called it. He had stockpiled dried meat and dried fruit. He had a small nook in which he built a fire, and a pot made of stone in which he cooked a simple broth for her.

"Why are you so good to me?" the Girl asked. She could not see him well now that they were inside, but she thought he was sitting next to her. Looking at her, perhaps. "Because I remind you of someone? Whom do I remind you of?"

The Shadow did not reply.

"Was it a woman? A wife?" the Girl asked. "You don't want to say?" She sipped her broth. It was warm and filling. "I won't ask about it if you don't want to say."

"Could you turn your head, please? Let me look at you that way." She did.

"Thank you. Now ask me something else, if you want," he said.

"Why can't I see you?"

"I lost my mind a long time ago. After a while, my body followed. A shadow is all that's left now."

"How awful."

"Yes."

"Can I touch you?"

"Touch me? I don't know. Can a shadow be touched?"

"Do you mind if I try?"

"Please. Please do."

The Girl put down her broth and turned to face the Shadow. She lifted her arm and caressed the smudged edges of his form blending into the darkness of the cave. Then she pushed her palm inward, toward his chest. Her hand was drawn to a warmth in his middle.

A soft sigh escaped his lips.

"Am I hurting you?" she asked.

"Yes. No," he said.

"Do you have a heart, Shadow?" she asked. She pushed her hand further towards the source of the heat, until she felt a pulsating core welcoming her fingers. "Is that your heart?"

Day after day, the Girl learned how to live in the cave-palace by the ocean. She grew accustomed to the Shadow's gaze, and could now tell when he was looking at her and when he was looking out at the waves, lost in his thoughts and memories. And as time passed them by, the Shadow started to find his body again under her touch, bit by bit; an eye first, a finger, part of a thigh, then a whole arm. And they lived as best they could, as man and wife. And when she opened her eyes one morning and found his returned head sleeping next to hers, was she really surprised to see her father's face? She wasn't, and it wouldn't matter if she had been, anyway. For she was walking her life's path as it was meant to be, and she had found it filled with love; and that, she thought, was all anyone should ever ask.

And the voices in the palace said:
Six years passed with no word from the Girl.
Six years before the war came to an end.
And on the seventh month of the seventh year,
the Snake came back to the palace.
His hair had gone grey from the grief for his lost wife,
and his eyes had gone darker from the sights he had seen,
but his teeth still flashed white and sharp like on the day he was born.
The Queen grew pale when she saw him,
because she knew she could not hide her lie from him.
And the Snake rejoiced, for his wife was still in the world.

"Are you angry, my son?" the Queen asked, shivering and frail.
"No, mother. I am happy. I am the happiest snake alive."
She looked at him, doubtful.
"Let me hug you, mother, to thank you for the good news you've given me, even if you did not want to."
The Snake approached her and put his arms around her, enveloping her small frame completely.
"Your embrace is too tight, snake," the Queen whispered, her breath leaving her body.
"Not tight enough, you said, mother?" the Snake asked.
And he tightened his embrace, until the Queen's life flickered and then was no more.

And the voices in the palace said:
So the Snake went looking for the Girl, once upon a time.
He followed the path that led from the pond into the dark woods, and from the woods into the great marsh that surrounded the kingdom.
He slipped and fell, and he got mud in his grey hair.
He reached the sea and wet his feet in the cold water.
He walked along the shore and saw smoke in the distance.
And just before nightfall, he found the Shadow's cave-palace, and entered.

And there was the King, once upon a time,
and the Girl, once upon a time,
and a path to be walked,
and a price to be paid.

"Let my wife go," shouted the Snake.

"And what if I don't?"

"Then I have to kill you."

"My Snake!" the Girl cried out. "Don't. This is our father you want to kill."

"What do you speak of?" the Snake asked.

"It cannot be," the Shadow said. "I never fathered any boys. And I've killed all the snakes. You are no son of mine."

"Let her go. How could you lie with your own daughter?" hissed the Snake, baring his white teeth.

"You married your sister. The woman whose milk you drank. How dare you judge me?" The Shadow picked up a stone and stared at his son, unmoving.

"Give her up. Let her go," the Snake said.

"Never," the Shadow replied. "She brought me back. I am lost without her. You left her. Leave her one more time," he said, and charged.

"Never," the Snake replied. "She made me. I am hers," he said, and ran towards the Shadow, his fangs dripping poison.

"Stop it!" the Girl shouted. She threw herself between them. The stone came down, striking her soft flesh. The teeth flashed white, her forgetful veins yielding under their poison.

Silence fell in the cave.

The Girl's body collapsed in their embrace, and they laid her gently on the stone floor. She had been without the Snake's venom for too long. Her body convulsed and a speck of blood appeared at the corner of her lips. She lifted her arm and caressed the Snake's mouth.

"My Snake, you came back to me. My brother, my child, my love," she said to the Snake.

His lips moved, but no sound escaped him.

"I know," said the Girl. "I know." She turned to the Shadow and put her hand on his chest, feeling his heartbeat. "Do you know your heart, Shadow? If only you knew how alike you two are."

And as she said these words, she was gone.

And then the voices in the palace said:
The Girl died, there in the cave, once upon a time.
And the Shadow wept for his lost daughter.
And the Snake wept for his lost love.

And they did not try to kill one another ever again.
They took her body back to the palace,
and they found it deserted and empty.
They buried her next to the dry pond, and they planted flowers
that soon withered and died, for there was no one to look after
them.
The Snake found his old shirts and put them back on.
He can be seen sometimes, sliding among the dead flowers
around her grave,
in the midday heat, when the snakes come out.
And the Shadow slowly faded away again,
and all that is left of him is spots of shade in sunny rooms.
And their voices still echo through the empty palace.
And their voices say:
Do you have a heart, Shadow?
Did you love her, Snake?
Does your heart break?
Does your heart break?

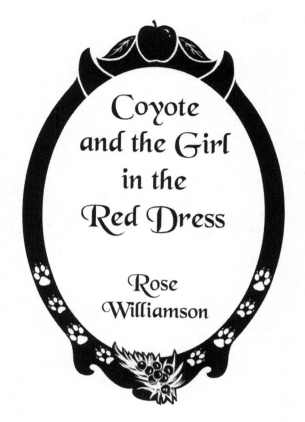

Coyote and the Girl in the Red Dress

Rose Williamson

Coyote moves into the city with his brothers because there is nearly no desert left. Man doesn't remember him very well, and has forgotten how to speak the language of the Animals, so the two have difficulty communicating. To remind Man of their ancient friendship, Coyote bears gifts of jackrabbits and kangaroo rats, which Man throws away in disgust. Man gives Coyote the gift of a bounty on his head: fifty dollars to anyone who shoots Coyote or his brothers within the city limits.

Coyote is annoyed. He gave Man fire and taught him to be clever like the Animals. Man should still be thanking him. Coyote hides himself in the city, living in dusty washes and in the shadow of the very tall bank. He strikes back by eating Man's domestic pets, and knocking over the trash cans with Javelina and her babies. Man is annoyed. Coyote is annoyed.

The girl in the red dress dances like she is alone. The men in the nightclub watch her like she is covered by the entry price. They are hungry.

The girl in the red dress has big, plump cheeks and lips. She has wide eyes that make her face wonder constantly. The men in the club watching her feel dirty because she can't be more than seventeen. Despite her fresh-faced youth, her hips swing like a woman's, and they appreciate that. She scares them. They like it.

Coyote feels like he owns the city at night. On Saturdays, he stalks the neighborhoods behind the bars and clubs. If he waits long enough, Saturdays are full of fallen food. He likes burgers best.

He paces back and forth in the empty alleyways, straining his ears for the vast silence that fills the streets after the bars shut. Coyote doesn't like the dull throb of noise from the clubs and the heavy scents which hang in the air on the weekends distract him from the things he has known for so many hundreds of years - the smell of a ripe prickly pear fruit, the sound of a mousey meal scurrying across the desert. But these things he has learned to live without, getting much fatter off Man's abundant and easy to catch trash. He likes it easy.

The girl in the red dress stops every once in a while, and, almost shyly, lets the hungry men buy her drinks. Her skin dries salty-sweet from the sheen of her glowy sweat. If they ask, she says she wants a gin and tonic. They are surprised at her old-fashioned tastes. They expect her to order a vodka and cranberry. Most girls do, to keep their figures. The tart cranberry juice is good for masking the taste of alcohol. The girl in the red dress isn't worried about her figure, and she likes the taste of gin.

She likes to imagine the process of turning tiny, pale blue juniper berries into gin. Giniper, she thinks, junigin. She wishes gin was pale blue like the fresh berries, or better yet, deep purple like the dried ones. She wishes she knew how to make it herself, and imagines the recipe is written out on parchment in fairy-tale calligraphy, like all lost arts must be. She imagines it overflowing from her bathtub right into little apothecary bottles that she would hand out at Christmas, affixed with handwritten labels noting particular facets of that year's batch.

She imagines tying sprigs of juniper berries to the necks of the bottles, letting people know just where their gin came from. Pretty little purple-blue berries.

She's glad she doesn't drink vodka. Imagining potatoes in her drink is vile.

She thinks all these thoughts while chatting to her suitors politely about nothing important. They don't realize she is somewhere else until the drinks are sipped away and she excuses herself. She doesn't invite them to dance with her; she doesn't give them the chance to ask. They are left disappointed.

She feels the gin layering itself in her veins throughout the night. Three drinks means she dances off-rhythm, four means she stops noticing.

Coyote laps up water meant for someone's chihuahua. He would lap up the chihuahua, too, but it's kept inside the house. It barks at him through the large screen door of the Arizona room. Coyote understands, but is slightly put off by the dialect.

"Hey jhou," yips the chihuahua, "Tha's mine! Comprende? Mine! Jhou keep out!"

Coyote bares his canines in a smile and slips out of the yard.

"I could just eat you up," grins a man at the bar. He is handsome and dark-haired. The girl in the red dress smiles at him. He feels invited and growls a low, friendly growl before wrapping his arm around her waist.

She steps away, but still feels his arm around her waist. She is slightly thrilled.

"Aren't you going to buy me a drink first?" She flutters her eyelashes. It looks strange on such big eyes.

He orders, not asking her what she wants. He drops drink names she's never heard of before. The bartender seems put out by the effort, but then looks proud when he sets in front of them two extravagant cocktails. Hers is in a martini glass, and garnished with a bright red cherry. His has a cherry, too, but already only the stem is left.

Coyote is pleased to see the taxi parade begin. He is only good at telling time when the sun is out, casting shadows. He likes the taxi drivers, who are, like him, opportunistic. They know the best times to gather, like two in the morning when the nightclubs shut. If Coyote ran the clubs, he would decree they be open all night. He would probably also add slot machines and poker tables, a little more opportunity for everyone, especially him.

Coyote's belly rumbles a little in anticipation. He can already taste the chemical meat of McDonald's and he licks his chops.

The girl in the red dress throws up in the bathroom. She doesn't remember drinking enough to make her as sick as she is, but she reminds herself she didn't eat much. It sounds like this: "Idiiiiiiiint eemahs."

She finds it difficult to walk. She finds it difficult to open her eyes. She likes the cool feeling of the bathroom tiles, but she also likes the warm, strong hands lifting her off them.

The girl in the red dress isn't sure where she is anymore.

What strong hands you have, she tries to say around tired, numb lips. "Whastrong hans yove."

Coyote inches closer and closer to the avenue of nightclubs and bars. They empty and empty until it is just a hardy few revelers and a troupe of weary bartenders left. He moves unnoticed behind buildings, smelling the old food in dumpsters and salivating for something fresh.

He smells a strange smell. It smells like fear, but muted and dull. It makes him anxious, and Coyote sneezes, trying to get it out of his nostrils. It doesn't go away.

Coyote tries to walk away from the smell, but it seems to cling to his fur and follow him. He gets turned around and around, until he is walking the direction he was walking in the first place. He can't tell where it is coming from, so he decides to find it and solve the mystery.

Coyote's nose brings him to the back of a club, where a man is carrying a girl in a red dress to a shiny car. He hangs back in the shadows and watches, sniffing the air. He sits back on his haunches and waits.

The girl in the red dress feels strange. She realizes she is in the air, above a dark parking lot. She floats along. She doesn't feel dead, but she isn't sure.

In the parking lot, a man is carrying her to his car. She wills her other self to stir in his arms, because something feels wrong. She tries to float to them and tear herself from his arms, but nothing seems to move the way she wants it to. She doesn't want to get in that man's car. She tries to scream. She is very afraid.

Coyote does not understand Man's courting habits these days. He remembers when the Animal Gods used to play a role. He liked doling advice and matchmaking when it was important. He had even had romances with the odd Woman now and again, revered and worshipped by her. Now Coyote must sidestep used condoms in the roads. He hears names of rock stars and actors said in the same adoring tone that Woman used to say his name. He wonders what has happened to Man.

His nose tickles with the smell of lust. It is Man's lust, heavy and hot and stale. There is no lust smell from the girl, which disappoints Coyote. He is still a male and he likes that smell, which is sweet and fragrant and pleasantly overwhelming. Instead, the girl in the red dress is the source of the stench of fear.

She does not want to be in that man's arms, Coyote thinks. He investigates further with his nose, and wonders how she can smell so sleepy and so frightened at the same time. Why doesn't she run? he thinks. He can smell alcohol on her, too, but underneath that fermented odor is something else that is unfamiliar and alien – poison.

Coyote's stomach rumbles again, but he decides this is more important.

The man drops his keys, and has difficulty bending over to pick them up with the girl in the red dress in his arms. He sets her on the pavement, and she slumps like a ragdoll. He has had a little too much to drink and accidentally kicks his keys under his car.

He swears and gets on his hands and knees. He can't see the keys, but he knows he'll find them, so he keeps looking. He figures he has a good hour to get his little treat home, and takes his time.

The girl in the red dress floats down to her body and pries her eyes open. She returns to the ground and tries to look around. The effort it takes to keep her eyes open and move her head is hard, so she just stares out straight ahead. All she can see directly across from her are the bright eyes of a wolf or a fox or something. She thinks perhaps it escaped from the zoo, but knows she cannot trust her own head in this state. Looking at it - its tongue lolling from its mouth dripping with saliva, its canines larger than life - she wishes it would attack her, because that would be better than the handsome man taking her home.

"Help me," she tries to mouth to the animal, because there is no one else around. She feels her eyes closing again, and she fights and fights to open them. When she can't, she puts her effort into speaking instead. "Help me, doggy. Help me, wolf. Help me, Coyote."

Coyote is surprised to hear his name come from the girl, even though he isn't sure her lips even moved. He is surprised to hear his name, but he is even more surprised because she is talking to him in the way Man used to talk to the animals, without moving his lips or making a sound, and how Coyote talked back.

He is not surprised that she wants to leave this man. Coyote hates the man's meaty smell, too, but he is not sure what to do. Coyote's powers are not strength or magic, but wit and cleverness, and he wonders how he can outwit Man without speaking to him. He feels a surge of tenderness for the girl, and she reminds him of his Navajo wife from many moons ago.

He creeps forward. The Man is distracted underneath the car, and the girl in the red dress asleep against the rubber wheels, and so Coyote lies next to her for a moment while he thinks of a plan.

"Girl," he says, "I want to help you."

The girl in the red dress doesn't know how to feel when the coyote speaks to her. She doesn't freak out, because it doesn't freak her out. It feels natural and strange at the same time. She can feel her reply rolling around densely in her mouth, as if her tongue could wrap around it and taste it. She pushes it against her soft palate and through her teeth, but she doesn't have to move her lips when she hears the words aloud.

"Thank you, coyote."

She knows, somehow, that he heard her, and she can feel him, warm and comforting, by her side.

"You smell poisoned," the coyote says-without-saying. His voice is loud and clear.

"I think there was something in my drink." Her voice is also clear, un-slurred and aware.

"It was stupid of you to drink poison, then."

"Why are you talking to me?"

"Why are you talking to *me*?"

She doesn't know the answer, but she knows that all this talking feels right. She lifts her heavy eyelids, which had closed once more, to listen to the coyote's calming voice. She sees him lying next to her, lithe and hairy and familiar. What used to be hard pavement around them is now sandy desert, the streetlights have become tall saguaros, and the car she was leaning against has transformed into a tremendous mesa. She smells herby creosote and sweet mesquite, and when she looks up into the sky, the stars are no longer dulled by the lights of the city, but fierce and bright and full of secrets she forgot she'd forgotten. She is amazed to discover that the night sky isn't hollow black, but deep, juniper purple. She reaches out and strokes the coyote's back, the hairs coarser than she expects. Then, she stands and looks around at the night desert, empty and free.

"We escaped," she says, "You saved me!"

"No, not yet," says Coyote. He is pleased by her pleasure in his spirit world, but aware of the danger that still waits in the real one. He wants to let her rest there, but she has a decision to make quickly. Coyote can see from the corner of his real eye that Man is stumbling angrily toward them, trying to chase him off, trying to keep his prey from a mangy, scavenging coyote. For now, Man is acting wary, but Coyote knows his resolve will strengthen, and he will soon attack.

The girl in the red dress - oblivious in the peaceful night desert - looks confused.

Coyote offers her three tales.

In the first, Coyote runs off, frightened by the man, because he is, after all, much bigger, and Coyote doesn't have the powers that he used to have. The man takes what doesn't belong to him quickly, right there on the pavement. He eats her up like he is a pack of wild dogs and leaves the remains. He scurries away. The girl in the red dress wakes the next morning, and wanders home barefoot, holding her shoes, her back scratched and bleeding. She forgets everything, and hurts all over.

Coyote feels ashamed. Man does not.

In the second, Coyote leaves her in the night desert. He doesn't let her see what happens to her real self - it is much worse than the first, but she doesn't know that - and he slinks off in the darkness to let her walk the spirit maze alone, over and over and over again.

He winces when he walks by that parking lot in the future.

In the night desert, following the labyrinth at her feet, she spins around in circles and dances through the twists and turns, drinking the nectar of the pink fairy duster flowers and eating sticky-sweet prickly pear fruit until a hundred thousand years pass and she turns into night desert dust.

In the third, Coyote howls. He howls for his brothers, and he howls for his home. The girl in the red dress howls, too, with the last of her energy. Together, they speak the same language, and the sound is magnificent.

Man is scared, because he thought she was asleep. He sees Coyote, and then he sees another coyote, and another, and they begin pouring out of alleyways and washes like a great wave. They seem to come from inside houses and yards, from behind the thick foreign trees and garbage cans. He didn't know so many coyotes were hidden in the city, and he thinks he is going crazy.

The coyotes gather, howling and yip-yipping. Man turns round and round and realizes they have circled him, like a knowing army ready to strike. He realizes that amongst the coyotes are his own pets, growling pitbulls and baying hounds and barking golden retrievers and even one tiny chihuahua, yapping endlessly. All the dogs in the city are lifting the latches on their gates and jumping their fences and joining the great circle.

Man throws his hands up in surrender, but too late. Coyote has already licked his lips, and grinned. The girl in the red dress stops howling and orders the attack.

Coyotes, in general, do not eat large animals, but tonight, his brothers are willing to make an exception.

Coyote does not allow himself to taste Man during the frenzy, but instead lifts the girl in the red dress onto his back. She can barely wrap her arms around his neck, but she buries her face in his fur and smells his desert smell and feels safe. Coyote thinks that, when she is better, he will ask her to be his wife. For now, he lets her sleep.

A Winter Evening

Sarah L Byrne

Once upon a wet November evening, I saw two moons in the London sky.

Me, Zara, twenty-three: named for a princess but grown-up a City wage-slave, soul stretched tight like all the rest. Getting off the train at the end of my usual commute, stepping out onto the platform where the rain slanted across the glow of the station lights. Starting up the steps to the bridge, jostled by the crowd, trying to avoid impaling myself on the spokes of someone's inconsiderately opened umbrella. And looking up, at what sky I could see between tower blocks and concrete walls.

That was when I saw the moon. High above to my right, bright in a gap between the clouds, and a fraction away from full - and then glancing to the left I saw it again. There were two moons, there was no mistaking it. Startled and wondering what trick the light and rain were playing, I looked from one to the other, and then.

And then. The world folded up as though snatched by a giant fist, and I was somewhere else:

A small round room, stone walls and a floor strewn with rushes. A fire burned in the round hearth in the centre, the smoke disappearing through a hole in the pitched ceiling. A low wooden stool to one side.

And nothing else. Except for the door, curved to fit the rounded walls. Walking over I tried the handle: nothing happened. I gave it a bit more of a shove, put my shoulder to it, but it was no good. I am a small woman, and it was a big heavy door, solid wood that looked like oak and smelled like a dark old church, mingled with the smoky scent of the fire. I walked around the perimeter of the room, running my fingers along the circular wall. I wondered if I should shout or call out, because surely that was the normal thing to do in these situations. But I've never really been one for doing the normal thing, and no words would come that did not seem foolish.

Eventually I sat down on the stool and stared into the fire. I started to think of home, and my boyfriend who would be missing me, and wondered what he would do when I didn't come home. I had no way of knowing how much time passed. My wristwatch did not seem to be working, the hands frozen at ten minutes past eight, and my phone was dead. After a long, long while I became so tired that I sat down on the rush-covered floor, folded my arms on the seat and rested my head on them. The fire was starting to burn low and the floor was cold. Eventually I got up, stiff and aching, and paced the floor. Up and down, three steps each way, over and over.

I froze mid-stride at the sound of the door creaking open, turned sharply. The fire had gone out and the room was dark, but in the open doorway a figure stood with a lamp or lantern. I struggled to see, lifting my hand to shade my eyes from the dazzling light.

"Don't be afraid, my child," the figure said, a low, grave woman's voice. That riled me.

"I wasn't afraid," I replied, though I could feel my heart pounding so hard I could barely get the words out, and my breathing was fast and shallow.

"Who are you, and why have you locked me in here?" I asked, trying to keep my voice steady.

She came in, closing the door behind her. I began to see her better as my eyes adjusted to the light. She was middle-aged, I guessed, and tall; she towered over me at least. I was not going to be easily intimidated though. I stood as tall as I could and looked her in the eye.

"Why have you brought me here?"

She looked at me as though I was slightly mad, which was not difficult for someone with such a condescending face.

"No one brought you here, child. You rode to the castle yourself to seek my wisdom. I have kept you waiting long, I regret, but if you wished to leave you had only to lift the spell on the door."

This was ridiculous. I spread my hands wide, hoping my face expressed the incredulity I was struggling to find the words for. As I was about to speak she cut me off with a gesture, pointed to the stool by the fire.

"Sit down child. I've kept you waiting long enough, let us begin."

I sat down and watched while she rekindled the fire with a taper lit from her lantern, tossed on a handful of what looked like dust that she took from a pocket of her grey robe. Kneeling she peered into the smouldering ashes and was silent for a moment. The she looked up at me again.

"Child, your suspicions were correct. A curse has indeed been placed on your prince, by a powerful witch. The curse is a subtle and long-acting one. You have done well to discern its presence so early. The signs must be trifling as yet."

I tried to speak again, but again she bid me silent.

"Every year this curse will strike, and each time it will take a piece of him. Small fragments to begin with, so that you will barely notice, but it will chip away little by little, as the years pass, until he cannot walk, nor see, nor -"

"Stop!" I jumped to my feet, angry and frightened because suddenly I knew what she was talking about.

And then I was back where I started, half way up the stairs to the railway bridge. Startled by the sudden transition, I tripped on the step in front of me and stumbled, bruising my knee and hand. Someone shoved past me, muttering in irritation, insistent feet nearly trampling me. That's London for you, of course, though actually I'd never been so pleased to see the wretched place. Hanging onto the handrail I struggled to my feet, wincing at the pain in my knee, and looked up at the sky. One moon, and barely visible at that, just a pale nebulous glow obscured now by cloud.

I walked the rest of the way home feeling numb and shaken, the rain quickly drenching my hair and clothes. The wind scattered dead leaves about my feet. I couldn't remember ever being so tired. Reaching my front door I fumbled for my keys and let myself in. I was greeted in the porch first by our dog - and I managed a bit of a smile despite myself at the sight of his wagging tail, briefly stroked his head and warm soft ears - then by my boyfriend with a kiss.

"Oh princess, you're soaking, you poor thing."

"I know, I know, give me a moment."

I pushed them both away, dropped the keys and struggled out of my wet coat and shoes, dumped my bag in the porch as well before coming inside properly. I pulled the door to, shutting out that strange rainy evening and immersing myself in the warm light surroundings of home. He was looking at me with concern; I could imagine what a state I looked.

"Are you OK? You're home late again."

"I'm fine. Just - work, you know? I might just go up to bed, I'm a bit tired."

He came and folded me in a hug, a big warm close hug despite my wet hair and obviously morose mood. He is a good and kind man.

"You sure? There's nothing wrong?"

I put my arms around him and leaned my head on his chest for a moment, taking in the reassuring familiar smell of him. In that moment, I considered telling him everything, but then I pushed myself away. I don't like to burden him with too many of my problems and neuroses. Instead I reached up and stroked his hair and the rough stubble of his cheek.

"Just tired, I've... had a long day. I'll see you in the morning, my love." He cupped his hand over mine.

"You don't want company? It's the middle of the month for you, isn't it? I saw the full moon just now. Maybe we should be, you know, *trying*?"

Then there was a piercing shriek through the wall, one of next door's kids, and I flinched away from his touch.

"God, do they never shut up?" I rubbed my hands over my face tiredly, and he looked at me with puzzled concern. "Not tonight, love" I said, and with that he had to be content.

Upstairs I stripped off my damp clothes and left them where they fell on the bathroom floor, rubbed my hair as dry as I could with a warm towel. I popped today's little gold pill from my hidden stash; poison me against the moon, like Tori used to sing, so much for *trying*.

Then I climbed into bed. It felt good to be there, so good. Sometimes I slept alone like this, I had restless nights full of thoughts and fears, and at those times I preferred solitude. I curled up on my side in the dark, pulling the duvet up tight around my ears, trying to get warm. Despite the tiredness I lay awake for a while, listening to the relentless drip drip of the rain outside, the baby still wailing next door. Some things you can't shut out.

Sleep came eventually though. It had been a long day.

But the woman's words preyed on my mind the next day, the way a disturbing dream lingers. Because I knew what she had meant. I've always been a worrier, a hypochondriac. You know the sort, always convinced they have cancer or a rare heart defect, every headache a potential brain tumour. It's something you get used to; I wouldn't know what to do with myself if I didn't have fantasies of playing the starring role in a medical textbook. But what you don't expect is what happens when you love someone. The worries about yourself fade into a background hobby, compared to that fear: what if Something Happens to them.

I'd worried about him a little always, of course I had. But lately the vague worries had coalesced into a specific fear. He'd mentioned little symptoms, aches and pains, maybe numbness here or an odd sensation there, and taken alone any of them would seem trivial, but together they all pointed to the early stages of a particular condition in my opinion. A disease, not a curse, but a cruel thing all the same, and it works much the way she'd described. Degenerative, progressive; terminal.

I knew I had to go back. Not easy, when you do not know the way. I spent the journey to work imagining that place, the world with the two moons, seeing it in my mind, closing my eyes and letting the hypnotic clatter and rumble of the train noise drown out any other thoughts. A couple of times I felt I was almost there, but could not quite slip through the barrier between the worlds.

At the station I let myself be swept along with the rush of commuters pushing off the train into the cavernous underground concourse, rode the escalator up towards the sky visible through the glass dome of the roof. I wished I could slow its progress, the way it was taking me inexorably towards the place I least wanted to go. I wanted to be back at home curled up in my warm safe bed. I wanted to be somewhere quiet and alone where I could think. I didn't think I could face the trading floor today, the bright light and shouting and bullying of it. I could barely face it on a good day. I wanted to be anywhere else but where I was.

I stepped off the escalator, feeling the chill morning air on my face, the damp wind blowing in off the river. I breathed in the usual morning smells of cigarette smoke and coffee and newspaper print. My steps slowed down, the knot of worry and sadness tightening in my stomach. I wished I'd just called and said I was sick.

I glanced up automatically at the scrolling financial news and share prices displayed on the big screens for those who can't wait to get to their desks. I only look out of habit, and that day I cared less than usual. But looking up I saw a white icy ghost of the moon in the pale sky and focused all my awareness and thought on that. I imagined there were two.

No. I was done with wishes and imaginings.

I made it so there were two.

And I was back there, back in that little room. I had no intention of waiting around this time. I strode over to the door, grasped the handle. It was locked again, of course, but this time I knew what to do. I closed my eyes and focused, willed it to open. A sharp click as the latch slipped out of place. I turned the handle and walked through.

Down a hundred spiraling stairs, then I ran into her in the long, lamp-lit corridor.

"Child, I have told you everything I know." She looked at me severely, though perhaps there was a touch of pity in her eyes. "There is nothing you can do for your prince. Go, and cherish the days you still have together in freedom."

It was not good enough.

Come on, I said. I know how this sort of thing works. Surely there's something I can do. Isn't there some riddle I can solve, a name to guess, a quest to go on? Or do I offer you some fraction of my soul in exchange for his freedom? My first-born child? I was never the maternal type anyway.

She stared at me coldly, raised an eyebrow. My flippancy did not amuse her. Nor me, really. I took a deep breath.

"Please." I couldn't let this happen. "I'll do anything."

She shook her head gently and turned to walk away.

"Tell me where she is!" I called after her, and she hesitated. "The witch who made this curse. Tell me where to find her."

"It's no use," she said patiently, as though I was a rather dull child. "A curse of this nature cannot be lifted, even if she wished to do so. And she does not."

"Just tell me where to find her," I insisted. I had the bones of an idea taking shape in my mind.

I hesitated a moment before walking into the witch's den, the little cottage in the woods outside the tower, its roof thatch warmed by two suns. I was afraid, but I wouldn't show it. I worked in an investment bank, after all. I faced worse than her on the trading floor every day.

I ducked through the low doorway and there she was, sitting in a wooden chair in the corner. She smiled at me, gestured me to come in. She didn't look terrifying - long fair hair pinned up and slightly disarrayed - she looked hardly older than I was myself, though I suppose you can never tell with a witch. But I didn't give it much thought. Looking around the room I saw the deep shelves lined with stone urns and glass jars of all sizes, and I shuddered slightly at what I thought I saw in those jars.

"I know your face," she said. "I've seen you at court. The princess in waiting. And I know what you have come to ask me for. It cannot be done. Even if I wished to - and I do not, for that handsome prince of yours deserved every word of it - I cannot unsay what I have said."

"I don't want you to lift the curse," I said. "Far from it. I want those body parts you take from him. The nerves, the muscles and the tendons, every one of them."

She laughed.

"What would you want with those things? Do you think to knit him back together and breathe life into him with your kiss? It cannot be done, I tell you, the curse cannot be averted or reversed, not by any means. Those are the laws of this world."

"And other worlds?"

She looked up, startled. That got her attention.

I told her everything, and when I was done she sat and gazed into the fire as though deep in thought.

"So, can it be done?" I asked her. "Can what you take from this poor cursed prince be passed between the worlds, and given to my love?"

She thought for a moment, then nodded her head, looked up at me.

"Yes, I can do it. Do you have something of his, something with a connection to him?"

That was easy. I slipped the sparkling ring off my third finger, left hand, and handed it over without hesitation. Later I'd tell him I lost it somehow.

She gave a brief nod of approval.

"Then it will be done. What this sickness destroys, I will replace, and your true love in the other world will have every chance of living out his natural years whole and healthy. You have my word."

I thanked her. I wanted to hug her. *Oh my love, I will keep you safe after all.* I turned towards the door, wanting only to go home to him now.

"Wait a moment." Her hand snaked out and caught my arm as I went to leave, jerking me back to face her. "Aren't you forgetting something? I don't do this for you out of the kindness of my heart. Indeed I've seen enough hearts to know they're full of muscle and stringy gristle but precious little kindness. What will you give me in return?"

I felt a chill run through me. Of course, it was never going to be that easy.

"Was the diamond not enough?" That ring had been the most valuable thing I owned.

"A shiny rock? You know life and health cost more than that." Her grip tightened painfully, fingernails digging into the soft inside of my wrist. "Life can pay for life."

Her blue eyes were terrible.

"My life?" I asked, my throat dry.

"Can you offer me something better? Your heart's desire for the love of your life, maybe?"

I wouldn't show her I was afraid, though she could feel it, of course she could, the panicked flutter of the pulse through my wrist. I kept my tone deliberately light.

"My first born child?"

To my surprise she nodded her head, let go of my arm.

"That would suffice. But you would not do it. No. Not once you've held him in your arms, smelled his skin, seen his little fingernails. Not even for your prince. No, you'd keep the babe and let him die in pain and horror while you held your little one close."

"I wouldn't," I insisted, rubbing my sore wrist. She laughed.

"You would. Every woman would. Do you think I haven't seen it often enough? What do you know about motherhood, girl?"

She was older than me, I could see that now, infinitely older. How could I have thought otherwise? She gave me a smile that made me shiver, and I looked away and found myself staring at the grisly jars on the walls. And then I knew.

"I'll *give* you my motherhood," I said, meeting her eyes straight-on. I gestured at the shelves. "Take my womb, ovaries, whatever you need. Grow the child yourself. My heart's desire, there."

She raised an eyebrow.

"A high price indeed. Well."

She stared at me intently as though she could see my thoughts, but she could not. Because motherhood was no heart's desire of mine, I really never was the maternal type. Oh, my soon-to-be husband would like a baby, I knew, hence the whole *trying* charade. But I don't care for children - I always did prefer dogs - and the thought of pregnancy and childbirth always horrified me. I'd have had that Essure sterilization done, except I'd have had to sell my engagement ring to pay for it, and that would hardly be right. But this?

Buy low, sell high, that's what the traders at work say. All their complex financial wizardry comes down to that in the end. Fertility came cheap to me, but was precious heart's-desire material to a witch.

She was still watching me.

"A barren princess, though?" She smiled, contemptuous. "What use would you be to anyone? He won't marry you, believe me. He'll put you aside when he finds out."

"He won't." *Will he?*

There was the true price, perhaps.

"I was never likely to be that kind of princess anyway," I said. "Do it."

She came towards me, and despite myself I flinched back then, imagining my body ripped open in bloody chaos. She held up her hand reassuringly.

"I will take what I need swiftly, painlessly. You will not even know it is gone."

My throat was dry, I forced myself to swallow, nodded my head firmly.

"Done," I said, holding out my hand for her to shake.

"Are you certain?"

"Yes." I was never more certain in my life.

She stretched out her hand too, but not to shake mine. Instead she reached towards my lower abdomen, so quick I hardly realized what she was doing. Suddenly I caught my breath, staggered back. The sensation was sickening and I closed my eyes involuntarily, screwing them tight shut. But she spoke the truth, there was no pain. When I opened my eyes she was fastening the lid of a stone urn like the dozens of others that lined her shelves. She looked up at me as I stood with my hands still pressed to my belly in shock.

"Then our business is concluded."

In bed that night, I curled my body protectively around him, smoothed back his hair and gently kissed the soft tip of his ear. I still felt a slight nausea and a crampy ache deep inside, but it would soon pass. It was nothing. No worse than the Essure procedure would have been. I snuggled close and the warmth of him eased the soreness.

There would be some difficult conversations to be had in the future, I knew. But I did it for him. He would understand. Wouldn't he? Isn't love supposed to conquer all? And we would never be short of something to love, not while Battersea Dogs Home overflowed with sad lonely strays.

"Love," I said to him softly. "Do you think we could find room for another dog?"

Enkesonnen

Alex Petri

When the boy came striding into the hall carrying the severed arm of a troll with the sword still in it, Felix choked. He knew without looking at him that Cyprian was shaken too - King Cyprian, now, he reminded himself. When he wore that startled look it was easy to forget.

In the ensuing hush all eyes in the hall turned to Cyprian, who said nothing, then to the Queen, who promptly fainted, then back to Cyprian again. Cyprian looked at Felix in panic. In moments like this, never mind the incrustations of almost ten years and the robes and the layers of court courtesy, Felix saw the nervous blacksmith's apprentice that Cyprian had once been - still was, enclosed within him somewhere nearer to the bone.

Once Cyprian had been a boy who hadn't known how to lift an enchanted sword, a boy too panicked by the noise of the approaching troll to notice that the sword was hanging in front of him. A boy who was about to pick up the brazier of coals and, Felix supposed, pelt the troll with them, until Felix had taken pity on him and said: "The flask. Drink from the flask and you can wield the sword." He'd been the boy who had halted a moment after downing the entire contents of the flask to say,

"But, horse, you talk," and then managed to run the troll through with surprising efficiency.

Now it was to the King that Felix murmured, "Greet him. And get rid of the arm," but the gratitude that flashed in Cyprian's eyes was familiar, although it surfaced less and less often in this new Cyprian - as seldom, Felix thought, as those enchanted seamen who swam up from the depths in certain moons that would tell you any truth if you caught them by the tail.

Cyprian gathered himself, catching his dignity like a mantle settled on his shoulders and said, "I bid you welcome, adventurer. Come and sit by me and tell how you came by this sword."

In a matter of minutes the boy was seated next to the Queen, who fainted again, and a page had been dispatched to do away with the troll's arm. The boy had been almost unwilling to part with it. He held the sword as tight as a child clutching a doll, face alight with excitement.

Cyprian beckoned Felix towards their end of the table.

Felix took the free chair next to the Queen, who still looked pale and greenish, like an unripe leek. The traveler gestured with the sword again, thwack of the bloody flat of the blade making the cups on the table dance. The Queen quivered all over.

He and Cyprian shared a glance. It was not only the blood, Felix suspected, that made the Queen look sick. Before she was the Queen the Princess had been the lover of a troll, and it had taken a great deal of time and some brutality to beat the enchantment out of her. It had sat ill with Felix. They said the only way to remove a troll's love was to beat it out with birch twigs, that certain unnatural loves curdled in the blood and formed a second skin - and something had appeared in the vat of milk that the old King's enchanter pronounced with excitement to be a troll-skin. Felix had not seen it. He had learned all of these details from Cyprian later, in the stables. What did it look like, he had asked, and Cyprian had shrugged and blanched, as though the memory were unpleasant, and run a hand thoughtfully along Felix's nose. "I don't suppose we can seat a horse at the wedding banquet," he had murmured, and Felix had shifted his weight among his hooves and murmured back that no, he did not suppose so either.

The cups danced again and the Queen shuddered.

"Traveler, you weary the Queen with blood, I think," Felix said.

The Queen took the hint and rose, gladly, looking gratefully at him. He was never certain what she thought of him. Since the day he had walked from the stables on two legs they had always been dancing around one another. He always seemed to be taking chairs she had just vacated.

Uncomplaining, she had borne Cyprian two princesses, one dark like him, one fair like her. Both girls had her small nervous mouth. Felix was teaching the elder, the fair one, to ride. Side-saddle, of course side-saddle, he'd assured the Queen's old mother, like a lady. But the girl was too impatient for that and he had begged britches for her off one of the stable boys. When she rode she reminded him of Cyprian.

Now he settled in the Queen's chair.

"Felix," Cyprian said to the boy, "was my companion in my adventures."

"I was his horse," Felix said.

"Nay!" the boy exclaimed.

"I used to be," Felix said. Cyprian guffawed, his blacksmith's guffaw that set plates rattling. Felix grinned at him.

The boy evidently mistook this for some elaborate jest, or perhaps his own tale burned in his pocket, for he asked no further questions and resumed – "Then I came to the glass castle."

"His father sent him and his elder brothers forth to seek their fortunes, saying that whoever returned with the most beautiful maiden would win the whole kingdom," Cyprian whispered. Felix nodded.

"And I knocked at the door of the glass castle," the boy said. "But no one came to admit me, and inside I found a cat drowning in a bucket of milk, mewling piteously, so I fished her out and said, 'That's not right,' and just then the troll who owned the place came roaring back, and there was I with not a weapon but my pocket-knife, and the troll as big as a mountain."

"How did he fit through the door?" Felix asked, and Cyprian grinned. The boy continued undiscouraged. "I am not sure. Perhaps there was a separate entrance, for he was the size of - many mountains."

"Many mountains," Cyprian said. "Naturally."

"Upon the wall were all manner of arms. I tried to lift them. I could lift none. And then - marvel! Marvel of marvels! - the cat, whom I had rescued, spoke: 'Drink from the flask,' said she, 'and you will lift the axe.' And so I did. I drank, and lifted it, and smote the troll a mighty blow – and I have just come thither."

"What became of the cat?" Felix asked, after a moment.

"The cat?"

"You said she spoke," Felix said. Cyprian shot Felix a glance.

"Miracle of miracles! She spoke, and saved my life. And I am hither come."

"Go," Felix said.

"What?"

"Put by the sword. Saddle a horse and go and find her."

"The cat? The talking cat?"

"There's no such thing as a talking cat," Felix said. "That's your maiden."

"The cat."

"Stop repeating 'the cat' like a blithering idiot," Felix said. He was angrier than he had been in a long time, and he knew that it was not entirely rational. "There are no talking cats. Cats do not talk. That was an enchanted maiden - she spoke, you said, 'she' - it has to be your maiden. These things do not happen by chance. These trolls are all enchanters. You saved her life. She yours. You left her. Did she say anything when you cut off the troll's head?"

The boy seemed to shrink a size. "I didn't," he said. "I ran him through."

"You are a blithering idiot," Felix said.

"Felix," Cyprian said, laying a hand on his arm.

"You left her there with him? And him bound to revive?" Felix was sputtering a little with inarticulate rage. The boy cowered, his fingers white around the handle of the sword. "After she saved you?"

"Felix," Cyprian said. "He didn't know any better."

"Not know better? Not behead a troll?"

"*I* didn't know any better," Cyprian said. "You had to tell me."

The boy looked appealingly at Cyprian. "Is he right?"

Cyprian sighed. "I have always found him to be so," he said quietly. "He does not know your circumstance All the same I think you had better go and see if it is not too late."

"Now?"

"Now," Felix said.

The boy got hastily to his feet, dropping the sword. It clattered against the dishes on the table.

"You'll need that," Cyprian said, then to Felix: "What horse should he take?"

"Give him Roan," Felix said. "She seems to understand haste." He felt obscurely that he ought to make an apology to the boy. "I am sorry to have spoiled your night," he said, his tongue heavy in his mouth. "But better your night than your quest."

Cyprian looked gratefully at him again - twice in an evening, Felix thought, this was almost like questing again, when Cyprian had whispered furtive questions into his neck about what sword to take and what rings and which treasure and could they stop yet for the night and what did the stars mean, and Felix had told him, hooves moving steadily over the ground, and when he had no ready answer he had lied.

After the boy's sudden arrival and equally sudden departure he drank a bit more than was wise. So did Cyprian, saying little, his dark eyes fathomless in the lambent glow of the rush lights. It was on nights like this that Felix's feet brought him to the stables without thought; there was a cold bed on the far side of the castle reserved for his use, he knew, but years of habit were hard to break. The smell of hay was soothing. Sometimes he still slept standing up. He wondered if Cyprian knew about the habit. He suspected he did. Once one of the stable boys had caught him sleeping in a corner and he had bribed him heavily, but he was not sure if it had taken.

At first he had loathed such places, he reflected while picking a brush off the wall and going to tend to a horse. The troll's stables were miserably cold and the troll placed a brazier of hot coals at his head and hay at his feet, so that he had to twist miserably to eat and his face was always scalded. That was before Cyprian had come and given him a puzzled look and set it right.

After Cyprian had killed the troll he had stood there, waiting patiently for his enchantment to wear off. As Cyprian made for the door he was still waiting. "Wait," he had said, and Cyprian had looked at him - a horse with curiously light human eyes, but if Cyprian suspected anything he had not looked any differently - "I don't suppose you need a mount."

"A mount's not all I need," Cyprian had said, taking the saddle down from its peg and fitting it on him before he realized what he had offered, because the other way out of the enchantment that he thought the troll had mentioned was too alarming to be real, too close to death, and perhaps the magic would wear off in time, as these things sometimes did.

As they trotted away from the castle towards the city Cyprian told him all that he needed besides a mount, and more - his whole biography, and whence he came, and tried to give him all manner of absurd horse names, and if he never asked how he had come to be a horse Felix supposed it should not have come as a shock; he had not asked how Cyprian came to be a blacksmith. Every so often he tried to tell him and the words turned leaden in his mouth. He had wondered whether his silence was an effect of the enchantment. The other possible request, the one the troll had suggested, the one that terrified him, lurked unsaid on his tongue. Without telling who you were how could you say the other thing?

He was still standing in the stables absentmindedly brushing the flank of one of the horses when he heard footsteps.

"I followed you in here," Cyprian's voice said, a bit thick from the wine still. "I didn't realize you still -"

Felix grinned. "To my shame," he said, "I find it easier to sleep in stables."

"No shame in that." Cyprian found another brush and joined him. "I used to sleep here with you."

"No shame for blacksmiths and their horses," Felix said. This tune was familiar enough. They had never played it to the end. "But for a king and - what did you call me?"

"I forget what I called you."

"It doesn't signify," Felix said.

Cyprian brushed very carefully, his tongue protruding slightly in concentration. "I remember this," he said. "It was soothing. It was easier with you telling me how to do it." His face clouded a little. "Most things were."

"I'm sorry for yelling at the boy," Felix said. "I never even got his name."

"It doesn't signify." Cyprian frowned. "I wonder if I started saying that because you said it or if you started saying it because I said it."

"It doesn't signifiy," Felix said. Cyprian's laugh was warm and dark in the stall. "You're a good king, you know."

"I would have made as good a blacksmith."

Felix grinned. "I doubt that, having seen your horseshoes."

"Worn, you mean. It's not seeing that's the problem." Cyprian finished with the flank and came around to Felix's side. "Do you really believe what you told the boy? About the cat?"

Felix watched Cyprian brush down the horse's flank in firm steady strokes. "I think so," he said.

"What made you so sure she was a princess?"

"I was," Felix said. "A prince, I mean."

Cyprian's hand faltered on the side of the horse. "You never said."

"Didn't I?" Felix said, very carefully, weighting each word like a coin dropped into a full glass. "You never asked."

Cyprian looked at him. Those looks were dangerous, Felix had found, like standing on the edge of a well gazing at your own reflection. It was unwise to lean too close. Cyprian had given him a look like that when he snuck back to the stables during his wedding feast and wreathed his horse neck with a wedding garland of white flowers, and at the bold simplicity of the gesture Felix felt something in his stomach sink. That was when he had made the impossible request.

"I should have suspected," Cyprian said now. "The things you know. The words you use. The way you walk. I thought it was a trace of horse still."

"It's that as well," Felix said, laughing.

Cyprian continued his scrutiny. "I like your laugh," he said. "It's the one thing you couldn't do when you were a horse."

Not the only thing, Felix thought, and then was ashamed of the thought.

"But you have a home."

Felix thought briefly and without regret of the cold palace, shrinking servants, and his father's stern eyes, of the crown that never fit.

Cyprian finished brushing down the horse. Felix watched his hands grow impatient for something to do. They were a king's hands now, not a blacksmith's hands, but they were still impatient.

"Why do you not go home?" He hung up the brush. He stroked the horse's nose. The horse whickered quietly. Felix remembered the warm touch of those capable hands - it was strange to have sense memories from a skin that was no longer yours. The thick neck Cyprian's arms had clung to, exhausted, on long rides, no longer existed.

"You have a way with horses," Felix said.

Cyprian turned to look at him. "Is that your answer to my question?"

He had tried not to make it sound like the answer to Cyprian's question.

Felix tried to think what he would say next. Cyprian would say, "It is proper for you to go home." Cyprian would say, "You should leave here. A prince, tending my stables! I will give you half my kingdom for all that you have done."

Felix patted the horse's nose. The horse shied from him. "He doesn't want anything else now," Felix said. "You've spoiled him."

"Do I have that effect?" Cyprian asked, quietly.

Felix wondered when Cyprian had become so adept at catching his meanings. But it was insane trying to pinpoint it. A day - an hour - but which, precisely, out of all their journeying? And had he been a man then or a horse? He tried to think. He remembered long roads and tired evenings under wan stars, walking slowly, Cyprian walking beside him, talking of nothing just to keep awake. He thought of all the perils they had passed to win the Princess, when she had been little more than an idea, a glorious idea that had been the wrack of every prior adventurer, in whose name the King had promised twice a kingdom. He remembered jumping over lakes of fire with Cyprian's trusting weight on his back - he remembered sneaking a cake out of Cyprian's hand, the delight of the taste of it, but how sick it had made him afterwards. He remembered the hush of the stable when he had come limping in and said, "I've got the ring the Princess wants," and Cyprian's sharp, "Never mind the ring, you're limping," and Cyprian's deft fingers tugging the thorn out of his hoof; he remembered the Princess riding behind Cyprian for the first time, the cruel tug in his gut that he attributed to the added weight. He remembered the wedding, the door of the stables left open so he could make out the occasional burst of applause, and Cyprian coming in afterwards with the garland and without the Princess.

Cyprian went back to stroking the horse's neck.

"I never thought I would like these stables," Felix heard himself saying.

"Neither did I," Cyprian said. "Which stall was it, where you made me - ?"

"The next one over."

"I thought you wanted me to kill you." Cyprian looked at him. "After the wedding, I mean. I thought that was what you were asking for."

Felix stroked the horse's neck. "If that cat turns out to be a princess she'll be very lucky," he said. "There will be the right number of pieces to the puzzle."

"I was worried that was what you meant," Cyprian said. "When you said you begged a boon."

Felix frowned. He remembered the startled light in Cyprian's eyes.

"Anything," Cyprian had said, too hasty. "I give you my vow."

And Felix said, steeling himself, startled that the words had finally reached his lips, "Cut off my head."

After that Cyprian had tried to retract the vow. "Must I do it today?" he asked. "Suppose I waited fifty years?"

But Felix had shook his head. Then he had a weeping Cyprian clinging to his neck and his mane was matted with tears and the broken petals of flowers, and he didn't know if the reassurance that he tried to offer was a reassurance or a lie.

When the ax bit through his flesh he was as startled to wake up with two legs and two hands and his old face and his old ears and thumbs - thumbs, of all things - as Cyprian was to find him there in an unkempt pile on the stable floor.

"Felix?" Cyprian had asked, very quietly.

"Yes," Felix replied.

"God is merciful," Cyprian had said, dropping to his knees.

Cyprian's mouth had tasted of cake and the kiss had been sloppy and desperate and sudden, a greeting, more to reassure Cyprian that he was alive and real than the product of any conscious thought. At least this was what Felix told himself, touching his lip nervously as Cyprian swept them into the banquet hall, waving his arms and introducing him to everyone in florid terms that made Felix wince. It had not happened again.

He had told himself that he would leave, but then the old King died and there were things to be done, and then a dragon was ravaging the countryside and there were more things to be done and then the Queen was with child and there was less to be done but Cyprian's eyes were pleading in a language of which he was not ignorant and he stayed, watching with Cyprian in the corridor long into the night, until the pale red eyes of morning squinted into the castle and Cyprian was giving him a baby to hold. And then there were more things to be done. In the process, Cyprian had grown into his title and everyone had grown accustomed to Felix.

In the darkness of the stable the horse whickered. Cyprian's restless hand slid over Felix's on the horse's flank. Their fingers intertwined.

"I hope the boy finds his cat," Felix said.

Cyprian was pensive, drawing nearer. "You were a prince, and you never said."

"Now that you know you will tell me to leave," Felix said.

The feel of Cyprian's hand on his neck was familiar but strange, the ghost of the same touch on another form, like hearing an old song on a new instrument. "I will tell you," Cyprian said, "yes, I suppose I will tell you."

"Now that you know I belong to someone or something, you will tell me to go back there."

"Why are you saying this?" Cyprian said.

"I have often thought of telling you," Felix said, "but I always heard you telling me to return where I belonged, that your stables were no place for a prince. After such revelations one generally gets removed from the garden."

Cyprian looked at him. "Do you wish to go home?"

"I am there already," Felix said.

The second kiss was nothing like the first one.

Felix watched the Princess cantering along the hillside, breathless, reckless, elated in new riding britches.

"You're trusting him too much," he yelled. "You can't give him so much rein."

"My father trusted you," she shouted back, merry. The more riding she did, the more sun she got, the less she resembled her mother, the more Cyprian blossomed in her, and he was always catching snatches of the King's insolent humor from her lips.

"That was a different circumstance," he yelled, pulling up.

"Pish tosh."

"You're just like your father."

"My father was a troll."

"He wasn't," Felix said. "That's idle gossip and you know it. Poison grows on wagging tongues."

The Princess pulled her horse up a little too sharply. "The same tongues say my father spends his nights in the stables."

Felix felt a swift kick in his stomach like pebbles clattering against a shield. "You should not listen to such talk."

"In your company." The princess looked at him. Her gaze was not malicious. Felix did not know what it was. "They say it is ill done. Some talk of sending messengers to my uncle in the country over hill, to see if he will rule."

"They said as much when your father took the crown," Felix said, guardedly. "They called him a blacksmith's apprentice, unfit for anything but the smithy."

The Princess looked at him, level.

"He was a blacksmith's apprentice," Felix admitted, "but not unfit."

"There is always truth to a story," the Princess said. "Mother says."

"Your mother is a wise woman," Felix said. The stones plinked against the pit of his stomach. "Sometimes."

"When I master jumping," the Princess said, switching subjects with an ease that Felix remembered from when Cyprian was young, "I shall ride to the kingdom over hill and see the country."

"And ask them to supplant your father, I suppose."

The Princess laughed.

"Just be careful they do not turn you into something," Felix said. "I hear the King over hill is an enchanter."

"There is no truth in stories," the Princess said, urging on the horse.

"We never did hear about the cat," Felix said, that night, at supper. He was pensive. Cyprian glanced over the Queen towards him. She was ill.

She had always looked like an unripe leek, but it was worse now. Felix could not remember when she had started to be ill, but he could hardly remember her well. It had come on by degrees. The younger of the two princesses did not seem to realize that it was serious, but the elder did, suddenly, curiously solicitous.

"No," Cyprian said. "We never did."

"That usually means it ended well," Felix said.

"Does it?" the Queen said, yawning.

"Those who succeed less often visit friends than those who fail," Cyprian said, grinning at Felix. It was one of Felix's lines. Felix lowered his gaze.

Sometimes he wondered if the Queen knew about him and Cyprian. There was usually a bitter confraternity among the people who always were looking at the same thing. But the Queen looked elsewhere, increasingly, not at Cyprian as he did - out the window, as though she were waiting for a ship to come sailing out of the sky. He had heard tales of flying ships. He did not believe them. He wondered if she were looking for the troll. Once he had tried to tell her he regretted their forced end to the enchantment. She had shrugged.

"There is enough to be contented with," she said, "in this skin."

"There are whispers," the Princess said, catching his arm as he made his way out of the banquet hall, about to turn towards the stables, "that before my mother di -" she blanched.

Felix nodded. "If anything should happen," he supplied. "Before it might."

"That -" The princess worried a nail. She had delicate hands, with traces of Cyprian's restlessness.

"You are not compelled to tell me," Felix said.

"You have always been kind," the Princess said. She did not look at him. "You are a horse no longer, but they say there is still an enchantment in you. That it must be rooted out. That you have worked vile magics on my father. That these vile magics have made my mother ill."

"What do they propose to do?" Felix said.

She worried the nail. "I do not - exactly know," she said. "But they are in the forest gathering birch switches, and I think they mean to find you in the stables."

Felix nodded. The nod seemed insufficient. He reached for the Princess's hands and squeezed them. "Do you think me a vile enchanter?" he asked.

She smiled tightly. "I think - I think all sorts of things, sometimes. I think you are kind."

Felix pressed her hands, warm competent hands that knew how to manage a horse, hoping the comparison would be enough to last him, and let them go. "Tell him not to come," he said, his voice flat. "Tell him you don't know what that refers to, naturally."

"Naturally," she said. "Gossip."

"Tell him goodbye."

He did not look back on his way out of the hall. The stables were empty. He picked a horse, a reliable mare that he knew the Princess did not especially favor, and goaded it out. As he rode he thought he saw dim shapes moving toward the road out of the woods, nearing the castle with birch twigs in their hands.

He rode aimlessly for several days until he came to the sea and had to think of somewhere to go. He pitched camp on the shore and made a makeshift net (his packing had been haphazard and his food stores dwindled) and spectacularly failed to catch several fish. The fish taunted him in the waning light until the moon hung low in the dark belly of the sky.

There was a splash in the distance - fin too big to be another of these despicable fish - and then another splash, nearer, and he waded curiously closer and when the fin splashed a third time, caught it and held on as best he could. Court life had softened him, compared to months when he could gallop miles and scarcely tire, and it took a great deal of effort to cling on, but finally, after he had swallowed a mouthful of seawater that made him cough, the tail stilled, subdued, and an old man's head, slightly barnacled, appeared at the other end, looking put-upon.

"Well," he said.

"I never know how much truth these stories have in them," Felix said.

"This one happens to be completely true," the old man said. "But I suspect it's not the truth you are most interested in hearing."

"No," Felix admitted.

"Ask your question, then."

"Just one question?"

"Unless you caught me twice."

Felix paused, pondering. Was the Queen yet dead, he wondered. Had the Princess mastered riding without him and was she visiting the city over hill? And Cyprian, what of him? Would they ever see each other again?

Instead he said, "What became of the boy and the cat?"

The barnacled face smiled. "He found her," the old man said. "Under a rose bush in the rain. He slew the troll, and followed her to her own kingdom, and when the year was up she followed him to his own land as his bride. Together they rule two kingdoms, his by the sea and hers in the mountains, where the moon's beam just pierces."

Felix squinted in that direction. "Are they there now?"

The old man frowned. "One truth," he said. "That was the bargain."

"Could you give me directions?"

The old man tugged his tail free and slapped the water with it. "I'd recommend swimming," he said. "It's much faster."

"Ha," Felix said.

The man shrugged. "Ride along the sea until the sea becomes the mountains, I would guess," he said. "I don't leave the water much."

Felix rode to the castle and discovered them there. He wondered whether the boy would remember him. But he did. His arrival proved sufficient cause for a feast, and he ate better than he had in days, the young Queen pushing more meat on him, laughing.

The boy would not stop thanking him. The Queen thanked him whenever the boy stopped to draw breath. They laughed together.

"Did you miss laughing?" he asked her, while the King shouted down the table. "I missed laughing."

She nodded. "But I miss - parts of it too, sometimes."

"I sometimes crave provender," he admitted.

She laughed. "Do you really?"

"I used to sleep in the stables," he said. "Standing up." He omitted to mention the rest of it.

She nodded. "I still wake up alarmed to be missing my tail," she added, blushing a little. "But on the whole I am much better pleased."

He nodded, mute.

"What became of your King?" the boy asked.

"I am not sure," Felix said. He finished his wine. They refilled his cup and he finished that too. Later, without consciously intending to, guided by some uncanny homing sense, he stumbled his way to the stables.

The Queen found him there in the morning and laughed, but her eyes were serious. "You have the looks of a long journey."

"Thank you," he said. "It is a long journey, and I am not sure where it will end."

"Rest here, then," she said. "Until you decide."

There was always something to do. He helped in the stables. He discovered that he was always looking out the window.

"Are you looking to see a flying ship?" the stable boys teased. Felix laughed, mechanically.

Sometimes he wondered if he did hope to see a flying ship, if the sight he hoped for were not exactly as marvelous as that.

Another prince came to the court with a troll's sword and a young dark-haired bride with bright laughing eyes and announced that he had won the maiden from the troll who kept her in thrall.

At this there was great hubbub. The Queen asked what was going on and they would not tell her. The court enchanter gathered the men together and murmured sternly and seriously about troll-hides, and in the castle courtyard they assembled with three vats of whitest milk and a hundred birch switches.

"No," Felix tried to tell them. "You will kill something in her. I do not know what. But it is something that should not be killed."

"She has a troll-hide still," the enchanter said. "Troll-hides must be beaten off."

The day of the enchantment-breaking dawned clear and cold and he felt his age for the first time, walking out to join the watchers.

His left leg troubled him. He realized that it was the hoof that had had a thorn in it, and then the memory of Cyprian's warm steady fingers plucking it free rushed over him and he felt lonely and cold.

The girl grew paler and paler as they led her out.

When they dunked her in the first vat of milk nothing happened. She laughed. Nothing happened in the second vat, and the crowd began to stir uncomfortably. This time she did not laugh. In the third tub when nothing happened they drew out the switches and began to beat her over the lip of the tub, and she began to scream.

"Stop!" she shouted, and when that availed her nothing, "It's not true," and when that, in turn, availed her nothing, "It is true! It is true I loved the troll!" and when that availed nothing she merely screamed, and he discovered without intending to that he had pushed forward through the crowd and interposed his body, and content enough to have something to beat they had fallen on him.

"Old fool," the enchanter said, staring down at him afterwards, "now the enchantment is not broken."

But with a lunatic courage he pointed at the vat. One of the townsmen reached in and drew out something black and red and wet and ugly, like the rind of a rotten human fruit.

They did not know what to do with him after that. He patched his wounds as best he could. The wedding went forward for the new adventurer.

He garlanded the horses, ruefully. His steps were slow. If he were still a horse, he thought wryly, they would have cut his head off in earnest.

The bride came to the stables and her eyes were sad, infinitely sad, but still lively. "Thank you," she whispered. "You taught me that you are not all terrible."

He smiled. "They are," he said. "I'm not."

She laughed.

"I don't think you ever had a troll-hide," he said.

"Don't you believe in them?"

"I don't know," he said. "No. Perhaps. Perhaps the one they found was mine."

But after they departed he resumed looking out the window. There were never any flying ships. He rode along the foothills and looked for them anyway. He would always see riders approach, and from a distance he would convince himself that they were Cyprian, but every time they drew nearer, they resolved themselves into strangers: merchants and messengers and knights errant and blacksmiths who had not become kings. Cyprian had the tiresome habit of becoming the world.

He had dreams, though. Uncomfortable slumbers always bred strange dreams.

In the stable he dreamed of a horseman who drew closer and closer and did not resolve himself into anything else except Cyprian, whole battalions of Cyprians - Cyprian young, Cyprian King, Cyprian with a white-streaked beard. They resolved and unresolved themselves until Felix saw that there was only one.

One morning he woke and led a horse out into the yard and back found a familiar stranger with a white-streaked beard staring at the castle, looking puzzled.

"Cyprian?" he said, faintly.

The man turned and Felix watched him in fervent prayer that he would not change. For what felt like hours Felix watched, and Cyprian did not change.

"God is merciful," Felix said, sinking to his knees.

Their hands found each other first, with as much relief as their lips did.

In the stables Cyprian explained everything, the story collapsing in on itself over and over again like a bad cake, telling him everything at once - you disappeared, Felix, and no one knew what happened, and the Princess disappeared and no one knew what had happened, and the Queen recovered (but she's dead now) and the end of it was the girl came back with a Prince (or a millers son I'm not sure) but they're happy and she says for a while she was made of cork, of cork of all things, horses I understand but not cork, but her Prince or miller figured it out and if he can figure that out then, bless him, he's the King and I'm a blacksmith. If you've any use for me, of course I knew I'd find you here, well no, I didn't know, I hoped I knew, and I did know. Now for God's sake tell me the news.

Felix laughed, extended himself on the hay, his leg protesting faintly. "Today," he said, "I saw a flying ship."

And Gold in Her Eyes

Maigen Turner

You were told stories, as a child, of women wed to monsters - sent down to dark beasts trapped in mazes, carried up to terrible, beautiful sons of gods. You were beautiful yourself, then. You dreamed of your marriage, of a queen's cloak and castle walls gold as grain. You dreamed strong sons and wise daughters, and you never wondered what children the lost brides, the lost-betrayed-sacrificed-forgotten, bore to the waiting night.

Your firstborn came out slime-slick and mewing, his claws already stretched to the world. His brother slid quick after, your second born, never patient.

"An easy birth," the midwife said, her voice fluting in a songbird's throat. She rubbed a towel rough over spotted fur, kitten-blue eyes, paws that already caught for feathers. She offered your sons to you.

You stared at them, your belly cramping against the afterbirth. Fighting to rid you of it, to free your body of those who took such easy possession. Mirror to each other, your sons, and mirror to their father. Bile burned your throat and you struck them away.

The midwife sang a soft note, a bird's sigh, and carried your children from the chamber.

Later, when your breasts ached milk-taut, you regretted it. You slipped down the tower stairs, through passages aglow with bowls of frozen flame - you thought this a place of wonders, once, when you still swallowed hope like a secret. Rushes sighed underfoot as you crept into the great hall.

A mist-grey wolf slept at the hearth. Her shoulder reached yours, standing, but that night a dozen small bodies nestled at her side. Little monsters, all of them: horned, scaled, furred, hooved. All hers, but for the cougar-cubs tucked behind one elbow.

The wolf raised her head and growled. You crouched, your breasts full but your middle hollow, empty and lonely as a drained pitcher.

The wolf kept growling. Her pups squeaked and squirmed, wakened. You spread a hand in appeal.

She opened her jaws, a gape large enough to crush a man's skull, and bent over the cougarlings. Your breath stuttered.

She licked each head, once, her green-ice gaze fixed on yours.

You rose in silence. Your empty middle spread until your heartbeat echoed in your fingertips, in the scars ridged down your spine, in every bone broken and reset. You'd lost your chance with your sons, if you ever had one. Perhaps monsters only loved other monsters.

The wolf's growl followed you from the hall.

Your sons were years old, their baby spots faded into sleek gold-brown pelts, when a minstrel stumbled into your lord's realm. His face looked so strange, the skin bare and soft. Human, and you could not tell if you pitied or despised him for it.

You would have eaten in your tower, but the lord himself summoned you to the hall. He watched you watch the minstrel, his eyes bright as coins. He observed you from habit, you suspected; he had already heard every cry, tasted every scream and sob and whimper he could draw from your throat.

You kept your face still and watched the minstrel play. His instrument had too many strings, and he sang in a choppy accent you strained to understand. Years had drifted through your tower, but centuries had passed in the world beyond.

The minstrel glanced at you, daring-smiling, and began another ballad. You untangled his words into the tale of a woman wed to a monster, a woman whose love and devotion earned the monster's heart in return.

You sipped your wine and ignored the amusement from the hall of diners. They understood the minstrel's tongue with ease; what hound did not understand the hare? You believed you might gentle their lord, when you first came to the hall. You believed if you were good enough, patient enough, beautiful enough, your suffering would at last earn a kind gaze and sheathed claws, a monster grateful for its taming.

You were a fool.

The minstrel sang on. He believed the lies of his ballad; you saw it in his prey-soft eyes. You hated him, a sudden rising heat in your chest, fury coiled from stomach to throat until your vision shimmered.

You stood, a knife hidden against your wrist. It dripped warm grease down your forearm as you stalked toward the minstrel.

The hall quieted, eyes of every shape tracking you. Curiosity perked the lord's ears. Always curious, that one. The minstrel faltered, perhaps finally glimpsing the place he had come.

You stepped behind him. It was harder than you expected, the resistance of muscle and sinew, but you had your reward in the rush of blood. You shoved the silenced minstrel from his chair and threw the dagger atop him. His instrument made a baffled, discordant sound as it struck the hearthstones.

You brushed your hands off, anger and satisfaction twinned snakes in your gut. A bear warrior rumbled. You looked up into the lord's brilliant stare, his shining-gold eyes.

It was then you realized the depth of your mistake.

He came to you that night, as he had not for weeks. You waited at your tower window, watching clouds chase and catch and shred each other across the sky. Blood stiffened the fine linen of your sleeves. You did not turn when the door slipped open and shut, or flinch as a soft-furred palm pressed, your throat.

"Why?" he murmured. His whiskers brushed your temple; his warmth heated the length of your back.

"A mercy," you said. "Better to die swiftly than torn apart in the hunt's teeth."

He chuckled, a vibration through both your chests. "You did not kill him out of mercy." A claw pricked the hinge of your jaw. "You are not so weak."

"No." The word tore fierce from your throat, and anger lashed you again. You spun in his arms, the claws slicing lines of pain.

He tilted his head. You caught his heavy muzzle in both hands, studied the dark-rimmed eyes that never held pity. They held none now, and you leaned forward and kissed him hard.

His face wasn't meant for such; whiskers pressed wiry against your upper lip, and short stiff fur tickled your chin. Fangs dented the corners of your mouth. You hadn't kissed him since you were a new bride, bold-shy and hopeful. Maiden no longer: you dug your nails into his muzzle and bit before he could. His blood coated your tongue like honey.

You paid for that night, with a swelling belly and new sets of wounds, but your daughter was born with a human face.

The midwife made no protest when you took her, though you hissed a warning anyway. This child you would not lose to the wolf. This child, daughter with your face, you would keep for your own.

She followed sweet and gentle at your skirts as she grew. You ignored the way her claws pulled and ruined her embroidery, and the gifts of dead mice she offered to soothe you if you lost your temper. She offered one to her sire, when she misplaced his favorite dagger.

He struck the mouse from her hands. She cringed, yellow eyes wide, and you forgot yourself enough to snap, "Let her alone."

The lord looked at you, then cuffed the girl into a table edge. She collapsed, tears welling, but made no sound. You clenched your fists and said nothing.

The lord lifted your daughter to her feet. His ears pricked, and alarm pierced your heart. Your daughter stood silent in his grasp, her face impossibly unbruised.

The lord traced a claw down her cheek. Pale skin split and bled.

Your daughter flicked you a swift, guilty glance. More tears wet her lashes, but the scratch sealed and disappeared.

"Well done," her father rumbled.

The smile lit her face like sun through ice, and you could not say which stung you more: that she would smile at him so, or that he stroked her ears with approval.

The lord caught your expression and laughed until the echoes chased you to your tower.

Your daughter laid twelve mice at your door, and one battered lark, before you could look at her.

Her face mocked you, but the pleading in her eyes roused your pity. If monster tainted the human in her, perhaps human tainted the monster. You ignored her father's sighs and comforted her when she came crying after his tests.

When he blinded her, you understood your cruelty.

She shook and sobbed in your lap, blood oozing between her fingers. Your sons fought in the courtyard, snaps and snarls; with a yelp one yielded the argument and quiet fell.

The lord glanced at them, then nudged your daughter. She shrunk away, tail tucked. He gave you a disgusted look.

"If she leaves the wound too long, she will bear it forever."

He stalked off. Panic clawed your stomach. You petted your daughter's ears and urged her to heal the damage, to repair herself as you knew she could.

She shivered and choked. Desperation grew, and a thorn of impatience. The scars pulled all down your back. You had survived worse, and you had no monster's blood; why did she not summon the will to do as she must?

Because you softened her. You tried to make her human, make her weak and slow, when she wore only a human mask over monster's bone and blood. What use is a monster unsuited to its labyrinth?

You gritted your teeth, furious at her, furious at yourself. She sobbed again.

You slapped her. "Halt your weeping. Are you woman or wormbait?"

She gasped, shocked to silence. You clenched your hand against the urge to strike her again. She swallowed, shivered once, and after a pause lifted her head. Her coin-gold eyes stared unblinking at you.

"Next time heal yourself in a prompt and sensible fashion," you told her.

You held to your resolve, over the next seasons, and ignored her as you did the others. It was for her own good, however much she begged your notice; a sharper light came into her eyes, and you often saw blood under her claws. You never inquired whose it was.

Only in winter's depth, when the lord dropped her flayed body on your steps, did you waver. You dragged your daughter inside, the bloody snow a banner behind. You collected her pelt from a drift. The lord had carefully cut hide from flesh, every inch but her face. You wondered how she had provoked him.

Your daughter bared her fangs feebly, as you returned. You started to wrap her skin about her, to aid her healing, then paused in consideration. With her fur removed, might she grow back human-skinned?

You laid her on your hearthstones and settled to wait. A log burned through before her raw flesh stopped oozing; soon a pink layer clouded the curves of muscle and fat and sinew. You held your breath.

You wept when the fur emerged, dust-gold and dark. Your daughter stirred at the sound.

You stared at the pool of blood she lay in, the pain still stretching her mouth. That you should condemn any child of yours to this life, this form -

You rose in silence and pulled your belt knife. It would be mercy, as you ought to have given years ago; the day she lay blinded, or perhaps the day she was born.

You knelt and shoved the knife into her chest.

She tried to dodge. The blade hit a rib, and she scrambled away; blood spread, a staining blossom, across the new fur of her breasts. She blinked at you, panting. "Why -"

"It's for the best." You reached again for her.

Your daughter tugged the blade free and crawled to a crouch. Her hand wavered, but the knife stayed pointed at you. The wound closed as if it had never been.

Your daughter's eyes narrowed, the color gleaming bright as her father's. You recalled your own thought, mercy. Shame heated your cheeks that you would be so weak, that you would offer a monster such a thing or think she might desire it.

No wonder she stared at you.

You stepped aside, face turned toward the wall. After a moment she dropped the knife at your feet and slipped out.

That spring you found a small embroidered flower on your tower steps. You grieved, for no monster should offer forgiveness.

Another human had come to the keep, you heard eventually. A wizard, not a minstrel, though both were prone to wandering. You caught sight of him one morning and indulged your curiosity.

He watched sharp-eyed as you approached, your slippers crunching on dry leaves. You wondered that he had chosen the autumn garden, when the spring and summer were ever full of blooms. He was older than you expected, broad-shouldered and scarred.

"I won't harm you," you said.

The wizard raised his eyebrows. Perhaps he took such remarks for empty courtesy, or perhaps not: his coat bore the repaired marks of teeth and claws. The hunting packs had brought him in, or brought him back.

"Do you believe in ballads?" you asked.

The air rippled and your daughter stepped from it. The wizard shifted, favoring one leg. Your daughter's gaze flicked between you, but you did not miss how it lingered on the wizard.

"Your pet is quite safe," you said, and showed your teeth. "Did you worry?"

She flicked her long tail. The wizard shifted again, muttering something you thought was an objection to being called pet. He moved stiffly under his leather coat, as if he had wrapped ribs. You raised your brows. He might dislike the term, but your daughter had already begun shaping him, working him into the form she pleased.

You smiled at both. Your daughter's eyes narrowed, but she ducked her chin. You caught her face with one hand. She stared back without flinch. No softness touched her gaze; her face matched yours, thin mask over darker truth. Your smile deepened.

"I'm sorry," you told the wizard, though you weren't. You dropped your hand and brushed past your daughter, your mirror, the child broken into your image.

It was the way a monster showed love.

Godmother Death

Kate O'Connor

She was born with her eyes closed and made no sound until the midwife slapped her little bottom. Even then it was only the tiniest of bird-peeps. At first, I thought I had been sent for her. She was pale and so very small. There was barely a breath in her tiny body. As I reached for her, a firm tug at my cloak stayed my hand.

The child's mother lay a short distance away, clutching at me with pain-clawed hands. Her hair was lank and stringy with sweat. Her dark eyes were dim in her fine-featured face, but they studied me with an intensity I was unused to. She was dying. I was there for her.

"How can I leave her without a mother to care for her?" She sighed, the weight of the richly embroidered blanket pushing the air out of her. Now that she had my attention, she was calm. "No matter how much I love him, my husband is not a strong man. He might not be able to look after her. Does it have to be now?"

"It does." These things could not be negotiated or changed. The room full of servants continued on without seeing me. Few ever did if they weren't dying themselves.

Her eyes fixed on me. She was beautiful in her pain, balancing on the tipping point between life and death. "Will you look after her?"

In my astonishment I answered without thinking. "I will, if that is what you want, but what could Death possibly have to offer a living child?" The living were usually desperate to spare their loved ones my company.

"You will never be far away. She should have a godmother who will never leave her." She smiled and closed her eyes for the last time. I kissed her forehead, reaching my hands through her physical form and gathering the threads of her life together, bright goodness twining inextricably with shadowy misdeeds. I tucked her bundled essence beneath my cloak and turned back to the luxuriously appointed room. I lingered for a while, watching my new goddaughter through the usual frantic activity. She slept quietly, alone in her basket as the servants tried vainly to revive their lady.

I picked the infant up and wrapped her in a blanket. Her tiny, perfect hand took hold of my finger and she cooed softly. The few wisps of hair on her head were the color of fading lilies. It was the first time I had held a child as it grew stronger and more alive. The warmth of her breath was the most beautiful thing I had ever felt.

"The child needs milk." One of the servants spoke, drawing my attention back to the room. The woman was looking directly at me. It seemed that while I held my goddaughter, they took me as one of their own.

"The cook has a babe and enough milk to spare for a second," another answered.

"I will take her," I replied, wrapping the tiny girl more snugly in her blanket as I stepped into the hallway. I brought her to the kitchen and sat with the young woman until my goddaughter was nursing, watching her pale cheeks begin to blossom.

"What is her name?" the woman asked.

"She has none," I answered, stroking the child's hair one more time as I got up to leave. The baby still had not opened her eyes.

She sat quietly on my knee while the physician examined her. She weighed scarcely more than grave mist. Her delicate doll's hands rested in her lap, too still for a real child's. Her father drifted in the background, sometimes moving forward to flutter at the physician's shoulder, sometimes staring out the window.

"There is nothing wrong with her eyes, my lord. She just doesn't seem to see the world in front of her." The doctor was young, fresh from his apprenticeship. His face said he was uncomfortable with his diagnosis. "You say she is not a frail child?"

"No." I answered when it became clear the lord of the house was lost in his thoughts, as he had been so often in the years since his lady's passing. The young man shivered at the sound of my voice. A man in his profession, even one so young, learned to feel when I was near, even if he saw only a lowly housemaid in front of him.

He studied my goddaughter more closely, clearly thinking the scent of death he caught came from her. He took her tiny hands in his, counting her heartbeat in the indigo veins decorating her thin wrists. The rhythm was strong and even. She said nothing, leaning back ever so slightly into my arms. This was yet another in a long line of such men who had examined her and she spoke rarely, even to those she was close to.

"Have you consulted with a priest?" the physician asked, sitting back on his heels and releasing her hands. "I can find nothing worldly wrong with her."

"Priests, philosophers, hedge witches. Each one sends me to speak to another." The lord finally joined the conversation. He ran a tired hand through his thick hair. "And they all say the same." Silence settled over the room again. My goddaughter's sightless eyes stared straight through the physician. Unlike so many of the others, he looked straight back into her blank gaze.

"I know it isn't my place to say so, my lord, but maybe the girl just needs a proper mother. Nothing can replace a mother's love." The young man began packing his bag.

"Perhaps you're right." I watched the idea take root in the lord's mind, growing rapidly into a light in his eyes. I tucked my goddaughter more tightly in my arms. Even so young, she had seen enough of me that the mortal world was nothing to her eyes. I hadn't known the effect my continued presence would have on her until it was too late, and now I knew of nothing that could cure her. A new mother would do her no good.

She stood in the garden, her slender fingers drifting idly over the sharp-thorned roses. She cocked her head when I approached.

"Are the ones you take with you frightened?" she asked. Her golden hair was tied in a neat knot at the back of her head. The faded dress she was wearing had been mended many times over by her careful needle and mismatched thread.

"At first," I answered, watching her hands find a pale pink blossom and explore its velvet petals. Her mist-blue eyes stared into the middle distance. Shortly after her father had married again, the attempts to cure her blindness had stopped. "Why do you ask?"

"The servants say that you'll be coming for Papa any day now."

"It will be tonight. Soon." I hadn't known until I said it. I hadn't been paying attention. I should have been, since it was her father. "Do you want to come with me?" I wanted her to see that it was gentle - that the fear was a passing thing. It would break my heart if she was ever afraid of me.

"Yes." She nodded, her fair face as smooth as it had been when she was a child. She never smiled and rarely cried. I thought perhaps it was my influence again. She had grown up with only one foot in the world of the living; my visits were an expected and welcome thing in her life.

We moved through the halls like a pair of shadows. The lady of the house had retired for the evening, taking her daughters with her. An old servant was asleep outside the door. His snoring continued uninterrupted as we entered the sick man's room.

Labored breathing filled the silence, deepening it until it was a solid weight. He moaned weakly, coughing his life away in thick, gagging heaves. I watched his pain settle on her, rounding her shoulders and stifling her voice. For long moments she stood there, saying nothing.

"It is hardest just before it happens." I moved towards him. His wet eyes widened and he turned weakly away from me. My hands slipped through his human flesh, past his failing heart and into his spirit. I searched for a moment and found the thread I was looking for. I pulled it free, tugging a filament loose and holding it out for her. "This is his love for you." It glistened in the dim room, illuminating the motionless corpse on the bed.

She took it in her hands, winding it through her fingers as carefully as if it were the finest silk. "Thank you." Her voice was serene and her face remote. It occurred to me that maybe I had made it worse, taken her further from the human world. Perhaps I should have left this last mystery until it was her turn to face it.

"The invitation arrived this morning addressed to all the ladies of the household. My stepsisters are going. The whole house is in a stir about it. They say the King is picking a new bride." She sat in the kitchen peeling a small mountain of potatoes.

"Will you be going with them?" There had been parties in the house before - the lord's second wife was fond of them - but my goddaughter had never cared to take part, preferring instead the quiet of her sewing or giving the horses a brushing.

"Of course not. Those invitations never mean to include the servants." There was a faint edge in her voice that I had not heard before.

"You are not a servant." Until becoming responsible for her, I had never noticed the differences in station in the living world. I wanted her to be cared for and happy. I wanted to see her take an interest in something, to grow and thrive. Here in her stepmother's kitchens, she moved from one day to the next as though sleeping.

"I might as well be. What does birth matter when I have dirt on my face and rough hands? Besides, somebody needs to keep this place running. The lady and my sisters have other things on their minds."

"Dirt washes off, my love. They are only mortal. They will rot with dirt over their heads just like the poorest cowherd." If I could have shortened the lives of her stepmother and stepsisters so much as one day, I would have done it, but it had never been within my power to name the time of a mortal's passing. With her father gone, they punished her for every lapse, real or imagined. She took it in silence, driving them to further acts of persecution.

"I forgive them." She shrugged her elegant shoulders, feeling for another potato.

"You have a good heart." I thought of it as a child's heart, clean and untouched by the world around her.

"No. If I weren't angry with them, there would be no need for forgiveness." Her short fingernails dug into the potato's thin skin, leaving tiny, pale crescents in their wake. "But I hear you, Godmother. I won't forget. Dirt is only permanent when we're dead."

I looked at her in surprise. Her emotions ran so deep and slow that I often forgot she had them. There was so much more that went on behind those blank eyes than she chose to share.

The evening of the ball came. I arrived at the estate, hoping to convince her to go. Mortal life was so short, and she had yet to really start hers. I found her in the back garden with an unattended basket of mending beside her. An air of sadness hung around her as heavy as a shroud.

"Godmother, do you think it will be wonderful?" she asked. The wistful question caught me off guard. It seemed even she was not as removed from dreaming of a better life as I had feared.

"Would you like to find out?" I wanted her to say yes. I wanted her to choose to reach for something different.

"No. I would just make a fool of myself. I couldn't find my way in the palace with all of those people. Which thread do I need for this?" She picked up a worn skirt, smoothing it across her lap and finding the tear by feel. There was the barest hint of tension between her eyebrows.

"This one, but leave that for the moment. I have something for you." I put my present into her outstretched hands.

She felt the package, unwrapping it delicately. I watched as her slender hands traced over the familiar shape. The crystal shoes glistened in the moonlight, clear and perfect as her face.

"You know I can't give you your sight, even for a night, but these will act as your guides. As long as you wear them, you can put no foot wrong." I had put a little of myself in them. The shoes would show her the shadows of the living world. With them on, she would see more clearly than those without her disability.

Hope bloomed on her face, then fell again as quickly. "I can't go. I have nothing to wear."

I smiled, though she couldn't see it. "I have borrowed everything you need." I dressed her in a gown a foreign princess had been buried in, adorning her with the crown jewels of a kingdom lost millennia before this one had even been a dream. "As long as you return to me by midnight, you will look like a queen." I waved my hand, fashioning a pale, glistening coach out of the low-lying mist.

She slipped the shoes onto her feet. "Why midnight?" There was something new in her voice - a fresh spring bud of excitement.

"I can only lend you these things until the world changes and moves towards morning. Death is only half the magic in the world. For the other half of the day I am only strong enough to take spirits. This requires more magic than that." A silver carp floated belly-up in the garden pond. I scooped it out of the weed-choked shallows and breathed on it; its scales drifted to the ground like dead leaves. I arranged its sharp bones in the patterns I wanted and stretched its rotting skin over the new shapes. With a thought, I sent them moving and growing until six silver horses stood ready at the front of the white coach.

That done, I looked my goddaughter over as she stood in the moonlight. There was something different about her as she stood in her finery. It was almost as though she were fading from my sight.

She put a trembling hand in mine and the distance between us was gone as if it had never been. "I'll go until midnight, then. So I'll have something to think on while I work." She spoke more to herself than me, squaring her shoulders as I helped her into the coach. A quiet ache started somewhere below my breast as the door closed behind her. Perhaps I had been mistaken to encourage her. Perhaps it would have been better to keep her home and let her live her life through dreams.

I walked behind her, invisible to all eyes. No one asked her name when she came to the gates of the palace. The wide-eyed footmen held the doors open as she walked towards them. The people she passed paused to bow low. She noticed none of them, drifting through her lonely twilight world.

The bright noise of the party washed over us as we came through the door and into the ballroom. She stopped at the top of the long stair leading down onto the marble floor. I felt the tremor that shook her slight frame as if it were my own. She half turned back towards the open door. A hint of deep uncertainty cracked through the crystalline façade of her composure.

I moved out of the way, staying out of sight. If she wanted to run, to return home, I would be the last to stand in her path. To my surprise, she caught her breath and turned to face the room again. Her face stilled abruptly and, for the first time, I noticed that we were not alone.

The King stood three steps below us with a compassionate half-smile on his young face. His eyes were sad, and the air around him was colored with recent loss. I knew him well. He had loved the Queen that illness - and I - had taken from him barely a year past. He had been a soldier before his father's death. I had visited him too often.

"It can be a bit overwhelming at first, my lady." He bowed, offering her his hand once he had straightened. She stared at it for a long moment through the shadows, then took it tentatively in her own. Something entirely mortal passed between them. Perhaps it was their shared loneliness, perhaps their losses or their wary dreams. Whatever it was, it made her lips turn up at the corners. The smile that blossomed on her face transfixed both me and the King. He had no way of knowing it was her first, but I watched it strike him as deeply as it split my own heart.

I stood back as they walked down to the waiting crowd below. She didn't spare another glance for the door and he not another for anyone else in the ballroom.

She was late home, returning in the worn dress she had been wearing for her chores. The shoes came off as soon as she was through the gate, though she cradled them to her chest. Something had changed in her. "I'm sorry, Godmother. I lost track of the time." She held the shoes out, her hands hesitating.

"Did you enjoy the party?" I ignored the offered shoes for the moment. She didn't need to know that I had gone with her.

"Yes. I suppose I did." Her answer came slow and unsure. "I danced with the King." The smile she had found earlier rippled across her face, awkward and lovely as a newborn fawn. "He knew you very well, Godmother. I didn't expect that of a king."

"Will you see him again?" I could see in her posture that she knew what I was asking. The whole kingdom knew he was looking for a new queen.

Her face was blank again and she was silent for a long time. "He needs a wife who can help him find a way to be happy. Who can help him run his kingdom and recover from the hardships his life has brought." She shook her head, frowning. "I know nothing about such things."

"Perhaps you should let him choose for himself what he needs." I saw mortal relationships all the time - hands entwined as they tried to hold me back, bonds of love that shone through the darkness I brought. There were long goodbyes and short ones as the threads that wove their spirits pulled tight together. I had seen love that let there be an end to pain and suffering and souls that would wait on the edge of peace until the other arrived to travel with them. The first gossamer fibers of it were there between my goddaughter and the king. It was little more than a wish right now, but given a chance, it could weave a lifetime for them.

"If he asks me, I'll go with him, but I will not chase after him hoping. Even if he does come, he will see what I really am and leave just as quickly. It was a dream, Godmother. A nice one, but nothing more."

I took the shoes from her still outstretched hands. "We will leave it there for now, then. You should get some sleep. Tomorrow is another day."

Many nights later, I left one of the shoes in a basket of carrots in her kitchen and made my way to the palace again. I passed through now-quiet corridors, unseen by the handful of alert guards who remained on duty. The door to the King's chambers was simple wood. He had moved from the royal suite the morning after I took the Queen. I had watched him go as the servants prepared her body.

I placed the second shoe on the floor before the door and knocked softly. The shoe would lead him straight to its match, if he wanted to follow where it led. There was no compulsion in it. The choice was his.

A true soldier, he was at the door within moments. He looked up and down the hall, eyes growing wary when he saw no one. Then his gaze dropped down and his face changed. He reached downwards with a shaking hand.

He touched the crystal slipper with light hesitancy, as though afraid it would vanish as thoroughly as its owner had. Rumor had it that he had been searching almost since the ball had ended, to no avail. She was unaware, scrubbing pots and washing floors, even more silent than usual. When the shoe remained solid, he scooped it up, cradling it to his chest as the first beginnings of hope made his face glow.

There was far more noise in the entrance hall than usual for this time of morning. She never looked up from kneading the bread dough. I sat by the fire, helping with the mending. There was flour on her face and hands and her hair was tucked under an old, faded rag. She did not hum or whistle. She scarcely seemed to breathe.

The noise from the hall faded further back into the house. It was odd that none of the servants had come down. If there were guests, the kitchen was usually bustling. Now, though, the only sound was the thump of dough on the board.

"My lady." His voice vibrated like a spring leaf in the empty kitchen. She turned towards it incredulously, her hands flying to her mouth to cover her gasp. He stood in the door, alone and tentative. I wondered how he had kept her stepmother at bay.

"You found me," she spoke with soft wonder.

He walked unsteadily across the small room towards her. He took in her flour-covered rags and mist-blank eyes as he caught her delicate hands in his. "I did." He spoke as softly as she.

"You're here." Tears came to her eyes and spilled down her face, tracing thin tracks through the flour on her cheeks: her first shed because of another mortal being. I watched the color of her eyes brighten and change as her mortal sight returned to her. She turned her wondering face up towards his. "I can see you."

"You always have." He touched her cheek, brushing away her tears even as his eyes glistened with his own. "Will you come with me?"

She looked at him with eyes turned the color of the summer sky and a bubble of joyous laughter burst from her lips. "I will."

He offered his arm, face radiant, and she took it.

At the door, she stopped and looked back. Her new eyes passed over me, though I made no attempt to hide from her. They were wholly mortal eyes now. "Godmother?" she asked and the uncertainty in her voice was a fresh heartbreak. Did she think I had abandoned her?

"You will see her again." The King put a strong, comforting arm around her shoulders.

"Yes." Her smile came quickly now. "Though perhaps not for a long time." There was hope in her voice, hope for a long life with the one she loved. Hope for a world where I was far away.

I sighed as she turned towards him, the throbbing ache of losing her a painful joy in my chest. I would watch her as well as I could as she moved towards morning.

Contributors

Alison Littlewood:

Alison Littlewood was raised in South Yorkshire, England, and went on to attend the University of Northumbria at Newcastle (now Northumbria University). She followed a career in marketing before developing her love of writing fiction. She now lives near Wakefield, West Yorkshire, with her partner Fergus. Her first novel *A Cold Season* (Jo Fletcher Books) was inspired by her winter commute to snowy Saddleworth, and was picked for the Richard and Judy Book Club. Her next novel, *Path of Needles* (2013) marked a return to her early obsessions – fairy tales, mysterious forests, and the things we can't quite explain – and concerns a killer who is bringing the darker aspects of fairy tales to life. Alison's short stories have been picked for the *Best Horror of the Year* and *Mammoth Book of Best New Horror* anthologies, as well as *The Best British Fantasy 2013* and *The Mammoth Book of Best British Crime 10*. Other publication credits include the anthologies *Terror Tales of the Cotswolds, Where Are We Going?* and *Never Again.*

alisonlittlewood.co.uk

Maigen Turner:

Maigen Turner was born in Southern California, to parents certain her destiny was to be a veterinarian. She did major in zoology, but always found animal behavior more intriguing than the details of anatomy. She is currently a dog trainer by day and a fantasy writer by night. The occupations dovetail surprisingly well - both involve imagining the inner workings of minds entirely different from her own (whether canine, character, or reader!).

spartezda.livejournal.com

Nadia Bulkin:

Nadia Bulkin writes stories and researches Southeast Asia in Washington, D.C. Her stories have been published in ChiZine, *Creatures: Thirty Years of Monsters*, Fantasy Magazine, and Strange Horizons, among other places. She has a B.A. in Political Science and an M.A. in International Affairs.

nadiabulkin.wordpress.com

Sarah L Byrne:

Sarah L. Byrne is a science writer and speculative fiction writer in London.

sarahbyrne.org

Angela Rega:

Angie's short stories have appeared in publications including *The Year's Best Australian Fantasy and Horror*, PS Publishing, Ticonderoga Publications, Fablecroft Press, Cabinet Des Fees and Little Fox Press. She is a lover of folklore, fairy tales and furry creatures and works as a Teacher Librarian in an inner city high school. She is a graduate of the Clarion South workshop and is currently studying for her Masters Degree in Creative Writing. She drinks way too much coffee and can't imagine not writing.

angierega.webs.com

Martine Helene Svanevik:

Martine Helene Svanevik is a fiction and games writer. Her work has been published in *Age of Conan: Secrets of the Dragon's Spine*, *Words With Jam*, and *Argument*. She lives in a tiny Oslo apartment with her fiancée and a growing assortment of dead plants.

Rose Williamson:

Rose Williamson is a desert dweller who has moved to rainy England in order to pursue her PhD in folklore and fairy-tale research at the University of Chichester. Her work will feature an exploration of baked goods and grains in fairy tales, and she consequently spends a lot of her free time learning to bake different breads. She recently completed her master's in creative writing, where she worked on a collection of stories inspired by fairy tales and mythology. This is her first print publication, though her short story *Bakkheia* was published in an e-magazine called The Jersey Devil Press.

David Turnbull:

David Turnbull is a UK based writer and a member of the Clockhouse London group of SciFi, Fantasy and Horror writers. His short fiction has appeared in magazines such as Lissette's Tales of the Imagination, Sword and Sorcery Magazine and numerous anthologies; including fairy tale inspired stories in *Time for Bedlam*, *Fangtales*, *Read by Dawn (Vol II)* and *Rapunzel's Daughters*. His children's fantasy novel about airships and dragon hunters *The Tale of Euan Recap* was published on the Pixiefoot Press Imprint of Wyvern Publications in March 2012.

tumsh.co.uk
clockhouselondonwriters.wordpress.com

Natalia Theodoridou:

Natalia Theodoridou is a UK-based media & theatre scholar. Originally from Greece, she has lived and studied in the USA, UK, and Indonesia for several years. Her writing has appeared or is forthcoming in The Kenyon Review Online, Clarkesworld, Strange Horizons, Spark Anthology IV (Grand Prize winner of Spark Contest Three), The Dark, and elsewhere. One of her poems, *Blackmare*, was recently nominated for the 2014 Rhysling Award. She is a first reader for Goldfish Grimm's Spicy Fiction Sushi.

natalia-theodoridou.com

Elin Olausson:

Elin Olausson was born in 1986 and grew up in a tiny village on the Swedish countryside, where she spent her childhood playing with words and making up stories. Now she lives with her boyfriend and two rather talkative cats, working as a librarian. Writing is still her life.

Ephiny Gale:

Ephiny is a writer, theatre maker and arts manager based in Melbourne, Australia. She is the author of several produced plays and musicals, and her short stories have appeared in publications including Daily Science Fiction, The Misfit Quarterly and Punchnel's. She is a past Secretary of the Green Room Awards Association, Melbourne's premiere performing arts awards, and is currently the Coordinator of the inaugural Container Festival, a multi-week, multi-venue arts festival.

Molly Pinto Madigan:

Self-proclaimed poet and songstress, Molly Pinto Madigan loves roses, old ballads, faery stories, and beaches, where she spends her days indulging her mermaid nature. In her spare time she drinks tea and writes novels about thinly-veiled versions of herself.

mollypintomadigan.wordpress.com

Caren Gussoff:

Caren Gussoff is a Seattle-based science fiction writer. Her first two books, *Homecoming* (2000), and *The Wave and Other Stories* (2003), were published by Serpent's Tail/High Risk Books, and her new novel *The Birthday Problem*, will be published by Pink Narcissus Press in 2014. Aside from that, she 's been published in anthologies by Seal Press, Prime Books, Evil Girlfriend Media, and Hadley Rille, as well as in Abyss & Apex, Cabinet des Fées and Fantasy Magazine. She received her MFA from the School of the Art Institute of Chicago, and in 2008, she was the Carl Brandon Society's Octavia E. Butler Scholar at Clarion West.

spitkitten.com.

Kate O'Connor:

Kate O'Connor was born in Virginia in 1982. She graduated from Embry-Riddle Aeronautical University-Prescott in 2009 and now lives (and occasionally works) in the New York area. She has been writing science fiction and fantasy since 2011. In between telling stories, she flies airplanes, works as an archaeology field tech, and manages a kennel full of Airedales.

Nicki Vardon:

Nicki Vardon - Dutch by birth, British by tea addiction. Writing is a hobby. A hobby that got horribly out of hand. In a good way. Throughout her life she's lived in three different countries, changed hair colour numerous times, bathed an owl, suffered malaria for cash, nursed and raised three nests of wild rabbits, had all her wisdom surgically removed, done a New Year's dive, and completed NaNoWriMo five times. She mostly writes stories with a speculative bent and especially enjoys settings based on historical eras with a twist. For short fiction she loves quirky pieces with unusual voices and unique concepts. When she writes novels, she tries to be a touch more conventional.

nickivardon.blogspot.com

Pat R Steiner:

As a child, Pat R. Steiner once found himself hanging from a nail pounded into a tree. Left there by his older siblings, he happily communed with the tree until his mother dragged the whereabouts of the missing youngster from the guilt-ridden children. Since then he has had a fascination with nature (including the human variety) along with its many mysteries. His writings and art are his attempts to explain these BIG QUESTIONS as well as those more mundane. Pat's stories have appeared in many small print anthologies. He is also a recent winner of the Illustrators of the Future contest. He lives in Wisconsin with his wife and two children.

patsteiner.com

Karen Heuler:

Karen Heuler's stories have appeared in over 70 literary and speculative magazines and anthologies. She has published three novels and two story collections with university and small presses, and her last collection was chosen for Publishers Weekly's Best Books of 2013 list. Permuted Press just published *Glorious Plague*, a novel about a beautiful apocalypse. She has received an O. Henry award, been shortlisted for a Pushcart prize, for the Iowa short fiction award, the Bellwether award and the Shirley Jackson award for short fiction. She lives in New York City.

karenheuler.com

Alex Petri

Alex Petri graduated from Harvard in 2010 and now writes a daily blog and weekly column for the Washington Post. Her writing has taken her from the campaign trail to the camps of Union reenactors to a whistling convention to the Deepest Wilds of the Internet. She is working on a book of essays for NAL/Penguin. Her writing can be found in two Scholastic Best Teen Writing anthologies, the Roz Wiseman book Queen Bees and Wannabes, and Daily Science Fiction.

"Then her
envious heart
was at rest,
as well as
an envious heart
can be at rest."

Snow White,
Jacob and Wilhelm
Grimm, 1857

Thanks

To London Burden and fairy godmother Sissel Berge

Belladonna
Publishing
belladonnapublishing.com

Made in the USA
San Bernardino, CA
29 June 2016